gen

KT-429-118

wld

GRAMPIAN
REGION
M007867

405787        F

SCHOOLS'
LIBRARY
SERVICE

Books should be returned on or before the
last date stamped above.

FRASERBURGH ACADEMY LIBRARY

M007867

The Collected Edition

ENGLAND MADE ME

Other books by
# GRAHAM GREENE

NOVELS
*The Man Within*
*Stamboul Train*
*It's a Battlefield*
*England Made Me*
*A Gun for Sale*
*Brighton Rock*
*The Confidential Agent*
*The Power and the Glory*
*The Ministry of Fear*
*The Heart of the Matter*
*The Third Man*
*The End of the Affair*
*Loser Takes All*
*The Quiet American*
*Our Man in Havana*
*A Burnt-out Case*
*The Comedians*
*Travels with my Aunt*
*The Honorary Consul*
SHORT STORIES
*Collected Stories*
(including *Twenty-one Stories,*
*A Sense of Reality* and
*May We Borrow Your Husband?*)
TRAVEL
*Journey Without Maps*
*The Lawless Roads*
*In Search of a Character*
ESSAYS
*Collected Essays*
*The Pleasure Dome*
PLAYS
*The Living Room*
*The Potting Shed*
*The Complaisant Lover*
*Carving a Statue*
*The Return of A. J. Raffles*
AUTOBIOGRAPHY
*A Sort of Life*
BIOGRAPHY
*Lord Rochester's Monkey*

Graham Greene

# ENGLAND MADE ME

WILLIAM HEINEMANN
&
THE BODLEY HEAD
LONDON

405787
F
M007867

None of the characters in this book
is intended to be that of
a living person

*First published 1935*
*All rights reserved*
Introduction © Graham Greene 1970
SBN 434 30551 0 (Heinemann)
ISBN 0 370 01425 1 (Bodley Head)
Printed and bound in Great Britain
by William Clowes & Sons Ltd, Beccles
Set in Monotype Plantin Light
*This edition first published 1970*
*Reprinted 1976*

*To Vivien*

'All the world owes me a living.'
*The Grasshopper and the Ant*
WALT DISNEY

# Introduction

I have always had a soft spot in my heart for this novel (a feeling which has not been shared by the general public), yet of the circumstances of its composition I can remember very little. I think of those years between 1933 and 1937 as the middle years for my generation, clouded by the depression in England, which cast a shadow on this book, and by the rise of Hitler. It was impossible in those days not to be committed, and it is hard to recall the details of one private life as the enormous battlefield was prepared around us.

When the story came to me, when Anthony and Kate, the brother and sister, clamoured for attention, and their incestuous situation (which was yet to contain no incestuous act) for exploration, I knew nothing at all of Sweden. I think it is the only occasion when I have deliberately chosen an unknown country as a background and then visited it, like a camera-team, to take the necessary stills. (Many years later I visited the Belgian Congo for something of the same purpose, but the Congo was a geographical term invented by the white colonists – I already knew negro Africa, in Sierra Leone, Nigeria, Kenya, the hinterland of Liberia.)

The photographs I brought back from Sweden were, I think, reasonably accurate, reasonably representative, and yet, now that I know Stockholm well and have learned to love the city in winter, spring, summer and autumn, I am a little afraid when I come to reread the book. That midsummer festival at Saltsjö-Duvnäs, a New Year's night when the melted lead formed a perfect question mark–such impressions are not to be found here, nor the swans gathering on the ice outside the Grand Hotel, the taste of akvavit in the Theatre Grill, the lakes of Dale-carlia, nor that island in the archipelago from which I rowed every morning to fetch water for cooking and a lavatory seat stood like a surrealist object all alone in a mosquito-noisy glade. These impressions are Sweden to me now, and it might be as distressing to read this novel as an ancient letter containing some superficial critical estimate of a woman met for the first time whom twenty years later one had grown to love.

I have few memories of that first visit with my younger brother in August 1933; the clearest, because they have not been overlaid by the later memories, are attached to the speckless miniature liner which brought us up the canal from Gothenburg to Stockholm (and which I imagined falsely would prove a background for the novel), of waking to the soft summer brilliance of midnight and the silver of the birches going by, almost within reach of my hands, and the chickens pecking on the bank. I remember that my brother and I carried on a harmless flirtation with two English visitors of sixteen and twenty; we went for walks in separate pairs when the boat stopped at a lock, and once, for some inexplicable reason, considerable alarm arose because my brother and the younger girl had not returned to the little liner at the proper time, and the mother – an intellectual lady who frequently won literary competitions in *Time & Tide* – was convinced that both had been drowned in the canal. One evening in Stockholm, on the borders of the lake, my companion of the canal slapped my face in almost the same circumstances as those in which Loo slapped Anthony's, for I had told her that I believed she was a virgin. Afterwards we sat decorously enough in Skansen, Stockholm's park, among the grey rocks and the silver trees. (Her reaction was the only characteristic she had in common with Loo.) But August is not the best time of year to see Stockholm for the first time – what with the heat and the humidity, and the formality of one dinner which we attended at Saltsjöbaden, we decided to move on to Oslo. I am amazed now at my temerity in laying the scene of a novel in a city of which I knew so little.

Would I have written the book any better now when I can easily find in my memories a model for Krogh, the industrialist, who so obstinately at that time refused to come alive? I doubt it. In most of my books, however well I have known the scene, there is one lay figure who obstinately refuses to live, who is there only for the sake of the story – Krogh in *England Made Me*, the barmaid in *Brighton Rock*, Wilson in *The Heart of the Matter*, Smythe in *The End of the Affair*, the journalist Parkinson in *A Burnt-Out Case*. The sad truth is that a story hasn't room for more than a limited number of created characters. One more successful creation and like an overloaded boat the story lists. This was the unexpected danger I encountered in *England Made Me*.

I was quite satisfied with my portrait of Anthony. Hadn't I lived with him closely over many years? He was a slightly idealised portrait of someone whom I knew very well, and I had shared many of his experiences. I had known Annette, the young tart whom he loved. I had walked up those forbidding stairs and found with the same emotion the notices – 'No milk this morning', 'Gone out. Be back at—' (no hour which would ever be recorded on the dial of my watch). I was satisfied too with Kate, Anthony's sister, who seems to me the woman I have drawn better than any other, with the possible exception of Sara in *The End of the Affair*. Anthony and

Kate were the heart of the book; Krogh was only there to manipulate their story, and the others, Loo, Hall, Hammarsten, young Andersson were background figures; no one else was needed. Then suddenly the boat listed because Minty stepped on board.

He was entirely unexpected when he emerged from the pre-conscious – this remittance man who woke up one morning in his Stockholm lodgings watched by a spider under a tooth glass – a late-comer at the end of Part Two. I suppose, for the purposes of Anthony's story, I had required, as a minor figure, some fellow outsider who would recognise – as only a fellow countryman can – the fraudulent element in Anthony, who could detect the old Harrovian tie and know at once that it did not belong. I had no intention of introducing into the story a sly pathetic Anglo-Catholic, a humble follower, perhaps, of Sir John Betjeman, who would steal all the scenes in which he played a part and have the last word, robbing even Kate of her curtain at Anthony's funeral. Oh yes, I resented Minty, and yet I couldn't keep him down.

The subject – apart from the economic background of the thirties and that sense of capitalism staggering from crisis to crisis – was simple and unpolitical, a brother and sister in the confusion of incestuous love. I found it odd to read once in a monthly review an article on my early novels in which a critic *disinterred* this theme. He wrote of the ambiguity of the subject, how the author himself feared or was even perhaps unaware of the nature of the passion between brother and sister. He quoted examples to show how the dialogue between the two broke suddenly at a dangerous moment into irrelevancies – I was shirking the true nature of my subject, so he wrote.

How dangerous it is for a critic to have no technical awareness of the novel. Surely the great prefaces of Henry James have marked one novelist's route indelibly – the route of 'the point of view'. There was no ambiguity in *my* mind; the ambiguity was in the minds of Kate and Anthony whom I had chosen for my 'points of view'. They were continually on the edge of self-discovery, but some self-protective instinct warded off, with false or incomplete memories and irrelevancies, the moment of discovery. Kate was nearer to knowledge than Anthony and both used their superficial sexual loves, Kate with Krogh and Anthony with Loo, to evade the real right thing. The cowardly evasions were not mine: they belonged to the doomed pair.

# PART I

She might have been waiting for her lover. For three-quarters of an hour she had sat on the same high stool, half turned from the counter, watching the swing door. Behind her the ham sandwiches were piled under a glass dome, the urns gently steamed. As the door swung open, the smoke of engines silted in, grit on the skin and like copper on the tongue.

'Another gin.' It was her third. Damn him, she thought with tenderness, I'm hungry. She swallowed it at a draught, as she was used to drinking schnaps; *skål*, *skål*, but there was no one to *skål*. The man in a bowler hat put his foot on the brass rail, leant his elbow on the counter, drank his bitter, talked, drank his bitter, wiped his moustache, talked, kept his eye on her.

She stared out past the dusty door pane into the noisy dark. Sparks leapt in the thick enclosed air and went out, sparks from engines, sparks from cigarettes, sparks from the trolley wheels beating on the asphalt. An old tired woman swung the door and peered in; she was looking for someone who was not there.

She moved from her stool; the man in the bowler hat watched her, the waitresses paused in their drying and watched her. Their thoughts drummed on her back: Is she giving him up? What's he like, I wonder? Jilted? She stood in the doorway and let them think: the deep silence of their concentration amused her. She watched the blue empty rails in front of her, looked up the platform to the lights and the bookstalls, then she turned and went back to her stool and was aware of their thoughts wilting again

1

in the steaming air round the urns; the waitresses dried glasses, the man in the bowler hat drank his bitter.

'It never rains but it pours. Take silk stockings for example.'

'Another gin.' But she left the glass on the counter, after barely touching it this time with her lips, and began hurriedly to make-up, as if it had been a duty she had been too excited to remember. Now, in the deep conviction that he would not come, she had one lonely hour for remembering all the things she had neglected: mouth, nose, cheeks, eyebrows. 'Oh damn,' she said. The pencil snapped, and she ground the charcoal end into the floor with her toe. 'Oh damn,' she said, caring not a hang that she was surrounded again by curiosity, alien and unfriendly. It was as if she had broken a mirror; it was unlucky; it was inefficient. Her self-confidence was shaken. She began to wonder if she would recognise her brother if, after all, he came.

But she knew him at once by the small scar under the left eye, the round face which had always looked as if only that day it had lost its freshness, like a worn child's, the bonhomie which even a stranger would not trust. 'Kate,' he was all contrition, 'I'm sorry I'm late. It wasn't my fault. The fact is——' and at once he became sullen, prepared not to be believed. And why, she thought, as she kissed him and touched his back to assure herself that he was there, that he had really come, that they were together, should anyone believe him? He can't open his mouth without lying.

'Have this gin?' She watched him drink it slowly and was aware how her own brain recorded unerringly his anxiety.

'You haven't changed.'

2

'You have,' he said. 'You're prettier than ever, Kate,' and charm, she thought, charm, your damnable accommodating charm. 'Prosperity suits you.' She watched him more closely and examined his clothes for any sign that the years had been less prosperous for him. But he always possessed one good suit. Tall and broad and thin and a little worn, with the scar under his lower lid, he was the mark of every waitress in the room. 'A bitter, please,' and a waitress tore along the counter to serve him, and Kate watched the automatic charm glint in his eye.

'Where shall we eat? Where are your bags?' He turned cautiously from the counter and one hand straightened his school tie.

'The fact is——' he said.

'You aren't coming with me,' she said with hopeless certainty. She wondered for a moment at the depth of her disappointment, for he belonged to this place, to the smoke swirling beyond the door, to the stale beer, to 'Guinness is good for you' and 'Try a Worthington', he had the bold approach, the shallow cheer of an advertisement.

'How did you know?'

'Oh, I always know.' It was true, she always knew; she was his elder by half an hour; she had, she sometimes thought with a sense of shame, by so little outstripped him in the pursuit of the more masculine virtues, reliability, efficiency, and left him with what would have served most women better, his charm. 'They aren't going to give you the Stockholm job then?'

He beamed at her; he rested both hands (she noticed his gloves needed cleaning) on the top of his umbrella, leant back against the counter and beamed at her.

3

Congratulate me, he seemed to be saying, and his humorous friendly shifty eyes raked her like the head-lamps of a second-hand car which had been painted and polished to deceive. He would have convinced anyone but her that for once he had done something supremely clever.

'I've resigned.'

But she had heard that tale too often; it had been the yearly fatal drumming in their father's ears which helped to kill him. He had not been able to answer a telephone without anxiety – 'I have resigned', 'I have resigned', proudly as if it had been matter for congratulation – and afterwards the cables from the East tremblingly opened. 'I have resigned' from Shanghai, 'I have resigned' from Bangkok, 'I have resigned' from Aden, creeping remorselessly nearer. Their father had believed to the end the literal truth of those cables, signed even to relatives with faint grandiloquence in full, 'Anthony Farrant'. But Kate had always known too much; to her these messages conveyed – 'Sacked. I am sacked. Sacked.'

'Come outside,' she said. It would have been unfair to humiliate him before the waitresses. Again she was aware of the deep listening silence, of eyes watching them go. At the far end of the platform she began to question him. 'How much money have you got?'

'Not a sou,' he said.

'But surely you've got a week's pay. You gave them a week's notice.'

'As a matter of fact,' he said, striking an attitude against his smoky metallic background, against a green signal lamp burning for the East Coast express, 'I left at once. Really, it was an affair of honour. You wouldn't be able to understand.'

4

'Perhaps not.'

'Besides, my landlady will give me tick until I'm in funds again.'

'And how long will that be?'

'Oh, I'll get hold of something in a week.' His courage would have been admirable if it had not been so feckless. Money, he had always been certain, would turn up, and it always did: a fellow he'd known at school noticed his tie in the street, stopped him, gave him a job; he sold vacuum cleaners to his relations; he was quite capable of selling a gold brick to an Australian in the Strand; at the worst there had always been his father.

'You forget. Father's dead.'

'What do you mean? I'm not going to sponge.' He believed quite sincerely that he had never 'sponged'. He had borrowed, of course; his debts to relatives must by now have almost reached the thousand mark; but they remained debts not gifts, one day, when a scheme of his succeeded, to be repaid. While Kate waited for the express to pass and shielded her face from the smoke, she remembered a few of his schemes: his plan to buy up old library novels and sell them in country villages, his great packing idea (a shop which would pack and post your Christmas parcels at a charge of twopence a parcel), the patent hand warmer (a stick of burning charcoal in the hollow handle of an umbrella). They had always sounded plausible when he described them; they had no obvious faults, except the one fatal flaw that he was concerned in them. 'I only want capital,' he would explain with a brightness which was never dulled by the knowledge that no one would ever trust him with more than five pounds. Then he would embark on them without capital; strange visitors would appear at week-ends, men older than

5

himself with the same school ties, the same air of bright vigour, but in their cases distinctly tarnished. Then the affair would be wound up, and astonishingly it appeared from the long and complicated pages of accounts that he had not lost more money than he had borrowed. 'If I had had proper capital,' he would explain, but he blamed no one, and no one was paid back. He had added to his debts, but he had not 'sponged'.

His face, she thought, is astonishingly young for thirty-three; it is a little worn, but only as if by a wintry day, it is no more mature than when he was a schoolboy. He might be a schoolboy now, returned from a rather cold and wearing football match. His appearance irritated her, for a man should grow up, but before she could speak and tell him what she thought, her tenderness woke again for his absurd innocence. For he was hopelessly lost in the world of business that she knew so well, the world where she was at home: he had a child's cunning in a world of cunning men: he was dishonest, but he was not dishonest enough. She was aware, having shared his thoughts for more than thirty years, felt his fears beat in her own body, of his incalculable reserves. There were things he would not do. That, she told herself, was the amazing difference between them.

'Listen,' she said. 'I can't leave you here without money. You're coming with me. Erik will give you a job.'

'I can't speak the language. And anyhow,' he leant forward on his stick and smiled with as much negligence as if he had a thousand pounds in the bank, 'I don't like foreigners.'

'My dear,' she said with irritation, 'you're out of date. There are no foreigners in a business like Krogh's; we're internationalists there, we haven't a country. We aren't a

6

little dusty City office which has been in the family for two hundred years.'

There were times when he did seem to share her intuition, to catch directly the sharp glitter of her meaning. 'Ah, but darling,' he said, 'perhaps that's where I belong. I'm dusty too,' he remarked, standing there with uncertain urbanity, with an uneasy smile, in his smart, his one good suit. 'And besides, I haven't a single reference.'

'You said you had resigned.'

'Well, it wasn't quite like that.'

'Don't I know it.' They stepped back to let a trolley pass. 'I'm damned hungry,' he said. 'Could you lend me five bob?'

'You're coming with me,' she repeated. 'Erik will give you a job. Have you got your passport?'

'It's at my digs.'

'We'll fetch it.' The lights of an incoming train beat against his face, and she could watch with hard decided tenderness his hesitation and his fear. She was certain that if he had not been hungry, if he had not been without five shillings in his pocket, he would have refused. For he was right when he remarked that he was dusty too: the grit of London lay under his eyes, he was at home in this swirl of smoke and steam, at the marble-topped tables, chaffing in front of the beer handles, he was at home in the one-night hotels, in the basement offices, among the small crooked flotations of transient businesses, jovial among the share pushers. She thought: If I had not met Erik, I should have been as dusty too. 'We'll find a taxi,' she said.

He stared through the window at the bicycle shops of the Euston Road; in the electric lights behind the motor

7

horns, behind the spokes and the tins of liquid rubber, autumn glimmered, lapsed into winter as the lights were put out and the bicycles were taken in for the night. 'Oh,' he sighed, 'it's good, isn't it?' Autumn was the few leaves drifted from God knows where upon the pavement by Warren Street tube, the lamplight on the wet asphalt, the gleam of cheap port in the glasses held by old women in the Ladies' Bar. 'London,' he said, 'there's nothing like it.' He leant his face against the glass. 'Dash it all, Kate, I don't want to go.'

He had used the one phrase which told her the real extent of his emotion. 'Dash it all, Kate.' She remembered a dark barn and the moon behind the stacks and her brother with his school cap crumpled in his hands. They had as many memories in common as an old couple celebrating their thirtieth anniversary. 'You've got to go,' and she watched him out of sight before she made her own way back to her school, the waiting mistress, the two hours' questioning, and the reports.

'You've got to come.'

'Of course you know best,' Anthony said. 'You always have. I was just remembering that time we met in the barn.' And certainly, she thought with surprise, he sometimes has his intuitions too. 'I'd written to you that I was running away, and we met, do you remember, half-way between our schools? It was about two o'clock in the morning. You sent me back.'

'Wasn't I right?'

'Oh yes,' he said, 'of course you were right,' and turned towards her eyes so blank that she wondered whether he had heard her question. They were as blank as the end pages of a book hurriedly turned to hide something too tragic or too questionable on the last leaf.

8

'Here you are,' he said, 'welcome to my humble abode.' She winced at his mechanical jollity, which was not humble nor welcoming, but the recited first lesson in a salesman's school. When the landlady smiled at them and told him in a penetrating whisper that he would not be disturbed, she began to realise what life had done to him since she had seen him last.

'Have you got a shilling for the meter?'

'It's not worth while,' she said. 'We aren't going to stay. Where are your bags?'

'As a matter of fact I popped 'em yesterday.'

'It doesn't matter. We can buy you something on the way to the station.'

'The shops'll be closed.'

'Then you'll have to sleep in your clothes. Where's your passport?'

'In a drawer. I shan't be a moment. Take a seat on the bed, Kate.' Where she sat she could see on the table a cheap framed photograph: '*With love from Annette.*'

'Who's that, Tony?'

'Annette? She was a sweet kid. I think I'll take it with me.' He began to rip open the back of the frame.

'Leave her here. You'll find plenty like her in Stockholm.'

He stared at the small hard enamelled face. 'She was the goods, Kate.'

'Is this her scent on the pillow?'

'Oh no. No. That wouldn't be hers. She hasn't been here for a long time now. I haven't had any money, and the kid's got to live. God knows where she is now. She's left her digs. I tried there yesterday.'

'After you'd sold your bags?'

'Yes. But you know when you once lose sight of a girl

9

like that, she's gone. You never see her again. It's odd when you've known a girl so well, been fond of each other, seen her only a month ago, not to know where she is, whether she's alive or dead or dying.'

'Then that other's the scent?'

'Yes,' he said, 'that other's the scent.'

'She's old, isn't she?'

'She's over forty.'

'Plenty of money, I suppose?'

'Oh, she's rich enough,' Anthony said. He picked up the second photograph and laughed without much amusement. 'We're a pair, aren't we, you and Krogh and me and Maud.' She didn't answer, watching him stoop again to find his passport, noticing how broad he had become since she had seen him last. She remembered the waitresses staring over the dish-cloths, the silence which surrounded their talk. It seemed odd to her that he should need to buy a girl. But when he turned, his smile explained everything; he carried it always with him as a leper carried his bell; it was a perpetual warning that he was not to be trusted.

'Well. Here it is. But will he give me a job?'

'Yes.'

'I'm not so bright.'

'You needn't tell me,' she said, sounding for the first time the whole depth of her sad affection, 'what you are.'

'Kate,' he said, 'it sounds silly, but I'm a bit scared.' He dropped the passport on the bed and sat down. 'I don't want any more new faces. I've had enough of them.' She could see them crowding up behind his eyes: the men at the club, the men in liners, the men on polo ponies, the men behind glass doors. 'Kate,' he said, 'you'll stick to me?'

'Of course,' she said. There was nothing easier to promise. She could not rid herself of him. He was more than her brother; he was the ghost that warned her, look what you have escaped; he was all the experience she had missed. He was pain, because she had never felt pain except through him; for the same reason he was fear, despair, disgrace. He was everything except success.

'If only you could stay with me here.' 'Here' was the twin dials on the gas-meter, the dirty pane, the long-leaved plant, the paper fan in the empty fireplace; 'here' was the scented pillow, the familiar photographs, the pawned bags, the empty pockets, home.

She said, 'I can't leave Krogh's.'

'He'll give you a job in London.'

'No, he wouldn't. He needs me there.' And 'there' was the glassy cleanliness, the latest fashionable sculpture, the sound-proof floors and dictaphones and pewter ash-trays and Erik in his silent room listening to the reports from Warsaw, Amsterdam, Paris and Berlin.

'Well, I'll come. He's got the brass, hasn't he?'

'Oh, yes,' she said. 'He's got the brass.'

'And there'll be pickings for yours truly?'

'Yes, there'll be pickings.'

He laughed. He had forgotten already the new faces he feared. He put on his hat and looked in the mirror and adjusted the handkerchief in his breastpocket. 'What a pair we are.' She could have sung with joy, when he pulled her to her feet, because they were a pair again, if she had not been daunted at the sight of him in his suspect smartness, his depraved innocence, hopelessly unprepared in his old school tie.

'What is that tie?' she asked. 'Surely it's not——'

'No, no,' he said, flashing the truth at her so

unexpectedly that she was caught a victim to the charm she hated. 'I've promoted myself. It's Harrow.'

## [2]

The fellows asked me to have another whisky. They all wanted to hear what I'd seen. For weeks before they had scarcely spoken a word to me, said I was lucky not to be turned out of the club, for claiming a military rank, they told me, to which I wasn't entitled. The sun beat down on the pavement outside, and a beggar lay in a patch of shadow and licked his hands; I can't think to this day why he licked his hands. The captains brought me another drink and the majors drew up their chairs and the colonels told me to take my time. The generals weren't there, they were probably asleep in their offices, because it was about noon. They forgot I wasn't really a captain, we were all commercials together.

A fishing boat rocking on the swell with a yellow light a man's height upon the mast, and a man kneeling and pulling at a bundle of nets in the pale light, with the sea and the dark all round him and we passing all lit up and a gramophone playing.

I told the fellows at the club how I was on the pavement when the coolie threw the bomb. A cart had broken down and the Minister's car pulled up and the coolie threw the bomb, but of course, I hadn't seen it, I'd only heard the noise over the roofs and seen the screens tremble. I wanted to discover how many whiskies they'd pay for. I was tired of being left out of every bridge four; I didn't know where to turn for a little cash. So I said I was badly shaken and they paid for three whiskies and we played cards and I won over two pounds before Major Wilber came in, who knew I had not been there.

Smell of whisky from the smoking-room, touch of salt on the lips. The gramophone playing, new faces.

So I went on to Aden.

Skinning a rabbit among the gorse bushes on the common, I shut my eyes for a moment and the knife slipped up through a fold of skin and stabbed me under the eye. They told me over and over again that I ought to have cut downwards, as if I hadn't known it all the time, and they thought I would lose my sight on that side. I was frightened and Father was ill and Kate came. Pale-green dormitory walls and the cracked bell ringing for tea, my face bandaged and I listening to the feet on the stone stairs going down to tea. I could hear how many waited by the matron's room for eggs marked on the shell with their names in indelible pencil, and the cracked bell ringing again before the boot-boy put his hand on the clapper. And then silence, like heaven, and I was alone until Kate came.

The man ran along the roofs and they shot at him from the street and from the windows. He dodged behind the chimney-pots and slipped in the rain pools on the flat roofs. He kept both hands clapped to the seat of his trousers because he had torn them in escaping and the rain beat on his head. It was the first rain we had had, but I could tell from the sky and the temperature and the sweat on the backs of my hands that it would go on now for weeks.

'Kate,' I said, and she was there as I knew she would be there, and we were alone in the barn.

Many things there are to consider over thirty years, things seen and heard and lied about and loved, things

13

one has feared and admired and felt desire for, things abandoned with the sea gently lifting and the lightship dropping behind like a small station on the Underground, bright at night and empty, no one getting out and the train not stopping.

I hoped it was the engaged tone, but I knew it was the ringing tone, and I rang up four times from a box in the Circus, while the faces glared at me through the glass as they waited their turn, and I remembered three times to press Button B and get my money back, but the fourth time when I knew there was no one there I forgot. So someone got a free call, and now I could do with even that twopence in my pocket. I might toss someone heads or tails and win the price of a drink. But they are nearly all Swedes on board and foreigners aren't sportsmen and I can't speak the language.

New faces and the old faces lost, dead or sick or dying, and the To Let board outside the block. When I pushed the button no bell rang, and the light on the landing had been disconnected. The wall was covered with pencil notes: 'See you later', 'Off to the baker's', 'Leave the beer outside the door', 'Off for the week-end', 'No milk this morning'. There was hardly one patch of whitewash unwritten upon and the messages were all of them scratched out. Only one remained uncancelled, it looked months old, but it might have been new, for it said: 'Gone out. Be back at 12.30, dear', and I had written her a post-card saying that I would be coming at half-past twelve. So I waited, sitting there on the stone stairs for two hours, in front of the top flat and nobody came up.

Feet on the stone stairs, running, scrambling, pushing, up to the dormitory; Kate gone and the room full and the prefects turning out the lights. Not a moment of quiet even at night, for always someone talks in his sleep the other side of the wooden partition. I lay sweating gently unable to sleep, forgetting the pain under my eye, waiting for the thrown sponge, the rustle of curtains, the hand plucking at my bed-clothes, the giggles, the slap of bare feet on the wooden boards.

Old faces, faces hated, faces loved, alive or dead, sick or dying, a lot of junk in the brain after thirty years, the prow rising to the open sea, the lightship behind, and the gramophone playing.

Down the stone stairs with money in my pocket meant for her; thirty bob to the good because she was not there; once gone, lost, not to be seen again. Fill the room with film actress photos, tear the portraits out of *The Tatler:* 'Will you sign this for an unknown admirer? One shilling enclosed for packing and postage.' Whores in plenty in Hollywood, but no whore like my whore. Unhappiness always makes a man richer: thirty bob to the good and no one to visit.

I knew at once of course what it was about when they said, 'The Manager wants to see you.' I'd expected it for days, so every morning I put on my best bib and tucker and cleaned my teeth extra well. I've forgotten who it was who told me once I had a dazzling smile, not knowing the practice before the glass, the constant change of paste, the expensive dentists for invisible fillings. A man's got to look after his appearance the same as a woman. It's often his only chance. Maud, for example.

Nearer forty than thirty, blonde, a little overblown about the blouse. 'There are things a man won't do,' I said, 'and one is to take money from a woman,' so she respected me and gave me presents and I popped them

15

when I needed some ready. We met on the Underground. All the way from Earl's Court to Piccadilly, eyeing each other down the length of the carriage; I had a hole in my sock and couldn't cross my legs. Slow. Slow approach. Meeting at last on the moving stair.

How quick with Annette. Ringing the bell of the flat, expecting another girl; then she opened the door and I thought, 'She's the goods.'

When I opened the door he pretended to be writing; it's a stale trick to make you feel inferior and it never fails to work. 'Oh, Mr Farrant,' he said, 'I want to ask you about a complaint I received from the shippers. I have no doubt that you can explain.' Well, if he hadn't any doubt, I had.

And so on to Bangkok.

Spit and hiss of water, the gramophone quiet. The lights out along the deck, nobody about.

Lectures, my God, how many lectures in a man's life? Only Kate, I think, never; simply said do this and that, never nagged. And Annette, content and quiet and affectionate behind the drawn blinds in the half-light. Maud lecturing, Father lecturing, managers lecturing. God in Heaven, I'm Anthony Farrant, as good as they are. I can add up two columns of figures in my head, multiply by three, take away the number I first thought of. Even the managers know that. 'Brilliant,' they say at first, 'a quite brilliant piece of work, Mr Farrant,' because I've put money in their pockets; it's only later when I put a little in my own that they ask me to explain.

Selling tea. Three hundred spoilt sacks they could do nothing with and shooting in the streets. I bought the lot from them for a song and sold them again at the full rate. There's always money to be picked up in a revolution.

But they looked at me askance after that. They never trusted me again.

Voices whispering in the dormitory: 'Someone has left a vest in the changing-room. Honour of the House', running the gauntlet of the knotted towels, noise over the roof-tops, paper screens trembling, spoilt tea, shooting in the streets, 'honour of the firm'.

And so on to Aden.

Everybody in bed; the night cold and the water invisible under the pale knife-edge of foam. The man in the lower bunk talking all night in a language I do not understand, and the new day grey and windy, the canvas of the deck chairs flapping, and very few people at breakfast; an unshaven chin, the dismal jocularity of stewards, a girl with hair like Greta Garbo's walking alone, a smell of oil and a long time till lunch, Kate thinking of Krogh.

How do I know that she is thinking of Krogh? How did I know that she would be waiting for me in the barn?

She said: 'We'll spend the night in Gothenburg,' and I knew she was worried.

I pretended I wanted to go to the lavatory and slipped out. I had my clothes on under my dressing-gown, carried my shoes and socks hidden, wore bedroom slippers. The cold of the stone steps crept through the torn sole. I left the dressing-gown in the lavatory and listened at the housemaster's door. It was all so easy. He had gone to supper and his window had no bars. But Kate sent me back and I trusted her: frost on the road and the smell of nipped leaves and a clear sky and I happy with everything behind; the hard ruts in the by-road and the noisy twigs snapping underfoot and the lamps of motorists on the main road and I miserable with everything the same as before.

Thinking of Krogh. 'Use Krogh's. Krogh's are cheapest and best.' That was ten years ago, no, fifteen years ago, twenty years ago, shopping with the nurse at the general stores, stooping in the doorway under the baskets, brushing against the tins of weedkiller, examining the mowing machines, while my nurse bought Krogh's. Now they are not the cheapest and the best. They are the only. Krogh's in France, in Germany, in Italy, in Poland, Krogh's everywhere. 'Buy Krogh's' has a different meaning now: ten per cent and rising daily.

And I might have been as famous and as rich as Krogh if I had been trusted as Krogh has been trusted, if I had been lent capital; they gave me a five-pound note and expected me to be grateful. There was a fortune in every one of my schemes, if they had trusted me. Could Krogh have sold a hundred bags of spoilt tea?

But I've never been trusted.

When Wilber came in, there were no more free whiskies from the fellows there; I was drummed out of that club; and so on to Colombo. Grey sea, the telegrams home, the bandit sheltering behind the chimney-pot, escape from school after the cracked bell had gone lights out, shippers' complaints, and the sound of the bomb rattling behind the roofs; a hundred bags of spoilt tea, the little Chinese officer in gold-rimmed glasses smoking Woodbines, the green dormitory walls and the grey sea and the canvas chairs flapping, Kate thinking of Krogh—Krogh like God Almighty in every home; impossible in the smallest cottage to do without Krogh; Krogh in England, in Europe, in Asia, but Krogh, like Almighty God, only a bloody man.

Kate heard Anthony's voice long before she was able to pick out his table. She listened with jealousy, affection, an irritated admiration, to the cheerful plausible tones. So he had found friends already, she thought: two hours alone in Gothenburg and he had found friends. It was an enviable and a shameless trait.

At first she had thought him a little daunted by the new northern country for which none of his tropic experiences could have prepared him. He had walked silently under the tall grey formal houses, beside the neat canals; when she registered her luggage at the station she watched him look askance at the beds of flowers behind the buffers. In the streets every lamp-post, every electric standard bore its bouquet like a *prima donna*. The air was liquid grey.

But he was only summing-up; he had been in more ports than she could count. When she said, 'I'll leave you now till lunch,' and gave him money and described the restaurant where she would meet him, he nodded abstractedly and immediately straightening the fallacious Harrow tie, with cocked chin and flat broad back, he was off and away, striding down the first street; he could have had no idea where it led to.

Apparently it had led to friends: he probably expected that. He had come to terms already with the new country.

'And then the bomb exploded,' he was saying. 'The coolie simply dropped it at his own feet. They picked him up in bits all over the city. My voice had frightened him.'

19

Kate came slowly up the steps to the terrace. The tables were stacked in the garden, and on a little stage opposite the terrace a man swept wet leaves off the boards. A big drum lay at the back with a rent in its skin.

'And the Minister?' a girl's voice said.

'Not a scratch.'

Anthony leant an elbow on the terrace rail; he had never looked better; he positively bloomed above a world falling away to winter. Seen across the restaurant floor he might have been a schoolboy in his teens. Three tourists hung upon his words; their chairs were pushed back from the table, their glasses empty, an elderly man and an elderly woman and a girl. The ravaged plate of *smörgåsbord*, the crumbs on four plates, told her that lunch was over.

'Why, here's my sister,' Anthony said. She was five minutes early; some easy adventurer's phrase withered on his lips as he saw her. Even his courtesy momentarily deserted him, so that while the three strangers rose he remained seated. He was screened from her by out-stretched hands and polite expressions and shifted chairs. 'Mr Farrant's been kindly showing us Gothenburg,' the elderly woman said.

Kate looked through them at his face, sullen and defensive and momentarily robbed of charm.

'He's taken us all over the port,' the old man said, 'he's shown us the warehouses.'

'And he's just been telling us,' the girl said, 'how he got that scar.'

'We thought,' the elderly woman said, 'that it might have been the war.' They were nervous and shy; they seemed anxious to assure her that they had no designs on her brother; they shielded him from the reproach that he had allowed himself to be picked up by strangers.

'But a revolution's much more exciting,' the girl said. Kate watched her closely, and a thought – Poor thing, she's fallen for him – touched her with pity, even while she assembled as evidence against her the large unintelligent eyes, the small damp badly tinted mouth, the thin shoulders, the patch of dried powder on the neck. She remembered Annette, and Maud swelling in a frame too small for her, the cheap scent on the pillow: he's always liked them common.

'They ought to have given him a decoration,' the girl said, 'saving the Minister's life like that.'

Kate smiled at Anthony shifting on his chair. 'But didn't he tell you? He's too modest. They gave him the Order of the Celestial Peacock Second Class.'

They took it with perfect gravity; it even hastened their departure. They were obviously unwilling to waste his time; it might ruin their chances of a further meeting. They hoped for one in Stockholm. Were they staying there long? the woman asked.

Kate said: 'We live there.'

'Ah,' the man said. He hesitated: 'We come from Coventry.' He was one of those men who are scrupulously fair in sharing information. He screwed his eyes up at her as if he were watching the movement of a delicate laboratory balance: another milligram was needed. 'Our name's Davidge.' His wife, a little behind him, nodded approval: the balance was correct. She sighed with relief at the delicate adjustment; she was able now to think of other things, to correct the set of her gown in the large mirror on the back wall, to tuck away a stray grey hair, to smooth her gloves, to hint with delicacy that they would soon be gone.

21

'Are you on a tour?' Kate asked, and noticed how the girl who shared none of their delicacies, who seemed a deliberate reversal of all the gentility they represented, protesting with badly chosen lipstick against their dim colours, their careful distinctions, had a sensibility which recognised her hostility, while they were aware only of her courtesy.

'An individual tour,' Mrs Davidge gently defined.

'I'm sure,' Kate said, with deliberate vagueness, 'we shall see you again.'

But the girl lingered. While her parents stepped with an exaggerated elderly care down into the little brown garden between the terrace and the split drum, she remained obstinately planted. She was like a small wood image, brightly painted, set to some vulgar use among the dining-tables; one looked for the ash-tray and the cigarette stumps.

'I can manage Tuesday,' she said.

'That's fine,' Anthony said, fiddling with a fork. Kate was sorry for her, for her crude innocence, but it didn't suit her purpose to have Anthony reminded of what he'd been saved from; the girl represented at that moment the lights behind the bicycles, the leaves on Warren Street pavement, the port in the Ladies' Bar.

'So you can manage Tuesday,' Kate said, watching the girl rejoin her parents among the stacked chairs. 'And you saved the Minister's life.'

'One's got to spin a yarn,' Anthony said, 'and they paid for lunch.'

'I paid for your breakfast, but I never noticed you spinning anything for me.'

'Ah, Kate,' he said, 'you know all my stories. Haven't I always written——?'

'No,' Kate said, 'you've written very seldom. Telegrams for Father; picture postcards; how many picture postcards; picture postcards from Siam, from China, from India; I don't remember any letters.'

He grinned. 'I must have forgotten to post them. Why, I remember a long letter I wrote to congratulate you when you got your job at Krogh's.'

'A picture postcard.'

'And when Father died.'

'A telegram.'

'Well, it cost more. I'd never spare expense for you, Kate.' He became serious. 'Poor thing, you've had no lunch. It was a shame to start without you, but they invited me. It was a chance of saving money.'

'Tony,' Kate said, 'if you weren't my brother . . . .' She let the sentence drift away over the crumbs and the soiled glasses unfinished, meaningless. What was the good?

'You'd be gone on me,' Anthony said, turning on her the same glance as he turned, she knew, on every waitress, calculated interest, calculated childishness, a charm of which every ingredient had been tested and stored for further use. The thought came to her: If I could put back time, if I could twist this ring Krogh gave me and abolish all this place, the big drum and the dropping leaves and that face of mine in the mirror there, it would be dark now and a wind outside and the smell of manure and he with his cap in his hand, and I'd say: 'Don't go back. Never mind what people say. Don't go back,' and nothing would be the same.

'She's a sweet kid,' Anthony said. 'She swallowed everything I said. Why, I could have sold her any pup I wanted to,' and she could watch him progressing in

23

thought up innumerable suburban pavements, ringing at doors, being sent round to the back. She was momentarily with him, watching the straightening of the Harrow tie, the adjusted charm, the adjusted hope, trying to distinguish what was courage, what was simply the conviction that something would always turn up.

And I have turned up.

The thought of what they could do together drove out her jealousy and fear. He was clever, no one had ever denied that he was clever, and she was stable, no one had ever dreamed of denying her stability. She had grip, she held on. Five years in the dingy counting-house in Leather Lane, then Krogh's, and later Krogh. 'I want a drink,' she said, 'I'm dry,' and when it came, 'To our partnership,' she said.

'You do put it down, Kate,' Anthony said, signalling to the waiter, running his tongue along his lips. He disapproved, he didn't believe in girls drinking, he was full of the conventions of a generation older than himself. Of course one drank oneself, one fornicated, but one didn't lie with a friend's sister, and 'decent' girls were never squiffy. The two great standards, one for the men, another for the women, were the gate-posts of his brain. She could see his lips tingling with the maxims of all the majors whom he had known lay down the moral law before smoking-room fires.

'Dear Tony,' she said, 'I love you.' He wriggled uncomfortably before her complete comprehension.

'All the same,' he said, 'it's wrong to drink on an empty stomach.' It was nearly admirable the way in which misfortune had never modified his slight pomposity; it would have been expelled from a man more self-conscious, less resilient, by the sense of inferiority;

24

in him disaster had only strengthened it. His shabbiest days, she could guess, had not been his least pompous; she imagined him preaching morality to Annette, abstinence to Maud. A frayed sleeve would only drive him to a Guards' tie.

She had been in Stockholm when their father died, but Anthony returning from Aden had spent his last pound on an aeroplane journey from Marseilles. He had behaved with a pomposity and a propriety that would have been applauded in every club from which he had been excluded. She remembered his telegram: 'Our father passed away quietly in his sleep on Saturday,' an orgy of expenditure on the magnificently trite phrase, followed by a series of economies and niceties of punctuation which left the rest of the telegram incomprehensible. 'Regret Case Mabel Damaged Transit Semi-Colon Discharged Servant Trouble Head Dash Gould-smith Affirmative.' He had told his father, she learnt later, that he had resigned, leaning over the bedpost, grinning and breezy and optimistic to the patient (the wiped tear for the nurse, the black suit for relations, the last clean collar for the priest and the solicitor). The human voice at last took up the theme so long confined to telegrams and postcards; he was home again and he had resigned; honour had really been involved, but he couldn't explain that.

'A penny for your thoughts,' said Anthony, and she saw that already he had recovered his poise and stood, as it were, on another doorstep full of hope and zest and the desire to exhibit his salesmanship.

'I was thinking,' Kate said, 'of Father.'

'Ah, Father!' Anthony said. 'How glad he would have been to see us here together.'

It was true. He had always regretted Anthony's long periods abroad; a brother, he believed, was a sister's natural protector until she married. And there was this, Kate thought, to be said for the old man: Anthony's ability to get out of a dangerous predicament had never failed. In a dive or a police court one could ask for no better guide or counsellor; he would be quite certain to know by instinct the back door or the right man to bribe. Nobody but Anthony would have come unscathed through so many shabby adventures.

Already he was looking round, measuring his surroundings, bright and eager and hopeful. 'What can one do in this place at night?' he asked. He added, with a deceit which took her unprepared: 'I mean, of course, flickers, music-hall. One's got to be so careful in a port,' and he gazed with sudden boredom at the small lonely garden, the abandoned stage, the broken drum, the leaves drifting, the brush sweeping them away. Then he turned on her his expression of blank innocence, polished and prepared.

'Oh, can't you be yourself?' Kate said. Tears of loneliness pricked behind the lids. She missed him painfully as he built up between them this thin façade of a fake respectability as she had missed him when he first went abroad: the cabin trunk on top of a cab, in the crammed tiny hall the suitcase rebelling against the locks, the trail of a pyjama cord across the carpet; good-bye between the umbrella-stand and the stained glass. At any rate then there was no deceit; they were as open to each other as they had been five years before in the darkness of the barn; he was white and frightened and ready to weep, as she told him that he must go, that he would miss his train, and kissed him quickly and felt her

26

brain divided as she watched him pull at the stiff cab door, half her body go with him drearily vibrating on the black polished cushions. But at least she believed that he would write, not anticipating the picture postcards, the 'This is a pretty place', the 'We bathed here', the 'My window marked with a cross', the growing bonhomie, the strange tricks of phrase protectively adopted, until at last there came the sense that he was irrevocably one of them, one of the seedy adventurers who had not courage enough for gaol. And now, she thought, raising her compact to hide her hopelessness, even a postcard would bring him nearer.

'Can't you be yourself?' she repeated, wondering what trick she might have learned from Annette or Mabel to surprise his sincerity. She said: 'Tonight we'll drink a lot and go to Liseberg.'

He winced at the suggestion. 'What sort of a place——?'

'Oh,' Kate said, 'it's quite respectable. Quite family. You can dance a bit or shoot a bit or jolt your liver on a switchback. I've no doubt it's dull compared with what you've seen, but if we drink first . . . .'

'You know,' Anthony said, 'we haven't had a serious talk yet.'

'What about?'

'Oh, Things,' Anthony said, 'Things. If you aren't going to have any lunch, let's find somewhere quiet,' and he raked the restaurant, the empty schnaps-glasses, the crumby plates, with austere disapproval. Nor, he declared, when she suggested that he might show the port to her as he had shown it to Miss Davidge, was it nearly quiet enough.

'How you keep on about that girl,' he protested, 'you

27

might be jealous the way you speak. Can't we get out of town for a little? Isn't there a park?'

For half an hour they sat on a wooden seat beside a pond watching the water-fowl, and boys pushed bicycles with brightly painted spokes up-hill away from Gothenburg; in the block of flats at the edge of the park the lights came out, one by one, brilliant and small and defined like matches struck in a cinema. A thin scum covered the water, and as the fowl pushed their way across, a few leaves clung to their flanks.

'You've brought me here,' Anthony said, 'and now. . . .' He was suddenly cold and hostile and discomposed. 'There's one thing I won't do. I won't sponge. I've never sponged.'

'Erik will give you a job.'

'You know I can't speak Swedish.'

'Swedish is not important in Krogh's.'

'Kate,' Anthony said, 'I'd be lost in a business like that. I'm used to something smaller. Listen. All the way across on the boat I was thinking, I'd be no good to Krogh. I wouldn't have a chance to show. . . .' A leaf circled down, touched his shoulder, fell between them on the seat.

'There,' Anthony said. 'Gold. You see, it missed me.'

'It's still green. It means nothing. Look,' Kate lifted the leaf and held it near to him in the darkening air, 'it's been nipped off. A squirrel. Or some bird.'

'Listen, Kate, when I was down there in the port this morning, I saw a notice. In English. They want a man with experience, an Englishman, at one of the warehouses. Book-keeping.'

'Yes, you could do that, I suppose,' Kate said.

'I've kept more books than I can count.'

'There wouldn't be a future.'

She had asked him, 'Be yourself;' now when she could hardly see his face in the quick cold dark, when she shivered and remembered, He has no coat, what has he done with his overcoat? between the thought of pawn-shops and old-clothes dealers, he came to her with complete sincerity, like a friend one has almost forgotten, catching at the sleeve. 'I haven't a future, Kate.'

He was quiet, he was sincere, he was completely himself, he was all that she had asked him to be, and it amazed her even while she tried to grasp the opportunity. She had known him to be unreliable, deceitful in small ways, hopeless with money, but she had not realised his self-knowledge.

He repeated, 'You know that as well as I do, Kate. I haven't a future.'

The water-fowl came up out of the water, feathers blown out against the cold. Distended like small brown footballs, they rolled up the slope of grass and disappeared, one after the other, flattening the leaves under their webbed feet.

'You have, you have,' she said; her fear of proving inadequate to her opportunity conflicted with her gladness that at last, as so many years ago, they were face to face without reserve. 'Trust me.' She thought: I have him now, this is Anthony, I must not let him go, but instead of the right word, she knew again a division of the brain and heart, so that it was she sitting there without a coat, without a future, without a friend, in a Harrow tie and an air. She would have taken him in her arms if he had not spoken.

'Of course,' he said, 'the luck may turn. Something may turn up.' She recognised at once that the moment had passed. He was as far away from her as ever he had been in the Shanghai Club, on the Aden golf-course. It had been less self-knowledge than a temporary break in the cloud of his self-deception. She had thought he needed help from her, but he needed only a breeze from the right quarter, a thought, a particular memory. 'Did I ever tell you about the spoilt tea?'

'I can't remember. It's cold. Let's go. About that warehouse. . . .'

But now the wind was set fair. He was ready to admit himself wrong, even to the extent of admitting that after all he had a future. 'I can see,' he said, 'you don't like the idea.' He laughed with an unbelievable freedom from care. 'I'll give your friend Krogh a trial.' He was like a man who has narrowly escaped a great danger. Relief made him hilarious, and hilarity made him the best of company.

And so he remained throughout the evening. He was tossed from one extreme to another; she had thought herself lucky to catch him in his moment of depression and truth, but it was a pleasure of another kind to catch him at his most joyous and his most false. He told her stories which began with a rather pallid veracity, but were soon as coloured as any he could possibly have told Maud or Annette or the Davidge girl.

'But I wrote to you about the General Manager's Fiat?'

'No, no,' Kate said, 'there was nothing about a Fiat on any picture postcard.' After two schnaps she was almost ready to believe what he told her. She warmed to him. She put her hand on his and said, 'It's good to have you here, Tony. Go on.' But before he could speak, she had missed his ring (the signet solemnly presented to each of them on the twenty-first birthday, or rather in his case sent out to him, she could not remember where, by registered post, 'Care of the club').

'What have you done with your ring? Didn't you ever get the ring?'

She could see how he measured her mood, calculated how much he could tell her. Is the evening going to be a failure after all, she wondered? I must break myself, oh, I must break myself quickly of this habit of asking questions. But after so many years of separation they left her tongue before she knew.

'Never mind,' she said, 'go on. Tell me about the car, the manager's car.'

Anthony said slowly, putting his left hand over hers, with a protective patronising gesture, bland and candid, 'But I should like to tell you about that ring. It's a long story, but it's interesting. Old girl, you just can't imagine what strange spots that ring has led me to.'

'No, no,' she said, 'don't tell me that. Tell me about the car. But first let's move on, we can't get another schnaps here.' It amused her to guide him through the intricacies of the licensing laws, to get a little drunk on schnaps, in spite of the regulations (two for a man, one for a woman).

'And now,' he said, 'Liseberg.'

After the canal, the rustle of water at the edge of the grass banks, the whisper of men and women sitting on benches in the dark, the suburban road with no one passing, a limping procession of sounds came round the corners; not music, but as if a tuner were touching the keys of a piano, one after the other, in no particular order in a house a long way away. Above the house-tops a succession of towers was drawn sketchily in white lights; the notes came together as a tune fretting the memory, became through the high-arched entrance the blast of a remembered rhythm (the Foreign Secretary in a high stiff collar replied with extreme formality to her *skål*, while Krogh trod across the terrace from the lavatory, bowing to this side, bowing to that, and the couples danced beyond the glass doors, jingling and twinkling like chandeliers).

'Come along, old girl,' Anthony said, 'let's shake a leg.' The more he drank, the further back he plunged in time. His slang began the evening bright and hollow with the immediate post-war years, but soon it dripped with the mud of trenches, culled from the tongues of ex-officers gossiping under the punkas of zero hour and the Victoria Palace, of the leave-trains and the Bing Boys.

A rocket spat and flared and failed to burst in the middle air, going damply out and the stick falling; in a square bounded by the stone pillars of dance-halls and restaurants an emerald fountain played into a wide shallow emerald pool: up, up like the spire of a tropical plant under a sky cold and deep and cloudless, down again in a green lustre, splashing from pool to paving, turning silver at the margin. An empty switchback shot above the roofs and out of sight, whining like a spent record. In the booths beyond ragged firing-squads shot off their pieces.

'This way. We'll go this way.'

A pirate ship floated on a still lake flecked with ciga-rette-cartons. A flower-lined path led in spirals to a little platform where two men in white overalls played chess against all comers at half a crown a game. Wherever you moved, through pink or green courtyards, through carefully contrived darknesses, you heard, beneath the music and the firing, the sizzling of the great concealed lights and saw the moths flock past to shrivel against the burning concave glasses.

Up into the light, down into the dark the switchback car; in an obscure booth a living fountain with pale-green skin and turban, water spurting out of scarlet stigmata on palms and feet; the cells of fat women, fortune-tellers, lion-tamers; the moths trooping by, like flakes of ash after a fire, going in one direction, not drawn from their course by the dim globes burning in the smaller booths.

Up above the roofs the switchback car; a rocket burst in mid-air, crowding the darkness with falling yellow fragments; the ragged squad loaded and fired.

'You are too drunk to dance,' Kate said.

'Listen,' Anthony said, 'one more drink and I'll take on the world at anything you like. Throwing rings. You've never seen me throw rings.'

Coloured ping-pong balls danced up and down on a column of water.

'Would you like a doll?' Anthony said, 'or a glass vase? I'll get you anything you like to name. What do I have to do, anyway?'

'Come along and throw a ring. You know you can't shoot. You get nothing unless you hit five balls in five shots. You never could hit a target when you were at school.'

'I've learned a thing or two since then.' He picked up one of the pistols which lay on the counter of the booth and tried to judge the sights. 'Be a sport, Kate,' he implored her, 'and pay for me.' He was excited, he felt the weight, he swung it in his hand. 'You know, Kate,' he said, 'I'd like a job with guns. Instructor to a school or something of the sort.'

'But, Tony,' she protested, 'you've never been able to hit a thing.' She opened her bag, but before she could find her money, he had fired. She looked up and saw a yellow ball stagger on the pinnacle of water.

'What luck,' she cried. He shook his head, too serious to speak, reloaded with a sharp feathered pellet, sighted quickly, swinging the pistol down to the level of his eyes, and fired. She knew before the ball dropped that he would hit it; she was attending perhaps the only performance at which he was supremely skilful, shooting at a fair. She did not see the balls struck; she watched his face, grave, intent, curiously responsible; his hands broad with bitten nails suddenly became like a nurse's, capable and gentle. He tucked a hideous blue vase under his arm and began again.

'Tony,' she said, 'what are you going to do with it?' as he laid a toy tiger at his feet. He paused in the act of opening the breech and frowned. 'What, what did you say?'

'This vase and tiger. What will you do with them? For God's sake, don't win any more prizes, Tony. Come and have a drink.'

He shook his head slowly; it was a long time before he realised what she meant; his eyes were continually straying back to the balls dancing in the fountain. 'A vase,' he said, 'it's always useful, isn't it? For flowers and things.'

'But the tiger, Tony?'

'It's not a bad tiger.' He wouldn't look at it, pressing the pellets into place. 'If you don't want it,' he said, 'I'll give it away.' He fired and loaded, fired and loaded while the balls cracked and dropped and a small crowd gathered behind. 'I'll give it to that girl on Tuesday,' he said, and sighed and pointed to a green tin cigarette-case marked with the initial 'A' and put it in his pocket and walked away with the vase under one arm and the tiger under the other. Kate had to run to catch him up.

'Where are you going?' she called behind him, and felt her brain stabbed with his home-sickness when he replied, 'Oh, Kate, I'd never get tired of doing that,' as he walked on hopelessly between the arc-lights. He said, 'One time, on Bank Holiday . . . I was never at home again on Bank Holiday.'

'What was the girl's name?'

'I've forgotten.'

She put her hand under his arm and the vase slipped and fell and lay in blue ugly fragments at their feet, like a broken bottle to mark the end of a night's drinking.

'Never mind,' he said gently, pulling her closer to his side, 'there's still the tiger.'

# PART II

## [1]

The bronze doors slid apart, and Krogh was in the circular courtyard, Krogh was surrounded by Krogh's. The cold clear afternoon sky roofed in the cube of glass and steel. The whole lower floors one room deep were exposed to him; he could see the accountants working on the ground floor, the glass flashing primrose before the electric fires. He noticed at once that the fountain was completed; the green shape worried him as he was not often worried; it accused him of cowardice. He had pandered to a fashion he did not understand; he would have much preferred to set in the fountain a marble goddess, a naked child, a nymph with concealing hands. He paused to examine the stone; no instinct told him whether it was good art or bad art; he did not understand. He was uneasy, but he did not show his uneasiness. His high bald face, like a roll of newspaper, showed at a distance only bold headlines; the smaller type, the little subtleties, obscure fears, were invisible.

He grew aware of being observed; he was watched through the glass by an accountant over his machine, by a director from his chromium balcony, by a waitress drawing the black leather blinds in the staff restaurant. The day faded quickly above his head, the lights began to go on behind the curved glass walls while he dallied beside the green statuary.

Krogh mounted the steel steps to the double doors of Krogh's. When his foot touched the top step, the doors swung open. He bent going in; it was a habit he had never broken; six feet two in height with a flat

36

aggressive back, he had been forced for years to bow in the doorway of his bed-sitting-room, his small flat, his first works. Waiting for the lift he tried to dismiss the statuary from mind.

The lift was unattended; Krogh liked to be alone. He was enclosed now by a double thickness of glass, the glass wall of the lift, the glass wall of the building; the office, like an untrustworthy man, emphasised its transparency. Moving slowly and silently upwards to the top floor, Krogh could still see the fountain; it receded, grew smaller, flattened out; as the concealed lighting went on all round the court, the brutal shape cast a delicate shadow, like a drawing on porcelain on the circular polished paving. He thought, I am neglecting something, with obscure regret.

He entered his room and closed the door; the papers he had demanded were stacked neatly on a desk which was curved to follow the shape of the glass wall. He could see the reflection of the log fire in the window; a log shifted and fell and a spray of pale heatless sparks rose up the glass. It was the one room in the building unwarmed by electricity. The gentle beating of the flames was a form of companionship to Krogh in his sound-proof room, in his Arctic isolation. Night was dropping into the court below like streamers of ink into a grey luminous liquid. He wondered whether he had been mistaken about the fountain.

He went over to his desk and put a call through to one of his secretaries. 'When will Miss Farrant be back?'

A voice replied from a microphone, 'We expected her today, sir.'

He sat down at his desk and idly spread his palms. A man is born with what is marked on the left palm; on

37

the right palm is what he makes of life. He knew enough of the doubtful science to recognise Success, Long Life.

Success: he was quite certain that he deserved it, these five floors of steel and glass, the fountain splashing beneath the concealed lights, the dividends, the new flotations, the lists closed after twelve hours; it pleased him to think that no other man had contributed to this success. If he died tomorrow the company would be broken. The intricate network of subsidiary companies was knitted together by his personal credit. Honesty was a word which had never troubled him: a man was honest so long as his credit was good, and his credit, he could tell himself with pride, stood a point higher than the credit of the French Government. For years he had been able to borrow money at four per cent to lend to the French Government at five. That was honesty – something which could be measured in terms of figures. Only in the last three months had he felt his credit not so much shaken as almost imperceptibly contracted.

But he was not afraid. In a few weeks' time the factories in America would have righted that. He did not believe in God, but he believed implicitly in the lines on his hand. His palm told him that his life would be a long one, and he believed that his life would not outlast his company. If the company failed, he would never hesitate to kill himself. A man of his credit did not go to prison. Kreuger, lying shot in the Paris hotel, was his example. He questioned his courage for the final act as little as he questioned his honesty.

Again he was obscurely troubled by the idea that he had neglected something. The statue in the court came back to worry him. On this building he had employed men whom he had been told were the best architects, sculptors, interior decorators in Sweden. He looked from the curved tuiya wood desk to the glass walls, from the clock without numerals to the statuette between the windows of a pregnant woman. He understood nothing. These things gave him no pleasure. He had been forced to take everything on trust. It impressed itself on him for just so long as it took the clock to strike the half-hour that he had never been trained to enjoy.

And yet the evenings had somehow to be passed until he was tired enough to sleep. He opened a drawer in his desk and took out an envelope. He knew what it contained, the tickets for the opera that night, the next night, all the week. He was Krogh; his taste in music had to be displayed in Stockholm. But he sat always in a small wilderness of his own contriving, an empty seat on either hand. It at once advertised his presence and guarded his ignorance; for no importunate neighbour could ask him his opinion of the music, and if he slept a little it was unnoticed.

He called his secretary. 'If I am wanted,' he said, 'I shall be at the British Legation for tea. Put through any long-distance calls.'

'The Wall Street prices?'

'I'll be back in time.'

'Your chauffeur, Herr Krogh, has just rung up. The car has broken down.'

'All right. It doesn't matter. I'll walk.'

He rose and his coat caught an ash-tray and spun it to the floor. His own initials were exposed, E.K. The monogram had been designed by Sweden's leading artist. E.K. – the same initials endlessly repeated formed the design of the deep carpet he crossed to the door. E.K. in the waiting-rooms; E.K. in the board-room; E.K. in the restaurants; the building was studded with his initials. E.K. in electric lights over the doorway, over the fountain, over the gate of the court. The letters flashed at him like the lights of a semaphore conveying a message over the vast distances which separated him from other men. It was a message of admiration; watching the lights he quite forgot that they had been installed by his own orders. E.K. flickering across the cold plateau a tribute from his shareholders; it was as close as he got to a relationship.

'Well, Herr Krogh, it's finished at last.'

Krogh lowered his eyes; the reflected light died from them; they focused with detachment on the figure of the door-keeper who beamed and rubbed his hands in hopeless bonhomie.

'The statue, I mean, Herr Krogh, it's completed, finished.'

'And what do you think of it?'

'Well, Herr Krogh, it's a bit odd. I don't understand it. I heard Herr Laurin say——'

He was irritated that a man who because of his youth and inexperience owed everything to him – for who would have dreamed of appointing Laurin, pale ineffective Laurin, to a directorship if he had not? – should disturb him for a moment with his doubts.

'Understand this.' He watched the little man's exuberance wither. 'That statue is by Sweden's greatest sculptor. It's not the business of a door-keeper to understand it; it's his business to tell visitors that it's the work of, of——get the name from my secretary, but don't let me ever hear you suggesting to visitors that the group's difficult to understand. It's a work of art. Remember that.'

He moved across the courtyard, then turned again; the light of his monogram flickered through the falling water. 'If it wasn't a work of art, it wouldn't have been commissioned by Krogh's.'

Across the sky stretched the hillside lights of Djurgården, the restaurants, the high tower in Skansen, the turrets and the switchbacks in Tivoli. A thin blue mist crawled from the water, covering the motor-boats, creeping half-way to the riding lights of the steamers. An English cruising-liner lay opposite the Grand Hotel, its white paint glowing in the light of the street lamps, and through the cordage Krogh could see the tables laid, the waiters carrying flowers, the line of taxis on the North Strand. On the terrace of the palace a sentry passed and repassed, his bayonet caught the lamplight, the mist came up over the terrace to his feet. The damp air held the music from every quarter suspended, a skeleton of music above an autumnal decay.

On the North Bridge Krogh turned up the collar of his coat. The mist blew round him. The restaurant below the bridge was closed, the glass shelters ran with moisture, and a few potted palms pressed dying leaves towards the panes, the darkness, the moored steamers. Autumn was early; it peeled like smoke from the naked thighs of a statue. But officially it was summer still (Tivoli not yet closed), in spite of cold and wind and soaked clay and the umbrellas blowing upwards round the stone Gustavus. An old woman scurried by dragging a child, a girl student in a peaked cap stepped out of the way of a taxi creeping up the kerb, a man pushed a hot chestnut cart up the slope of the bridge towards him.

He could see the lights in the square balconied block where he had his flat on the Norr Mälarstrand. The breadth of Lake Mälaren divided him from the work-men's quarters on the other bank. From his drawing-room window he could watch the canal liners arriving from Gothenburg with their load of foreign passengers. They had passed the place where he was born, they emerged at dusk unobtrusively from the heart of Sweden, from the silver birch woods round Lake Vätten, the coloured wooden cottages, the small landing stages where the chickens pecked for worms in soil spread thinly over rock. Krogh, the internationalist, who had worked in factories all over America and France, who could speak English and German as well as he could speak Swedish, who had lent money to every European government, watched them of an evening sidle in to moor opposite the City Hall with a sense of something lost, neglected, stubbornly alive.

Krogh turned away from the waterside. The shops in the Fredsgatan were closed; there were few people about. It was too cold to walk, and Krogh looked round for a taxi. He saw a car up the narrow street on the right and paused at the corner. The trams shrieked across Tegelbacken, the windy whistle of a train came over the roofs. A car travelling too fast to be a taxi nearly took the pavement where Krogh stood, and was gone again among the trams and rails and lights in Tegelbacken, leaving behind an impression of recklessness, the sound of an explosion, a smell. In a side street a taxi-driver started his car and ambled down to the corner where Krogh stood. The explosion of the exhaust brought back Lake Vätten and the wild duck humming upwards from the reeds on heavy wings. He raised his oars and sat still while his father fired; he was hungry and his dinner depended on the shot. The rough bitter smell settled over the boat, and the bird staggered in the air as if cuffed by a great hand.

'Taxi, Herr Krogh.'

It might have been a shot, Krogh thought, if this were America, and he turned fiercely on the taxi-driver: 'How do you know my name?'

The man watched him with an air wooden and weather-worn. 'Who wouldn't know you, Herr Krogh? You aren't any different from your pictures.'

The bird sank with beating wings as if the air had grown too thin to support it. It settled and lay along the water. When they reached it, it was dead, its beak below the water, one wing submerged like an aeroplane broken and abandoned.

'Drive me to the British Legation,' Krogh said.

He lay back in the car and watched the faces swim up to the window through the mist, recede again. They flowed by in their safe and happy anonymity on the way to the switchbacks in Tivoli, the cheap seats in cinemas, to love in quiet rooms. He drew down the blinds and in his dark reverberating cage tried to think of numerals, reports, contracts.

A man in my position ought to have protection, he told himself, but police protection had to be paid for in questions. They would learn of the American monopoly which even his directors believed to be still in the stage of negotiation; they would learn too much of a great many things, and what the police knew one day the Press too often knew the next. It came home to him that he could not afford to be protected. Paying the driver off, he felt his isolation for the first time as a weakness.

He could hear the siren of a steamer on the lake and the heavy pounding of the engines. Voices came through

43

the mist muffled, the human heat damped down, like the
engines of a liner flooded and foundering.

Krogh was not a man who analysed his feelings; he
could only tell himself: 'On such and such an occasion
I was happy; now I am miserable.' Through the glass
door he could see the English man-servant treading
sedately down marble stairs.

He was happy in Chicago that year.

'Is the Minister in?'

'Certainly, Herr Krogh.'

Up the stairs at the servant's heels: he was happy in
Spain. His memories were quite unconcerned with
women. He thought: I was happy that year, and remembered the small machine no larger than his suitcase that
began to grind upon the table of his lodgings, how he
watched it all the evening, eating nothing, drinking
nothing, and how all night he lay on his back unable to
sleep, only able to repeat over and over again to himself:
'I was right. There's no serious friction.'

'Herr Erik Krogh.'

The room was full of women, and he experienced no
pleasure at the way they watched the door with curiosity
and furtive avidity (the richest man in Europe), their
faces old and unlined and pencilled in brilliant colours,
like the illumination of an ancient missal carefully
preserved under glass with the same page always turned
to visitors. The Minister attracted elderly women. He
was absorbed now by the little silver spirit-lamp under
the kettle (he always poured out the tea himself), and a

44

moment later, after a nod to Krogh, he was picking up slices of lemon in a pair of silver tweezers.

'This is a great day, Mr Krogh,' a hawk-like woman said to him. He had often met her at the Legation and believed that she was some relative of the Minister's, but her name eluded him.

'A great day?'

'The new book of poems.'

'Ah, the new book of poems.'

She took his arm and led him to a fragile Chippendale table in a corner of the room furthest from where the Minister poured out tea. All the room was Chippendale and silver; quite alien to Stockholm it was yet like a cultured foreigner who could speak the language fairly well and had imbibed many of the indigenous restraints and civilities, but not enough of them to put Krogh at his ease.

'I don't understand poetry,' he said reluctantly. He did not like to admit that there was anything he did not understand; he preferred to wait until he had overheard an expert's opinion which he might adopt as his own, but one glance at the room had told him that here he would wait in vain. The elderly women of the English colony twittered like starlings round the tea-table.

'The Minister will be so disappointed if you don't look.'

Krogh looked. A photograph of de Laszlo's portrait faced the title-page: the sleek silver hair, the rather prudish quizzing eyes netted by wrinkles, the small round appley cheeks. '*Viol and Vine.*'

'*Viol and Vine,*' Krogh said. 'What does that mean?'

'Why', said the hawk-faced woman, 'the viola da gamba, you know, and – and wine.'

45

'I always find English poetry very difficult,' Krogh said.

'But you must read a little of it.' She thrust the book into his hands and he obeyed her with the deep respect he reserved for foreign women, standing stiffly at attention with the book held at a little distance almost on the level of his eyes – 'To the Memory of Dowson' – and heard behind him the Minister's voice tinkling among the china.

'I who have shed with sorrowing the same roses,
   Drained desperately the tankard and despaired,
   Find, when I come to where your heart reposes,
   Ghosts of the sad street women we have shared——'

'No,' Krogh said, 'no. I don't understand it.' He was embarrassed. Correctness was the quality he most valued: the correctness of a machine, the correctness of a report. It was necessary at times, he thought coldly, for men to go with women as it was necessary at times not to disclose certain assets, to conceal the real value of certain shares, but there was a way of doing these things, and he watched with astonishment and suspicion the Minister nibbling the edge of a macaroon. A tiredness touched him at manners he could not understand and words he did not appreciate, and he thought for the second time that afternoon of his bed-sitting-room in Barcelona and the little model that ticked him into fortune: into great wealth, into great influence, into this weariness and this anxiety. He had entered the American market, he had to be prepared for American methods.

He thought of Chicago. He had been happy in Chicago, a Chicago quite untouched in those days by gang warfare. It was a long time ago, before Barcelona; he could not remember now why he had been happy. He could remember only these things: ice on the lake, a room in an apartment-house with a hammock bed, the bridge on which he worked and how one night when it snowed he had bought a hot dog at a street corner and ate it under an arch out of the wind's way. He supposed that he had friends, but he could not remember them, girls, but there was no face left him. He was a man then still unconditioned by his career.

Now he was hopelessly conditioned by it: even here in the light airy white-walled room, catching the Minister's eye over the spirit kettle. He knew that presently he would be suffering the usual cross-examination: did he see any hope at all for rubber? what were the chances of a boom in silver? Saõ Paulo coffee, Mexican railways, Rio improvements, and finally the thank-offering, the patronage: I told my broker to buy two hundred of your last flotation, as if Erik Krogh should be grateful to the author of *Viol and Vine* for the loan of two hundred pounds.

The voices came towards him in waves, breaking where the Minister stood above his Rockingham china, rippling towards him, dying out several yards away, receding in a rush, to rise and fall again over the tea-table. Even the hawk-faced woman had retired; no more than the others did she feel capable of talking financially; not all his patient vigils at the opera, his stately foxtrots with Kate in conspicuous places, his evening parties in the presence of collected editions, had served to convince them that he was a man who cared for the same things as themselves. And certainly, he thought, opening *Viol and Vine* again at random, they are right: I don't understand these things. If only Kate were here.

The man-servant opened the door and padded to his side. 'A long-distance call from Amsterdam, sir.' The phrase braced him, and he was momentarily happy, following the servant from the room, down the bright pictured passage to the Minister's study. He waited till the man had gone before he lifted the receiver. 'Hullo,' he said in English, 'hullo. Is that Hall?' A very small, very clear voice replied, scraped and cleaned and polished by the miles between: 'It's me, Mr Krogh.'

'I'm speaking from the British Legation. Tell me. What happened on the Exchange?'

'They are still dumping stock.'

'You bought, of course?'

'Yes, Mr Krogh.'

'You kept the price steady?'

'Yes, but . . .'

Yes, but – it was the same doubting voice, with the faint Cockney intonation, that had inserted itself into the bed-sitting-room at Barcelona. I tell you there is no serious friction. Yes, but—— He thought of Hall with irritation: the man had no quality but fidelity. It was odd to think how they had once spoken on such level terms that they had been Jim and Erik (not Hall and Mr Krogh), borrowing each other's boiler-suit, drinking together at the wine shop near the Bull Ring.

'Go on buying. Don't let the price fall more than half a point.'

'Yes, Mr Krogh, but——'

If he had been less trustworthy he would have been a director now and not Laurin. Hall and Kate. Kate and Hall. 'Listen,' Krogh said, 'the stock is nearly worthless. Much better for it to be in our hands. We don't want questions.' One had to explain things to Hall as to a child.

'If the I.G.S. can afford it . . .'

'Of course it can afford it. We have Rumania now, in a week or two America.'

'Money's close.'

'I can always get money.'

'Three-minute call up,' the exchange said.

'One moment,' Hall said, 'one thing more.'

'What's that?'

'Three-minute call up.'

'Dongen's . . .' Hall's voice was snipped in two like a piece of tin; the telephone whistled and moaned, a fading voice said: 'Une femme insensible,' and then silence and a gentle tapping at the door.

'Come in,' Krogh said.

'My dear fellow,' the Minister put his head round the door, entered on tiptoe, 'I don't want to disturb you, but I must snatch a moment away from these harpies. A disgusting woman has just chipped one of my cups. Oh dear, I see you are still 'phoning.'

'No,' Krogh said, 'I've finished,' and he hung up the receiver.

'What a life,' the Minister said, 'tied to the end of a 'phone. Money, figures, shares, morning till night. You weren't even at the opera yesterday, were you?'

'No,' Krogh said, 'I had meant to go, but something intervened.'

'You know,' the Minister said, 'the other day I took some of your last issue.'

'You could do worse,' Krogh said.

'Of course, I never really expected to be able to get any. I am so slow about these things. I was quite astonished, my dear fellow, to find that the lists were still open. After twelve hours.'

'Money is more close than it was.'

'Of course, I don't speculate. Really it's because I regard Krogh stock as gilt-edged . . .' He flitted, a grey worried phantom, from door to window, from window to bookcase. There was something on his mind.

'Not gilt-edged at ten per cent, Sir Ronald.'

'I know, I know, my dear fellow, but one trusts you. As a matter of fact, I've done – will you have a whisky? – something which a few years ago I might have thought rash, Krogh. I've put a lot of money, a damned lot of money for me, into this last flotation. It's sound, isn't it?'

'As sound as the parent company.'

'Yes, of course. It must seem odd my asking you like this, but I've never put so many eggs into one basket before. Damn it, Krogh, a man at my age should not have to worry about money. My father never had to worry. Consols were good enough for him. But today one can't even trust Government stocks. Labour governments, moratoriums, everything is so uncertain. Do you know, Krogh, in the last year two friends of mine have been ruined? Really ruined, I mean. Not a question of selling the car or the hunters, but left high and dry with about twenty pounds a week. It makes one think, Krogh, it makes one think.'

'You have a few Metallic Industries, haven't you?'

'Yes, a couple of thousand. They've been doing very well. Not Krogh stock, of course, my dear fellow, but still very fair.'

'If you will let me advise you,' Krogh said, 'I should get into touch with your broker first thing in the morning. I think they will pass a hundred and twenty-five shillings tomorrow, they may even reach a hundred and thirty, but tell him to sell as soon as they reach a hundred and twenty-five shillings. They'll drop to eighty shillings before the end of the week.'

'That's very good of you, very good of you indeed. Now if only your list hadn't closed, I really believe that a few more eggs in the basket——'

'Ring up my secretary, Miss Farrant, tomorrow. I think I might be able to spare you a thousand or so at par. For friendship's sake,' he said with an icy attempt at geniality. The Minister pattered up and down the room in excitement, swinging his monocle, talking of rubber, of Rio Improvements, recurring again and again to Metallic Industries; there was something fawn-like in his greed; it was robbed of half its grossness by his manner, childlike and inexpert. Krogh watched and listened with faint irritation; he stood stiffly against the bookcase which contained a few of Sir Ronald's own works: *Silverpoint* and *Once at the Mermaid* and *A Pilgrim in Thessaly*. Part of his stiffness was pride, part the dislike he could not disguise for the amateur in finance, and part was simply the gawkiness of the poor past: the wooden cottage and the nights on the lake, the wild geese and the Chicago bridge.

'When did you last see the Prince?' Sir Ronald asked.

'The Prince, the Prince,' Krogh said, 'oh, it was last week, I think.' A little chiming clock told out the hour. 'I must be off,' he said, 'the Wall Street prices will be through.' But after twenty years of prosperity he was still uneasy, still afraid of a slip in manner which would betray his peasant birth. He watched the other man with a hungry anxiety – whether to bow, or to shake hands, or simply to smile and nod; for the moment he was absorbed as deeply as over a question of finance.

51

'Then if I telephone——' the Minister said, whirling his monocle.

Suddenly, from out of what distant past Krogh could not say, a joke emerged of the crudest indecency; it came with the warmth of an ancient friendship renewed; it surprised him into a smile of rare humanity.

'What's the joke, my dear fellow?' the Minister asked with astonishment.

But the joke, like an old friend, could not be passed on: it belonged to a different, a harsher, shabbier, friendlier period. He was ashamed of it now, he could not introduce it to new friends, not to the Minister nor to the Prince nor even to Kate. Give it food secretly and money, and pack it away; it at least would never come back for blackmail; but it left him with a sense of loneliness, of dryness, as if his life now were narrower instead of infinitely enlarged. 'And when they got to the bawdy house . . .'

'It was nothing. A thought. I must be going.'

But the telephone rang. The Minister took up the receiver, then passed it to Krogh. 'Yours, my dear fellow. I'll leave you to it. Ring the bell when you've finished and Calloway will show you out.' He pressed Krogh's arm affectionately and tiptoed away. Once he put his head back to remind Krogh: 'I shall ring up tomorrow at eleven.'

'But it's impossible,' Krogh was saying. 'We've got informers in every department. What were they doing?' When he heard the Minister speak he said, 'I'll be back immediately. Get hold of Herr Laurin; he knows how to talk to these men.' He was impatient; he started for the door; he did not want to wait for Calloway, but in the passage the delicate sound of tea-cups, the sight of the gold-framed dignitaries restrained him. He stiffened and went back and rang the bell.

'Not a nice evening, sir,' Calloway said, pulling at his coat. 'More of that nasty mist we had yesterday.'

'A taxi, please.'

He watched Calloway standing in the middle of the road with two fingers raised and thought: he wanted to talk to me; even Calloway, I suppose, buys shares. Or perhaps he only wanted to gossip about the weather. How does one speak to people? How does one address a man with different interests, different standards? A troop of cavalry rode between him and Calloway; the bald man in the short black jacket was momentarily hidden by a moving grove of brass and plume. The officer saw Krogh on the steps of the Legation and nodded and waved his white-gloved hand; the horses tossed their heads and stepped lightly under the lamps, waving their chestnut tails. Everyone on the pavement stood still and watched them go by, smiling at the troopers, as if something young, lovely and irresponsible were passing. Only Calloway seemed unmoved, as he looked this way and that way and signalled for a taxi.

The monogram over the entrance to the court was unlit. The ring of small blackened bulbs reminded him of a tarnished steel brooch. He said sharply to the porter, 'Why are the lights here not turned on?'

'Herr Laurin sent a chit the other day. The lights were to be turned off after six.'

'Turn them on immediately,' Krogh said.

On his desk was a typed list of the Wall Street closing prices; outside the tape ticked like a sewing machine.

'Is Miss Farrant back?'

'Not yet, Herr Krogh.' Her substitute, thin, grey,

53

with a nervous tick in one eyelid, waited by his desk.

'This strike: when did news come of it?'

'Just after you left the office, Herr Krogh.'

'And it's called for tomorrow?'

'Tomorrow at noon.'

'At how many factories?'

'Three.'

'The leader?'

'Our informant at Nyköping reported Andersson . . .'

'Was it a dismissal,' Krogh asked, 'or a mere matter of wages? This must be settled tonight.'

'The report from Nyköping – it is there, Herr Krogh, by the flowers – suggests that there's American influence . . .'

'Of course,' Krogh said, 'that's obvious. But what's the excuse?'

'They have some story about the low wages you are offering in America; undercutting there, unemployment.'

'Why should they trouble about what happens in America?'

'This man Andersson passes as a Socialist . . .'

'You must get Herr Laurin here. Immediately. We can't waste time. He knows how to speak to these people.' It was the one thing Laurin was good for; he had promoted him to the Board for no other reason than this: there were times when one needed a man of no particular qualifications except amiability, the power of getting on with his fellow men.

'I tried to get Herr Laurin. But he's not in Stockholm.'

'He must return.'

'I rang up his house. He's ill in bed. Shall I ring up Herr Asplund, Herr Bergsten?'

'No,' Krogh said, 'they would be no good at all. If only Hall were here.'

'Should I send a car for Andersson? You could see him here yourself, Herr Krogh. It would only take ten minutes.'

'Your suggestions,' Krogh said sharply, 'are useless. I shall have to go to the man myself. Have the car ready in five minutes.'

He turned his eye to the Wall Street prices and tried to read. He had no idea of what to say to Andersson. E.K. on the ash-tray; E.K. on the carpet; E.K. flashing on above the fountain while he watched, above the gateway; he was surrounded by himself. It seemed to him that he had always been so surrounded. What could he say to Andersson? He could offer him money, but if he did not want money . . . He had to be friendly, he must reassure him, he must speak to him as man to man. It seemed a cruel injustice that Laurin, whom yesterday he had forgotten so easily, Laurin whom he despised, should find no difficulty in talking to these men. How would Laurin start? He had watched him often at his game. He made a joke and put them at their ease.

I too, Krogh thought, must make a joke. He tore a leaf off his memo pad and noted and underlined the word 'joke'. What joke? 'And when they came to the bawdy house. . . .' At the Minister's the remembrance had made him smile. It had come out of a secret past and carried with it the pathos and beauty attached to something from an unhappy youth that had never been quite forgotten. He found that he could no longer smile; he was touched by a sense of shame and melancholy at the thought that he must use even that story for the sake of his career; he could remember no others.

And then, he wondered, what next? What would

Laurin have said next? Perhaps he should inquire after the man's family. He rang for the secretary and presently noted on the same slip of paper, below the word 'joke', 'a wife, two sons, one in the factory, a daughter aged ten'. He wrote the words carefully, he underlined them; then he tore the paper up and dropped the pieces on the floor. One couldn't plan a human relationship like a graph of production. He tried to encourage himself: this is good for me, I have been too taken up by finance, I must enlarge my scope – the human side. He told himself: there must have been a time when I was at ease with other men, and tried to remember, but he could recall only the water dripping off the oars, his father silently waiting, the early light, the weary return.

The riveters on the bridge, he thought, they were my friends. But eating the hot dog out of the wind's way he had been alone, in the hammock bed alone (he couldn't remember one girl's face); only a bawdy joke remained of all that companionship.

But later there was Hall; we used to drink cheap red wine together near the Bull Ring and talk; once Hall wore a paper nose during a *festa*; we used to talk till midnight and after; of what? The machine, the friction, the expansion of metals were the only subjects he could remember.

'Your car, Herr Krogh.'

He picked the price list from his desk and pretended to read it. Why should I go?

| | | |
|---|---|---|
| Air Reduction | $94\frac{1}{2}$ | $94\frac{3}{4}$ |
| Alaska Juneau | $20\frac{1}{4}$ | $20\frac{1}{2}$ |
| Allied Chemical | 148 | 148 |
| American Woollen | $13\frac{1}{2}$ | 14 |
| Bethlehem Steel | $40\frac{1}{8}$ | $41\frac{3}{4}$ |

He took in very little of what he saw.

'Your car, Herr Krogh.'

'I heard you. I'm coming.'

| Chile Copper. | 14 | 14 |
| Colgate-Palmolive-Peet | 15½ | 16⅛ |
| Continental Can | 76 | 77 |

He turned to the end of the list. U.S. Industrial Alcohol, U.S. Leather, U.S. Rubber, U.S. Steel. He thought grimly, quite without amusement: I'm a shy man.

| Woolworth Co. | 49¾ | 50⅜ |
| Worthington Pump | 24½ | 25½ |
| Youngtown Sheet and Tube | 26½ | 27½ |

It no longer gave him any pleasure to think that soon a new company under his control would be quoted there, as already he was quoted in Stockholm, London, Amsterdam, Berlin, Paris, Warsaw and Brussels.

A joke, he thought, an inquiry after his family; ought I to offer him a cigar or a cigarette?

[3]

'There should be speed-boats,' Anthony said. 'Are you sure there aren't speed-boats?'

'Listen,' Kate said, 'is that the lift?' She could not disguise her anxiety; she had planned everything, her voice plainly told him, but with Krogh even she could not be certain of the result.

'What will you do,' Anthony asked, 'if he won't have me?'

'What will *you* do?'

'Oh,' Anthony said, 'I'll scrounge along. Why worry,

57

anyway?' He was like a native campaigner accustomed to travel vast distances with the lightest food; one didn't starve; one didn't die; in the kind of war he fought, survival was the greatest victory. Kate stood with strained pale face between Krogh's bookcase and Krogh's door, and he knew that she was afraid for him. He would have liked to explain to her the baselessness of her fear, but he lacked the right words. 'I've been on my uppers before,' he said, but the phrase even to himself failed to convey the idea of his success. This was victory: somehow to have existed. Happiness was an incidental enjoyment: the unexpected glass or the unexpected girl. It was perhaps the only lesson he had thoroughly learned at school, the lesson taught by the thirteen weeks of overcrowding, tedium and fear. Somehow time passed and the worst came to an end; there were breaks, there were moments of happiness: sickness, tea in the matron's room, punishments which carried with them a momentary popularity. One even after a time adapted oneself to circumstances, learned the secret of being tolerated, wore with conviction the common uniform.

But Kate he recognised was different: she had ambition, or perhaps the greater difference (for he had ambition too: his patent hand-warmer was a sign of it: the ambition to have money to spend) was that she had hope. Behind the bright bonhomie of his glance, behind the firm hand-clasp and the easy joke, lay a deep nihilism.

When he spoke again it was with a note of patronage as if she were a child for whom he was responsible, an imaginative child, a child with ideas. 'Don't worry, Kate, about what he'll say. Really, you know, it doesn't matter. We may as well amuse ourselves. Show me the place. Are those books his?'

'Yes.'

'Does he read them?'

'I don't think so.'

'And through here?'

'His bedroom.'

She was ill at ease; for the moment he felt himself older, more responsible, more knowledgeable than she. He was in his element, accustomed as he was to filling up time, better able than anyone to banish apprehensions. There had been a period, lying in cubicle beds, tossed in the narrow bunks of liners, when he had waited in fear of the hand plucking at the sheet, of the man in white drill from the office coming on board with the customs. But the years had trained him to be thankful for the moment, not to look forward. Now at this instant I am alone in the cubicle, now at this instant I am happy in my bunk, now for the moment only I am with Kate, with a friend. He pushed the door of the great sliding cupboard and disclosed a dense forest of suits.

'Like a second-hand clothes shop,' he said. 'Does he buy them wholesale?' He began to count them, but when he reached twenty he stopped. 'The cloth's good, but the pattern—— This red stripe's a bit loud, don't you think? And the ties. He seems to have plenty, but the colour——' They dangled row upon row like bright dead tropical fish. 'I wouldn't be seen in one of them,' Anthony said. 'The trouble is these foreigners don't know how to dress. Don't you help him choose?'

'No, he has a special buyer.'

'There's the job for me,' Anthony said. 'What a commission one could draw! But doesn't he see the cloth before it's bought?'

'He won't even have a fitting,' Kate said. 'He hasn't

59

had his measurements taken for two years. The suits come up in loads like this. Once every six months.'

'But why?'

'Of course he always bought ready-made clothes before he was rich. I don't suppose he ever went to a tailor. I believe he's afraid of them.' She hesitated. 'He's a shy man. He hasn't many interests.'

'What a jest,' Anthony said, 'to take him in hand. First of all we'd get rid of those ties.'

'No,' Kate said suddenly, 'no.' She stood in the doorway between the two rooms; she dissociated herself carefully from his easy intimate stroll of inspection. He noticed that her lips needed making-up; they were too pale; they did not match her dress. He thought: Is he one of those old boys who disapprove of paint and powder? What right has he to dictate to her? and continued in a quick rage of jealousy: 'We'd clean out all this stuff.'

'Leave him alone.'

His anger went as quickly as it came; he listened to her voice raised in Krogh's defence with melancholy as if someone he had known well many years ago had failed to recognise him in the street, had passed on through another world of consciousness in which they had no memories in common. Kate standing beside his bed while the cracked bell rang for tea, Kate in the crowded hall saying: 'You will miss the train. You must go now,' Kate borrowing money for him, Kate planning, Kate deciding: he wondered how far these memories were excluded by Krogh on this occasion, Krogh on that. He looked at the suits, at the ties, at the steel and the glass of the bed; he noticed for the first time her platinum watch, her expensive ear-studs.

'Oh,' he said, 'he'll do without me. I shall be asking for my fare home tomorrow.'

'He'll have to take you,' Kate said.

'Because you love him?'

'No,' she said, 'because I love you.'

'Dear thing,' Anthony said, 'I've never met anyone quite like you. Blood must be thicker than water after all. How you'd hate me if I weren't your brother.'

'It's not true,' she said.

'Think: the cheap lodgings, the pawnbrokers, the jobs I lose, the dreadful friends I'd bring home to share the convivial kipper. No, no, old thing, you've risen in the world. You don't know what's meant by love when you say you love me.' He laughed at her serious attention. 'It's just family affection, Kate darling.'

'No,' she said, 'I love you. I'll come back to London with you tomorrow if he won't give you a job.'

'I wouldn't want you,' he said. 'You'd quarrel with the landladies. What happens through that door? His study?'

'No,' Kate said, 'that's my bedroom.'

Anthony put out his hand quickly and set the coats swinging. 'My God,' he said, 'that red stripe. It hits you in the eye. Those ties. How anyone can wear such things! If I were a shareholder, I'd never trust a man like that.'

'And what about Erik,' she said, her anger struck like a match to flare and go out and burn her own fingers, 'do you expect him to trust a man in a fake tie who's been sacked from more jobs than I can count?'

'Stop it,' Anthony said, 'stop it.' He came close to her. 'If I'd wanted to I could have made plenty of money in your way.'

She struck at his face quickly with her clenched hand, and he caught her wrist with a readiness which came from long practice, but with pain he wondered: how often has this happened before, how often, damn it all, and with whom?

'You are quite right,' he said gently, releasing her hand, 'there's Maud.' He admitted himself wrong according to the formula he had always ready. 'I was jealous of the blighter. I must love you, Kate, it's the only explanation.'

'Family affection,' she said sadly. He let it pass. Life was too short for quarrels, and now he directed at her his whole technique of appeasement. He forgot Krogh; he even forgot Kate, she was a blurred, composite figure, she was Maud, Annette, the barmaid at the 'Crown and Anchor', the American girl in the *City of Nagpur*, his landlady's daughter that year in Edgware Road. 'Darling,' he said, 'I like your lipstick. It's a new shade, isn't it?' and immediately he remembered that she was wearing none; he should have mentioned her clothes or her scent.

But 'Yes,' Kate said, 'yes. It's a new shade. I'm glad you like it,' and he slipped back through the years to find the appropriate slang. 'Kate, you're a stunner.'

Then at the sound of a key turning in the hall door he momentarily lost his confidence. This was the price he had paid for his freshness, his schoolboy air of knowing a thing or two; he lived in the moment and was never prepared for the sudden crisis, the stranger's face, the new job. Before he followed Kate into the drawing-room he looked hopelessly round, plumbing the possibilities of the bed, the wardrobe and the door beyond.

Composure came back with his first sight of Erik

Krogh; even his jealousy wavered. The man was only a poor bloody foreigner after all. He wore a suit with a mauve stripe which was much too prominent, his check shirt was crude, his tie didn't tone. And there was nothing in his physical appearance to rival Anthony's. He was tall and might have had a good figure once, but he had put on flesh badly; he hadn't worn well. He was the kind of man who looked better in public than in private. Anthony began to bubble with bonhomie behind Kate's back. Here was someone to touch for tin, someone who didn't know too much and had lots of the ready. It was astonishing, almost unbelievable, that this was Erik Krogh, and again the thought came to him, as it had come after every failure, before every possibility of success: the whole damned thing is luck. What a laugh. Look after number one.

'I'm glad you're back, Kate,' Krogh said. He retreated back into the hall, he didn't even take off his hat, he watched Anthony with apprehension, he was too tired to be polite. His tiredness welled from him like an ectoplasm in the darkness of the hall. Little noises came from the passage through the chink of the door, feet moving away, the closing of the lift gates, somebody coughed, a sea bird mewed outside the window, and the tiredness flowed out of him as if at a séance, restless with the shaking of tambourine, the creak of table.

'Where have you been, Erik?' He closed the door carefully, nipped out the thin glitter from the passage.

'There's a reporter waiting about.'

'What does he want?'

The flow of weariness for a moment ceased; he said with sharp vitality: 'A series of great Swedes.' Then he was as tired as before, feeling for somewhere to put his hat. 'Somebody's set them at me. I don't know why.'

'This is my brother. You remember. I wired you something——'

He came out again into the light of the room and Anthony saw how his hair receded from his temple, giving the impression of more brow than most men have. 'I'm pleased to meet you, Mr Farrant, we must have a talk tomorrow. You must excuse me tonight. I've had a tiring day.' He waited stiffly for Anthony to go; the impression was not so much one of rudeness as of awkwardness.

'Well, I'll be pushing along to the hotel,' Anthony said.

'I hope you had a good journey.'

'Oh, it wasn't so dusty,' Anthony said.

'Electrification,' Krogh began and stopped. 'Oh, you must forgive me. Dusty. I had forgotten the expression.'

'Well, good-bye,' Anthony said.

'Good-bye.'

'Can you amuse yourself, Tony?' Kate said.

'Oh, I'll find a flicker,' Anthony said, '—or the Davidge perhaps.' He let himself out and closed the door behind him very slowly; he was curious to know how they greeted each other when they were alone. But all he heard Krogh say was, 'Dusty. I'd quite forgotten,' and a moment later, 'Laurin's ill.'

Through the glass lift-shaft he could see the hall far below him, glittering with light; the porter's bald head bent over the visitors' book sailed slowly up towards him, two men sitting on either side of the hall uncurled like watch-springs till he could see their waistcoats, their legs, their shoes, till they faced him through the door of the lift. He got out and closed the door. When he turned again they were on their feet watching him. One of them,

64

a young man, came forward and said something to him gently in Swedish.

'I'm English,' Anthony said. 'I don't understand a word.' He looked over the young man's shoulder to the smile which dawned on the other's face. Small, wrinkled, dusty, with a stub of cigarette stuck to his lower lip, he advanced with outstretched hand. 'So you're English,' he said. 'Isn't that lucky? I'm English too.' There was something in his manner, cocky and ingratiating, which Anthony remembered well. It was the shabby badge of a profession, as unmistakable as a worn attaché case, a golf bag hiding the detachable parts of a vacuum cleaner.

'I don't want to buy anything,' Anthony said. The Swede stood at his elbow, his head a little on one side, listening carefully, hoping to understand.

'No, no, you're wrong,' the man said. 'My name's Minty. Have a cup of coffee. The porter will oblige. I'm not a stranger here. Ask Miss Farrant about me.'

'Miss Farrant's my sister.'

'I ought to have guessed it. You take after her.'

'I don't want a cup of coffee. Who are you anyway?'

The man peeled the stump of cigarette off his lip; it was stuck as hard as sticking-plaster and left a few yellow shreds behind it. He ground the rest under his heel on the black glass floor. 'Ah,' he said 'you're suspicious. You don't trust Minty to do the right thing by you. But you won't get a better price in Stockholm for a story.'

'Oh,' Anthony said, 'you're journalists, are you? Do you always follow him around? Have a cigarette?'

'He's News,' the little dusty man replied and helped himself to two. 'If you only knew how little news there is in this place, you'd understand how close I have to stick. I'm a space man. Nils here, he's all right. He's on the staff, but I can't afford to miss a thing.' He coughed, a long dry cough reeking of tobacco. 'He's board and lodging to me,' he said, 'he's cigarettes, he's coffee. My one fear is that he'll die first: a couple of lovely blessed columns for the funeral, the wreaths and all; half a column of tributes every day for a week – what an orgy – and then, silence, good-bye to Minty.'

'Well,' Anthony said, 'I must be going now. Won't you walk along with me?'

'I daren't,' he said. 'He might come out again. He was at the British Legation this afternoon and left early, much too early, and caught me napping. I'd popped across the bridge for a bite and Benediction. I can't lose him again today.'

'He won't come out again,' Anthony said, 'he's dog-tired.'

'Dog-tired? I wonder why.'

'Perhaps,' Anthony said at random, 'because Laurin's ill.'

'Oh no,' he said, 'it wouldn't be that. Laurin's of no importance. No one cares about Laurin. He didn't, did he, say anything about a strike? There are rumours——'

'He was too tired,' Anthony said, 'to discuss things with me properly tonight. I shall be seeing him to-morrow though.'

'We might perhaps,' Minty said, '– have you a match? Thank you so much – come to some arrangement. I can always do with a little intimate story. What exactly are you? You are new here, surely?' He smoked while he talked, never taking the cigarette from his mouth; his face was grey with inhaling; sometimes the smoke blew up and burned his eyes.

66

'Yes,' Anthony said, 'I've only just joined the firm. I shall have a confidential position.'

'That's fine,' Minty said. 'We'll work together. Give Nils a cigarette. He's a good boy.' He searched the pockets of his shabby suit. 'Well, well, I've come out without a card, but I'll write my address on this old envelope.' He sucked a stump of pencil and looked up at Anthony's tie with sudden bright interest, a sparkle among the dust. 'I see you were at the old place,' he said. 'Those were the days, eh? But Henriques would have been before your time, and Patterson. I don't suppose you'd remember old Tester (six months for indecent assault). I try to keep up with them. Whose house were you?'

'Oh,' Anthony said, 'he would be since your time. We called him – Stodger. But shall you wait here all night, Mr Minty?'

'I shall give up at midnight,' Minty said. 'Then it's home and a hot-water-bottle for Minty. Have you been back lately, Mr Farrant?'

'Back? Oh, you mean Harrow. No, not for a long time. Have you?'

'Not for donkey's years.' The eyes were clouded with cigarette smoke; they emerged bloodshot and full of tears. 'But I keep up with the place. Every now and then I organise a little dinner. The Minister's a Harrovian. He writes poetry.'

'You see something of each other then?'

'Ah, he tries not to recognise Minty,' he said in a voice that seemed to Anthony as cracked as a boot-boy's bell, swung from dormitory to dormitory, and then the hand on the clapper, the boots heavy on stone, climbing down to the cupboard beneath the stairs.

Minty added shrilly, as though searching in vain for the old intonation, the jargon of gymnasiums and changing rooms: 'He's a beastly æsthete.'

'I'm tired,' Anthony said, 'I must go. I'll see you again.' He held out his hand and he saw how Minty noticed at once the frayed patch on the cuff. 'For a good story,' Minty said, 'I'd pay you in advance. But it's got to be exclusive. You'll have plenty of others after you if you've joined Krogh's. Don't touch them. They're just a lot of foreigners. I've lived here for twenty years now and I know what I'm talking about. Harrovians ought to stick together anyway. You don't get your pickings unless you stick together.' He turned away quickly as someone rang for the lift from an upper floor and watched its sparkling crystal progress with tired greed. The young smart Swede stood at his elbow watching where he watched, turning where he turned, with the devotion of a page in an Elizabethan play who has followed a monarch into poverty and exile. So Anthony left them.

Passing through the flat doors he came immediately to the Visby quay. Lake Mälaren licked gently the last stone steps; the rail of a small steamer stuck above the level of the pavement. The light of a street lamp reached just far enough to touch the water sliding back and forth over the stone; in the saloon two sailors played at cards. Anthony stood on the pavement and stared at them through the glass pane, across the padded velvet settee, to the polished oblong table.

Cards, Anthony thought, I could just do with a game of cards. He rattled the few coins in his pocket and stared, trying to make out the game they played. The boat gently rubbed the quay, and a black cat moved up and down on the deck, sharpening its claws between the boards. He could hear the tram bells by the City Hall, and while he watched the card players a tram came by and glittered like low late sunlight into the water. One of the players looked up at him and smiled.

Anthony turned up the collar of his coat and went on to his hotel. This place, he thought, will do as well as another; it's better than Shanghai; I can get along with Minty and earn enough to keep me for a while. I'll stay a week, even if Krogh won't have me, and opening a window he leant far out into the cold wet evening air and saw a gull cruising on wide wings down the narrow street between the hotel backs, and he thought Tuesday, I must get some money from Minty or Kate or Krogh. What shall I do with her? I'll give her the tiger, she's a sweet thing. She believed everything I told her about Gothenburg, we'll find some kind of a park, that sort of entertainment's dirt-cheap. Her name is Davidge and she comes from Coventry. The gull folded its wings and came to rest on an hotel garbage can. Kate doesn't want the tiger and the vase is broken.

Kate and Krogh, he thought, and me and Maud. He shut his eyes in sudden pain and when he opened them again the gull had gone. We were in the barn and she said to me, 'Go back.' She was right, of course, after two years I was as popular as anyone. She was by my bed and I was happy and in great pain and I was going to lose my eye. In the hall I felt nothing, I scratched my hand upon a nail turning to take my bags and I felt nothing; I was ill for six days on board with the poison; and I sent a postcard when we got to Aden. We were never together again; she used to know when I was in pain and I used to know if she were miserable. They said that was the curse of being twins, but I think we were happy, knowing what the other thought, feeling what the other felt. This is the curse, the ceasing to know.

Krogh is with her now.

He began quickly to unpack. With each thing that he took from the bag she had bought him in Gothenburg it was as if he were re-affirming his belief that certain things were inevitable, that certain things were past, that you had to take life as you found it, success and ignorance, failure and the stranger in the bed: the rather torn photograph of Annette which he had stripped from its frame (he leant it against his tooth mug), the ties which he had crammed into his pocket at the lodgings, his new pants, his new vests, his new socks, *The Four Just Men* in a Tauchnitz edition, his dark-blue pyjamas, a copy of *Film Fun*. He turned out his pockets: a pencil, a half-crown fountain pen, an empty card-case, a packet of De Reszke cigarettes. He did not keep much in his pockets; his good suit had to last. He had bought a tie-press in Gothenburg and now very carefully he draped in it his Harrow tie; the others could wait their turn. He hung his coat upon a chair and arranged his trousers under the mattress. Then he lay for a while in his pants and shirt; he was tired, he had passed through the fear of the new faces and reached the inevitable stage, of studying where his profit lay. He had lain thus more times than he could count on a strange bed, without ever finally tiring of so much thought, so many hopes, with so little result.

It will have to be half and half with Minty unless I get a good job.

He closed his eyes and suddenly, without warning, with all the old clarity he became aware of Kate's

70

thoughts beating in his brain. It was as if in the ravaged country between them, over the dynamited bridges, through the unfriendly villages, past the old entanglements, a spy had crept and at the frontier, joining two wires, had put them again in touch, so that she could tell him that all was for the best, that again she had managed things, that she was in control, above all that she loved him.

But love, he thought, that means me and Maud, you and Krogh. 'That is my bedroom,' she had said when he pointed at a door and a little later she had tried to strike him with her fist.

Anthony got off the bed and began again to undress. But the room was cold (he shut the window), it was bare. He tore the coloured cover off *Film Fun* and stuck it against the wall with a piece of soap: a girl with large thighs dressed in a green bathing-suit sat in a swing with her knees apart. He tore out a photograph of Claudette Colbert in a Roman bath and balanced it on his suitcase. Two girls playing strip poker he put above his bed with more soap.

Well, he thought, that's a bit more comfortable, and stood in the middle of the room wondering what to do next to make the room like home, listening to the hot-water-pipes wailing behind the wall.

[4]

I awake and Erik sleeping and his hand cold on my side. All settled. He said to me, 'Laurin's ill,' but I knew it was not that. So tired he was. Never seen so tired now asleep so cold his hand. Anthony asleep now, the scar below the eye, the knife slipping upwards suddenly

71

through the rabbit's fur, the scream, he went on screaming, no control the matron said. I woke in the middle of the night hearing him fifty miles away. Knew he was in pain. Father ill. They wouldn't let me go. The French exam all that day long the irregular verbs and twice the supervisor went out with me to the lavatory. I spoke to her and she said to me: 'You mustn't speak until you have handed in your paper.'

Like an old married couple after thirty years. A silver copper what d'you call it golden wedding.

Erik said: 'The strike's off. I managed it as well as Laurin could have done.' He said: 'I told him a joke, asked after his family, gave him a cigar.' I said: 'Was that all you gave him?' He said: 'I gave him a guarantee that the wages in America would not be lowered.' I said: 'Did you write it down?' He said: 'No. I just gave him my word.' How tired he was.

Awake sleeping hand cold all settled.

He said: 'What can your brother do?' Postcards from Aden, the vacuum cleaner, the waitresses listening, 'you made me love you,' that day in the music-hall he bought me a drink in the bar, the first I'd ever had, and Father said: 'Where have you been all day?' and he said: 'Walking in the park.' I was hopeless. I said: 'He was always good at arithmetic.' Erik said: 'There's nothing I can do for him. Tell me yourself. Is he good for anything?' I said: 'He's good for nothing except winning tigers.' He thought I was cracked. He said: 'Winning tigers?' I said: 'He was emptying the shooting booths last night at Gothenburg until I stopped him.' I never thought that would appeal to Erik, not in his nature, joke, enquiry, cigar, cold hand against my side. He said: 'I'll give him a job.'

72

'I'll give you a job,' he said to me. The little dusty office in Leather Lane. He sat up very stiff in the only other chair with his gloves on and Hammond scraped and scraped to him. Pince-nez falling off the pointed nose, nibbling voice, rat face. He said: 'She's always given satisfaction,' and upset the ink on his desk rising too quickly to open the door. A friend of my father's he felt responsible. The business bought up and the office in the hands of the breakers and my father dying.

When I left England my father said, 'I wish Anthony were with you.' He said I must be careful, there would be temptations. But he had never been tempted, he didn't know what the word meant, lying there in his bed dying slowly, knowing nothing. The smell of medicine, the nurse at the door, the stained glass in the hall, in the mahogany bookcase a complete set of *Punch* in blue cloth bindings; his uncle had known Du Maurier and he remembered how people were shocked at *Trilby*. And he said to me one year: 'I don't like Miss Mollison. A girl should not be seen at a play with her employer.' Honour the dead, these were the maxims he lived by, a little bit of England, Anthony wrote that he must have marble, I said, 'devoted, devoted children is too strong,' but Anthony said devoted was four letters cheaper and anyway it was seemly. But these were his maxims. Do not show your feelings. Do not love immoderately. Be chaste, prudent, pay your debts. Don't buy on credit. 'Devoted' was too strong. On Mother's grave 'affectionate husband', he did not grudge five letters in the good cause of accuracy.

He read Shakespeare and Scott and Dickens and did acrostics all the days of his life. A little bit of England. He was disliked by his servants. He was an honourable man. His palm was warm as mine is warm. He may have loved Anthony too in his own way. Why did I dislike him so?

These were the reasons. I will be precise and remember clearly. He would have appreciated that. It is the dead hour of night when graves give up their dead. He did not care for *The Bride of Lammermoor*. He said it was exaggerated, the work of a sick man. And *Troilus and Cressida* was not, he was certain, by Shakespeare, for Shakespeare was not a cynic. He had a profound trust in human nature. But be chaste, prudent, pay your debts, and do not love immoderately.

These were the reasons. Anthony learning (the beating in the nursery, the tears before the boarding school) to keep a stiff upper lip, Anthony learning (the beating in the study when he brought home the smutty book with the pretty pictures) that you must honour other men's sisters. Anthony learning to love with moderation. Anthony in Aden, Anthony in Shanghai, Anthony farther away from me than he had ever been, Anthony making good; yes, he loved Anthony and he ruined Anthony and he was tormented by Anthony until the end. The telegrams, the telephoned messages, the face grinning over the bed-rail: 'I've resigned.'

Now in the darkness be fair, Erik sleeping, hand cold on my side, all settled, only the Strand, a strip of water and a street between us – seem standing darker than last year they stood and say we must not cross, alas, alas.

He said: 'Winning tigers,' he said: 'I'll give him a job.' I cannot understand. I would wake him and ask him but he is tired, he would think I want him. Only once I wanted him, an ambassador to dinner, and I drunk and the first secretary pulled at my dress while they talked business in the other room. I said, 'What's the good? How can we? They'll be back any minute. Have some more brandy?' He was as tall as Anthony, Erik's height, he had a duelling scar under his right eye (in the mirror over the mantel it was the left eye), he taught me to swear in his language and we laughed; I wanted to let him do what he wanted to do, but they were talking business in the next room, and I said, 'Do you skin rabbits?' and he thought I was cracked. That night I wanted Erik, I wanted anyone, I wanted a man I could see from the window while I undressed sheltering at the quayside. Erik said, 'They'll take the loan, they'll take the loan,' and he couldn't sleep and I couldn't sleep, and soon we were happy and tired together because of that man's scar and the other man's loan. And that night.

Anthony near Marseilles, father dying, the electric light burning until seven in the morning under a heavy shade, the nurse reading, the kettle boiling, the sterilised swabs ready in a basin covered with gauze. My year in hospital. Putting the iodine where the vaseline should have been.

The blue vase broken and Anthony said, 'But still we've got the tiger.' Would it have been the same tonight to Erik if I had said: 'Winning blue vases, winning cigarette-cases marked with an initial A,' would he have said, even then, 'I'll give him a job?' Tiger burning bright in Tivoli, immortal eye, the hand against my side, feet touching mine; even there the women watched him when he turned, when he smiled, what shoulder and what art, to see the rockets throwing down their spears. I saw the girl's eyes on him in Gothenburg, the badly-painted face, the trust, the innocence, the cunning that asks to be betrayed. Those we love we forget, it is those we betray we remember. Did she smile her work to see? He said: 'I'll give her the tiger.' And when my heart began to beat in the Bedford Palace in Camden Town (he told Father 'we were walking in the Park') I loved him more than I had ever done before. The days of oranges were over, but he bought me peanuts.

And I watched with twisted sinews of the heart, with jealousy, the female tumbler falling towards the boards, the tights, the toothy smile, peroxide queen. It was my sixteenth birthday; I stared at the clock; and when it showed 6.43 I said: 'It's my birthday,' and when it showed 6.49 I said: 'Many happy returns.' A comedian came on the boards wearing check trousers drawing a toy lamb.

These memories one turns over like an old couple after thirty years, who have shared first love first hate first drink first treachery when I said, 'You will miss your train.' The bitter draught. He couldn't drink the beer, spluttered, turned away, face saved by rising curtain, but the sherry I drank and held my breath and never made a sound. Afterwards eating apples at Mornington Crescent to take the smell away.

Father deceived again. Affectionate children. But there was such sweetness in the deceptions we did together.

That year I was in the hospital being trained he came to see me and asked whether the matron would buy a vacuum cleaner. Down from the ward, the tables washed with ether, the swabs counted in the right basin, the gauze, the shaded lights, to Anthony waiting, the winter sun on the pavement going west, he whistled a new tune. I had fifteen shillings and he had five. The cinema, the club in Gerrard Street, the last drink, he wouldn't let me have another, nice girls don't drink. Dear fool. The matron said unsuited to nursing, and when he went abroad I went to Leather Lane. Book-keeping, short-hand, the prize for speed presented by himself, by rat-faced Hammond. From that moment, I might tell my biographers, I never looked back. Plotted for this, planned for this, saved for this, that we should be together again.

Awake hand cold all settled. You may sleep now.

No new issues the market steady. You may sleep now. The early firmness maintained, averages higher, more interest, it's rising, response to call, it's rising, returned to favour, rising, it's rising, no reacting, rising, Anthony our bond, our bond Anthony, what profit taking, our bond, our futures are steady, the new redemption, rising, rising.

Don't be afraid. Don't hesitate. No cause of fear. No bulls on this exchange. The tiger bright. The forests. Sleep. Our bond. The new redemption. And we rise, we rise. And God Who made the lamb made Whitaker, made Loewenstein. 'But you are lucky,' Hammond said that day in Leather Lane, 'Krogh's safe. Whatever comes or goes people will always everywhere have to buy Krogh's.' The market steady. The Strand, the water and a street between us. Sleep. The new redemption. No bulls, the tiger and the lamb. The bears. The forests. Sleep. The stock is sound. The closing price. We rise.

# PART III

## [1]

Minty knew the moment he got up in the morning that this was one of his days. He sang gently to himself as he shaved: 'This is the way that Minty goes, Minty goes, Minty goes.' Although he had a new blade he did not cut himself once; he shaved cautiously rather than closely, while the pot of coffee, which his landlady had brought him, grew cold on the washstand. Minty liked his coffee cold; his stomach would bear nothing hot. A spider watched him under his tooth glass; it had been there five days; he had expected his landlady to clear it away, but it had remained a second day, a third day. He cleaned his teeth under the tap. Now she must believe that he kept it there for study. He wondered how long it would live. He watched it and it watched him back with shaggy patience. It had lost a leg when he put the glass over it.

Above his bed was a house-group, rows of boys blinking against the sun above and below the seated figures of the prefects, the central figure of the house-master and his wife. It was curious to observe how a moustache by being waxed at the tips could date a man as accurately as a woman's dress, the white blouse, the whalebone collar, the puffed sleeves. Occasionally Minty was called on to identify himself; practice had made him perfect; there had been a time of hesitation when he could not decide whether Patterson seated on the housemaster's left or Tester standing rather more obscurely behind, his jaw hidden by a puffed sleeve, best acted as his proxy. For Minty himself did not appear; he

78

had seen the photograph taken from the sickroom window, a blaze of light, the blinking blackened faces, the photographer diving beneath his shade.

'This is the way that Minty goes.' He picked a stump of cigarette from the soap-tray and lit it. Then he studied his hair in the mirror of the wardrobe door; this was one of his days; he must be prepared for anything, even society. The scurf worried him; he rubbed what was left of the pomade upon his scalp, brushed his hair, studied it again. Minty was satisfied. He drank his tepid coffee without taking the cigarette from his mouth; the smoke blew up and burned his eyes. He swore so gently that no one but himself would have known that he swore. 'Holy Cnut.' The phrase was his own; always, instinctively, like a good Anglo-Catholic, he had disliked 'smut'; it was as satisfying to say 'Holy Cnut' as words that sullied, Minty believed.

Minty put on his black overcoat and went downstairs. It was Tuesday, the twenty-third. A letter from home was due. For nearly twenty years Minty had fetched his monthly letters from the General Post Office; it prevented embarrassment. On occasion it was necessary to change a lodging without the usual notice. He found the sun quite hot in the square by the station, but he always wore a coat when he went to fetch his letters. He parked his cigarette outside in a spot where a beggar was unlikely to find it. Presenting a dog-eared card at the Poste Restante counter he believed that, as an Englishman and an old Harrovian, he honoured Stockholm by choosing it as his home. For no one could deny that he was a gentleman of leisure who might have lived in any place with a post office and scope for personality.

To his surprise there were two letters; this was

something which had to be celebrated with another cup of tepid coffee. He chose a leather arm-chair facing the street in the lounge opposite the station and sat there waiting for his coffee to cool. He was so certain that this was one of his days that he ground out the stump of his cigarette and bought a packet. Then he tried a little coffee in a spoon, but it was still too hot.

On the point of opening one of the letters he paused, his eye caught by an unusual activity at the station. Several men were running across the road with movie cameras. He saw Nils darting by outside and waved to him. He remembered what it was all about. 'The film star's return home.' He had earned sixty crowns a few days ago translating into Swedish all the dope he could discover in the movie magazines. 'The screen's greatest lover.' 'The mystery woman of Hollywood.' A number of people (were they hired by the hour? Minty wondered) began to cheer, and several business men, with port-folios under their arms, stopped on the pavement and scowled at the station. They obscured Minty's view. Minty stood on his chair. It was just as well to keep an eye open even if it was not his own pigeon. The actress was not very popular in Sweden; something disgraceful might happen; something which someone would want hushed up. If, for example, she was hissed . . .

But nothing happened. A woman came out of the station in a camel-hair coat with a big collar; it was just possible to see that she was wearing grey flannel trousers; Minty had one glimpse of a pale haggard humorless face, a long upper lip, the unreal loveliness and the unreal tragedy of a mask like Dante's known too well. The movie cameras whirred and the woman put her hands in front of her face and stepped into a car. Somebody threw an expensive bouquet of flowers (who paid for that? Minty wondered) which missed the car and fell in the road. Nobody took any notice. A little woman in heavy black weeds and a black veil scuttled into the car and it drove away. The newspaper-men came together in front of the station and Minty could hear their laughter.

He opened the first letter. Scott and James, solicitors. *Enclosed find money order for £15, being your allowance for the month ending next September 20th. Please sign and return the enclosed receipt.* Reference GL/RS. GL, Minty pondered. I haven't had those initials before. New blood in the old firm. After twenty years it amused him to find the smallest variation in the letter's form. Before he opened the second letter he drank his coffee for luck.

Holy Cnut, it's Aunt Ella. I'd quite forgotten the old – the old woman (be careful, Minty) was alive.

*Dearest Ferdinand.* The name checked Minty. He had not seen that particular arrangement of letters for a very long while. One signed one's Christian name on cheques, of course, but somehow Minty carried off the burden of the name. *Dearest Ferdinand.* He laughed and stirred his coffee; that's me.

*It seems a long while since I heard from you.* A long while, Minty thought. I should think it is a long while: the best part of twenty years. *I happened to come across an old letter of yours the other day when I was clearing out my drawers preparatory to my latest move. It had got pushed to the back of a drawer where I keep my old sketching-blocks. The thought came to me that we are the last of the immediate Mintys. Your cousin Delia's family, of course, still go on, and there are the Hertfordshire Mintys, but we have never had much to do with them, and there is your mother of course, but she is only a Minty by marriage. I suppose – an odd thought, isn't it? – that we are all only Mintys by marriage. Anyway, there was your letter, and it was such a pleasure to read it over again. Characteristically it is undated, so I cannot tell how long it is since I received it. It must be some years now, I expect. I see that you say that you enjoy Stockholm and hope that is still true. I can't quite remember now why you went to Stockholm, I must remember to ask your mother when I next see her, her memory, poor dear, is not what it was, and it would not surprise me at all to hear that she had forgotten what position it is that you occupy. It must, at any rate, be satisfactory financially or you would not have stayed away from England all these years. I notice that my brokers have just bought me some Norwegian State Bonds; rather a coincidence, isn't it? Curious – I am reading your old letter as I write – I see that you ask me for the loan of five pounds; it must indeed have been written many years ago when you were first starting whatever work it is you do. Doubtless I sent you the money, but I wonder whether you ever repaid me. However, we'll be charitable and take it for granted that you did. It's an old story now, anyway. You'll be wondering what news there is of home, but you will have heard about Uncle Laurie's death and the affair of Delia's twins from your mother. She'll have told you everything important. I saw a Harrow boy on Fakenhurst platform the other day; another coincidence.*

*Your loving Aunt,*

*Ella.*

Well, Minty thought, this is indeed a proud day. To have heard from the family. How long this coffee takes to cool. I've a good mind to write to Mother on the strength of it. 'Aunt Ella when she last wrote mentioned. . . .' What a start it would give the dear woman to see my handwriting on an envelope. Not sweet enough. Another lump. But I don't know her address, and if I sent it to the solicitors they would return it. Reference GL/RS. Cool enough now. I could send it under cover to Aunt Ella and ask her to stamp and forward it. My handwriting under an English stamp. What a surprise for mother, but cautious, Minty, cautious. Your imagination runs away with you, Minty. Nothing must endanger the fifteen pounds a month so regularly and gracefully paid. Reference GL/RS.

'I see you, Nils,' Minty said, wagging his finger roguishly at the young man on the pavement, 'you knew it was pay-day and you want a cup of coffee. And you shall have one. This is a special day. I have had a letter from the Family.'

Nils came up the steps from the street, shy and graceful as a young fawn pressing its nose against a fence and seeing life go by behind the rails. Minty was life, Minty sipping his cold coffee, Minty yellow about the lips, 'Have a cigarette,' Minty munificent.

'Thank you, Mr Minty.'

'Quite a commotion at the station.'

'Yes, Mr Minty. She is a fine actress.'

'Did she pay for the bouquet?'

'No, I do not think that she did, Mr Minty. The card fell off. I have it here.'

Minty said, 'Give it to me.'

'I thought it might be useful to you, Mr Minty.'

'You're a good lad, Nils,' Minty said. 'Take another cigarette. Put it in your pocket.' He looked at the card. 'Take the whole packet.'

'No, really, Mr Minty.'

'Well,' Minty said, 'if you won't;' he put the cigarettes quickly into his pocket and got up, 'business calls. Bread and butter. The squalid necessity of earning money.'

'The editor,' Nils said, 'wants to see you.'

'Trouble?'

'Yes, I think so.'

'I can face him,' Minty said. 'I have fifteen pounds in my pocket; I have heard from the Family.' He walked boldly out and round the corner; his shortness, his long black coat made him ridiculous, people smiled at him and he knew why they smiled. It had been poison to him once, but that was many years ago. He had taken the poison so often in small doses, dodging between side street and side street, that now like Mithridates he was immune. He could come out into the main streets, he could stand and talk to himself and plume his dusty image in the windows of haberdashers, minding the smiles hardly at all; only a little malice stirred in his veins, moved with the blood stream.

It stirred, after the long stairs, the machine-room, the opening and closing of glass doors, at sight of the editor. He resented the red military moustache, the curtness, the efficiency; one might as well work in a factory and have done with it. 'Well, Herr Minty?'

'I was told you wanted to see me.'

'Where was Herr Krogh yesterday evening?'

'I just went to snatch a cup of tea. There was no reason why he should leave the Legation like that.'

The editor said, 'We are not receiving very much from you, Herr Minty. There are plenty of men we can employ for outside work. I think we may have to try

84

someone else. You haven't a trained eye for news.' He blew out his chest and said suddenly, 'Your health is not good enough, Herr Minty. That cup of tea. A Swede would not have needed a cup of tea. Poison. You probably take it strong.'

'Very weak, Herr Redakteur, cold, with lemon.'

'You should exercise yourself, Herr Minty. Have you a wireless set?'

Minty shook his head. Patience, he thought with venom, patience.

'If you had a wireless set you could exercise as I do every morning under a first-class instructor. Do you take a cold bath?'

'A tepid bath, Herr Redakteur.'

'All my reporters take cold baths. You cannot be efficient, Herr Minty, with a bent back, an undeveloped chest, poor muscles.'

But this was the familiar poison. He had been slowly broken in by parents, by schoolmasters, by strangers in the street. Crooked and yellow and pigeon-chested, he had his deep refuge, the inexhaustible ingenuity of his mind. He blinked his scorched eyes and said with brave perkiness, 'So I'm discharged?'

'The next time you let slip an opportunity . . .'

'I would rather leave now,' Minty said, 'when I have something to sell.'

'What have you to sell?'

'A friend of mine, Miss Farrant's brother, has joined the firm. A confidential position.'

'You know very well that you get the best price from us.'

'For that,' Minty said, 'but for this?' and he snapped a visiting-card on to the desk. It was stained with mud.

85

'She never got the flowers,' Minty said. 'They just fell in the road. That's what comes of employing athletic reporters. They can't throw straight. You ought to have come to Minty.' He wagged his finger and left the room; he was quite drunk on two cups of coffee, his monthly cheque, on Aunt Ella's letter. In the reporters' room he saw Nils. 'I put him in his place,' he said. 'He won't trouble me again for a while. Has Krogh left the flat yet?'

'No. I've just rung up the porter.'

'He's late,' Minty said. 'Re-union, eh, Nils? A Night of Love. We're all human,' he said, sucking in his cheeks, shivering in the draught from the wide window, seeking malevolently for a stray cigarette-packet on an empty desk and finding none. 'It's turning cold. It's going to rain again,' and while he searched the rain came; a great blown cloud from over the lake drifted like a derelict airship above the roofs, bringing shadow, bringing the first slow deliberate drops which stung the window-sill, broke and ran down the wall.

[2]

The shower caught the people sitting outside the restaurant unawares. It had been hot in the sun before the cloud came up from Mälaren. Anthony was entangled in the rush for shelter. Dusk fell unwanted and for a long while no lights went up, because the sun was expected any moment to reappear. Then the waiters reluctantly turned a few lamps on, but they gave no real light and were presently extinguished one by one. The rain tapped on the tables outside, soaked through the brown leaves in the square, washed across the pavement. Anthony ordered beer.

86

He had no coat and no umbrella. It was just as well for him to stay where he was. He did not want to move: he would get wet while he was on the way to Krogh's and spoil his only suit. He thought of economy, he thought of health, he thought of the nursery they had had one year in the crescent, the year before he went to school. The umbrellas passed like black and dripping seals; a foreign language he could not understand fretted his nerves. If he wanted to ask for a match, to ask the way, he would not be able to make himself understood. The waiter brought his beer; it seemed to establish between them the elements of companionship because the man had understood at least that much. The pale lamps burning in the daylight dusk, the waiter who had served him, his chair, his table, 'some corner of a foreign land that is for ever England', he dwelt on them with a lush sad sentiment. His manner momentarily had a touch of nobility, of an exile's dignity as he stared into the outer world through the splashed glass and thought of nothing so immediate as Krogh's, of Kate waiting to tell him whether she had found him work, but of rain falling on untended unmarked graves, soaking through the clay.

'How wet it is,' he said to the waiter. 'The trees——'
He wanted to establish his corner of England a little more securely by talking about the weather; he wanted to tell him how soon the leaves would all have fallen if the rain continued. He wanted to hang his corner with the conversational equivalents of Annette's photograph, the pictures from *Film Fun;* he did not want to have to move from here for hours. He would have all his meals here and they would get to know him.

The waiter did not understand. *'Bitte?'* he asked

anxiously, '*bitte?*' The head waiter came. '*Bitte?*' he said, '*bitte?*' He went away and fetched a woman who was cleaning the stairs. 'What do you want?' she asked him in English. He could think of nothing to say; he had to order another beer while his glass was still full. He could see the waiters talking about him at the other end of the restaurant.

The trouble, in a way, was that they were waiters; if they had been waitresses it would have been so much easier to establish his English corner. Although he had travelled half-way round the world in the last ten years he had never before been far away from England. He had always worked in places where others had established the English corner before he came: even in the brothels of the East English was spoken. There had always been the club (as long as he retained his membership), bridge-parties, the neo-Gothic Anglican church. He stared out through the foreign glass at the foreign rain and thought: Krogh won't give me a job, I'll go back tomorrow. Then he smiled and forgot his resolution because he saw England staring back at him through the glass with coat-collar turned up and dripping hat.

'Minty,' he called, 'Minty,' to the surprise of the waiters.

Minty came in cautiously, looking this way and that up the rows of tables. 'I don't come here as a rule,' he said. 'The fellows from the Legation – we don't get on well together.' He sat down and laid his hat under his chair. He leant forward and said confidentially: 'The Minister sets them on me. I'm certain of it. He doesn't like me.'

'What do they do?'

'They laugh,' Minty said. He looked at the beer-bottles: 'Are you expecting someone?'

'No,' Anthony said. 'Have a bottle?'

'Well, frankly,' Minty said, 'I'd rather have a cup of coffee. I don't like any form of strong drink. No moral objection, but my stomach won't stand it. It was the operation I had ten years ago, almost exactly ten years ago. August the twenty-first. The feast-day of St Jane Frances Fremiot de Chantal, widow. I hung between life and death,' Minty said, 'for exactly five days. I always put my recovery down to St Zephyrinus. But I'm boring you.'

'No,' Anthony said, 'no. It's very interesting. I had an operation in August ten years ago.'

'Your eye?'

'No. That was – a wound. An explosion. I had appendicitis.'

'Mine was in that neighbourhood,' Minty said. 'But they didn't remove the appendix. It was far too dangerous. They made an incision and drained me.'

'Drained you?'

'Yes, drained me. You would never believe the amount of pus they removed. It would have filled a milk-jug, a large milk-jug.' He blew on the coffee the waiter had brought him. 'It's good to have a fellow-countryman to talk to. And what a coincidence that you were at the old place, too.'

'The old place?'

'The old school,' Minty said, stirring his coffee, squinting upwards with sudden malicious amusement. 'Kicking a fug about, eh. What a life. Were you a fez?'

Anthony hesitated. 'No,' he said.

'And whose house did you say——'

Anthony looked at his watch. 'I'm sorry. I've got to be off. I have to be round at Krogh's this morning.'

'I'll come with you,' Minty said. 'I'm going that way myself. But you needn't hurry. Krogh's only just arrived at the office.'

'How do you know?'

'I had the porter on the 'phone a few minutes ago. One has to have an eye on these things. I lost him yesterday.'

'Is everything he does news?'

'Very nearly,' Minty said. 'And anything he does secretly is headlines, special editions, wires to England. I'm a religious man,' Minty said, 'and it's good to think that Krogh – the richest man in the world, who controls the market, lends to governments, takes our money and turns it into – Krogh's, millions of money converted into Krogh's you can buy for a few pence in any general store, it's good to think he's merely one of us, that Minty keeps an eye on him, watches, records, perhaps now and then puts a drawing-pin on his chair (I wonder if you remember Collins who taught history?). Well, Farrant, it makes Minty feel all evensong, all *vox humana* – "and He shall exalt the humble and meek". Partridge used to say – you know whom I mean, of course——'

'Partridge?'

'The senior chaplain. He only retired a year or two ago. How curious that you don't remember Partridge.'

'I was thinking of something else,' Anthony said. 'It's stopped raining. I must get to the office before it begins again. I haven't a coat.'

He walked very fast to the office, but Minty kept up, indeed Minty showed the way, a hand on the sleeve here, a check there, a direction across a street. He talked the whole time about the use of chasubles. He seemed to have quite forgotten Harrow. Only at the entrance to Krogh's he suddenly reverted to the school. 'I'm trying to organise an Old Harrovian dinner here,' he said. 'Of course you'll take a ticket, and later I'll ask you to approach the Minister. The Minister doesn't like Minty, and if Minty were a swearing man, what names,' he raised his yellowed fingers episcopally: 'Oh, Holy Cnut.'

Anthony looked back and England was again outside, keeping a watch on him through the iron patterning of the gateway, one bloodshot eye on each side of a tender branching iron plant. He knows about Harrow, Anthony thought, he wants me to admit it; great heavens, he thought, turning suddenly to escape from Minty's gaze, that statue, fountain, what you call it, they have queer tastes in Krogh's; you wouldn't find a thing like that off Mincing Lane, what is it meant to be? inhuman. Following the porter through the glass door into the glass lift, he forgot Minty in the familiar pain of being a supplicant. There was nothing he hated more than asking for a job, and it looked like being his life-work. Already he felt a grudge against Krogh for refusing him, for taking him. If he takes me, it'll be charity for Kate's sake. What right has he to be charitable? At least, no one can say I'm inhuman. The fountain slipped away below him, damply dripping into the grey basin, and he thought with pride: I'm human. I may have my faults, but they are human faults. A glass too much, a girl now and then, there's nothing much wrong with that. It's human nature, I am Human, and he blustered out of the lift with his shoulders squared to find Kate waiting for him on the landing, Kate smiling, Kate welcoming him, Kate quite ready to embrace him in front of the lift-man, in front of the clerk hurrying by with a portfolio of papers, and I am human, his spirit whispered weakly, faintly, dying out in gratitude, like a band of street musicians moving away down a long street, while another band approached playing more loudly, with a more urgent appeal: Good old Kate, she's always done her best, she's never let me down.

'You've come at last,' Kate said.

'I got caught by the rain. I had to shelter.'

'Come to my room for a moment.' He followed her across the landing, a steel chair, a glass table, a bowl of yellow roses; on the walls a succession of charts made of inlaid wood, showing the time of day in every capital of the world, showing the mailing dates to every country, showing the movements of liners. In her own room, the same steel chairs, the same glass tables, the same yellow roses, she turned back to him. 'You've got a job.' She clapped her hands together once; she looked ten years younger. 'I've always worked for this.' She watched him with an undisguised devotion that startled him, a devotion of the blood, not of the brain. 'Oh, Anthony, how good it'll be to have you here.'

He tried to respond with the same intensity. 'Good. I should just think so.' He wanted her to enjoy his triumph, he was grateful, but his love was blurred, was dispersed, was thinned out like pastry over a large area. Love was not gratitude, love was not this dependence of the brain, this thought-reading, this inconvenience of shared pain, this was the unfortunate trick of being twins; love was fun, love was a good time, love was Annette, was Mabel. 'What's he making me do, Kate darling?'

'I don't know. But listen. You needn't worry. It's a real job, not charity. He wants you.'

'Of course it may not be quite my cup of tea.'

'Oh, but it will be, Anthony, I'm sure of it. Give it a trial, anyway. I want you here. Listen. We'll be able to do things together, see things, go to places.'

'That'll be fine, won't it?' Anthony said, smiling at her, 'but don't forget I shall be doing a spot of work now and then. Where will it be, do you think? At the factory perhaps. I've always been interested in machinery. Do you remember the old car I put together and did twenty miles an hour in it down the Brighton Road? But I suppose it'll be book-keeping. That's where I've had all my experience.'

'And it'll be no longer you in China, me in London, you in India, me in Stockholm.'

'We'll see plenty of each other. You'll see too much of me perhaps.'

'No.'

'It's never been like this before since we were small. There was always school. Holidays never seemed to last long.'

'I'm only afraid that this will be the same,' Kate said.

'How do you mean?'

'That this won't seem to last long either.'

It occurred to him with astonishment and pain that he had been wrong just now, that this after all was love, that he had been damned to bad luck from birth: she was his sister. He was conscious of a great waste, a great disappointment. Nobody, he thought, can put it over her on looks, she's got class, she's swell. The inadequate words fumbled at his heart. She says what she means,

93

she knows what she wants, she does what she likes, a fellow can trust her. He wanted to tell her that he loved her, but a light went on above a door, and she said: 'That's Erik. He's ready for you.' The opportunity had gone, leaving a sense of guilt, of melancholy, of opportunities lost, as if, hearing the limping music of the lame band fade round the corner of the street, one had to admit want of charity and indecision. The pennies had been there, he wouldn't have missed them, and who knew what luck might have been his in return for one spontaneous gesture?

'I'll go in. Am I all right? No smuts on the nose, a close shave——'

'You're all right. Erik wouldn't notice, anyway.'

Erik this and Erik that, he thought, and tried to feed his envy by imagining Krogh's face triumphant because Kate was his, but saw only the stone stairs to a familiar flat, the whitewashed wall, the pencilled messages. 'Back at 12.30.' 'No milk today.' He has this and I have that; we divide the world between us.

Kate opened a door. He touched her as he passed. Brother and sister, affection, she knows me and I know her, the deep comfort of no pretence. Why should I envy him? he wondered, remembering love, remembering the bell ringing in the empty flat, the search for messages, entwined hearts, 'Gone round the corner to the pub', 'Back at 12.30', 'No milk today', the stone stairs slippery with soap going down, first the good time and afterwards the despair.

'Well, Mr Krogh,' he said, 'it's good of you to see me.' He was frightened, he was breezy, he was bitterly happy because after all this was the end, one couldn't go lower by any club standard than to ask for work from your sister's lover. He turned on Krogh the deep deceptive candour of his gaze.

But it was wasted. Krogh didn't look at him. He nodded at a chair, 'Sit down,' he fumbled with a lighter. Anthony thought with incredulity: He's shy.

Krogh said: 'I hadn't thought at first there was any job I could offer you. Our accounts department is fully staffed. I think that was where you have had most experience?'

'Yes,' Anthony said.

'You understand I don't know the details of all these things. I depend on my manager's reports. He was dissatisfied with no one. You can hardly expect me to get rid of an experienced man who has given satis-faction——'

'Of course not.'

'I felt sure you'd understand,' Krogh said. 'But on the other hand, I want to do something: you are Miss Farrant's brother. Miss Farrant is——' he searched for a word; he lifted a dry passionless, for some reason anxious, face towards his secretary's door. He looked at the light switch on his desk; he seemed on the point of finding out from Kate herself what the word was he required. 'She's invaluable to me,' he said at last, and hurried on. 'Do you know America?'

'I was in Buenos Aires once.'

'I mean the United States?'

'No,' Anthony said, 'I was never in the States.'

'I have interests there,' Krogh said. Again he was at a loss for words. 'A cigarette?'

'Thanks.'

Krogh held out his lighter and began in a loud uneasy voice which withered at once in the rather close air between the sound-proof windows and the sound-proof

95

door: 'The suggestion I've got to make may seem odd. You may not want to accept it.' He was painfully embarrassed. He said, as if he had forgotten that he had explained nothing, 'It's not a thing I can go to the police about.'

Anthony said gently, 'What do you want me to do? Steal something?'

'Steal,' Krogh said, 'of course not.' He fidgeted, swallowed, took the plunge. 'All I want is a personal guard. I thought yesterday – I know that it was nothing but a car back-firing, but it gave me a shock – how defenceless I am against any really unscrupulous. . . . It must seem fantastic to you, but these things are done in America. I had trouble only yesterday at the factories. You may not believe——'

'But of course I do,' Anthony said. He did not hesitate a moment; only a certain vacancy behind his earnest gaze indicated that the mind was away in Buenos Aires, in Africa, in India, in Malaya, in Shanghai adapting an old story to new needs. 'Why, I remember meeting a fellow once who had been a bodyguard of Morgan himself. It was in Shanghai. He told me they all had them. He told me——' Anthony stopped. 'Why, it's common sense. Even the film stars have their bodyguards.'

'But here in Stockholm. . . .'

'You've got to move with the times,' Anthony said. He was quite confident now; he was selling himself as he had sold silk stockings and vacuum cleaners; the eyes fixed, the foot inside the door, the rapid patter which never ceased to be that of a gentleman ('He was quite the gentleman,' they would say in excuse displaying unwanted purchases to their husbands). 'And you've come to the right person, Mr Krogh. I could show you cups I've won, silver plate.' He did not even forget the touch of pathos which would supply the purchaser with another excuse – 'poor fellow, he'd seen hard times'. 'But I've sold most of them, Mr Krogh. Times when I was on my uppers. I've pawned a lot in my time and dropped the ticket in the nearest dustbin. I've never regretted anything so much as a silver *épergne* I won at the Singapore Club; I had something to compete against there; they were all crack shots. It was a lovely *épergne*.'

'So you'll take the job?' Krogh asked.

'Of course I'll take it,' Anthony said.

'You'll be free as long as I'm at the office, but outside the office I shall want you with me.'

'You ought to do this thing in style,' Anthony said. 'Bullet-proof glass, steel shutters.'

'I don't think that's necessary in Stockholm.'

'All the same,' Anthony said, eyeing the glass walls with undisguised distaste, 'anyone could lob a bomb into this building. Not that it could do any harm to the fountain.'

'What do you mean?' Krogh said quickly. 'Don't you like the fountain?'

'I ask you,' Anthony said, 'could anyone like it?'

'It's by the best modern sculptor in Sweden.'

'Of course it's highbrow,' Anthony said. He went to the window and scowled down at the fountain, at the green stone dripping with water under the grey sky. 'It's in a fine situation,' he said encouragingly.

'But you think – it's bad?'

'I think it's horrible,' Anthony said. 'If that's the Swedish type of beauty, give me the Edgware Road type any day of the week.'

97

'The best judges,' Krogh said, 'they've all told me——'

'Ah, but they all have an axe to grind,' Anthony said. 'Ask the common people. After all, it's the common people who buy Krogh's.'

'You like this ash-tray?' Krogh asked.

'Oh, the ash-tray's fine,' Anthony said.

'The same man designed it.'

'He's good at knick-knacks,' Anthony said. 'The trouble is, you shouldn't have given him all that stone to play about with. Something smaller.'

'Your sister likes it.'

'Dear Kate,' Anthony said, 'she always was a bit highbrow.'

Krogh joined him at the window. He stared down with gloom into the court .'The porter didn't like it,' he said.

'Of course, if you like it . . .'

'But I'm not sure. I'm not sure,' Krogh said. 'There are things I don't understand. Poetry. Something your Minister wrote. I haven't had time for these things.'

'The same with me,' Anthony said, 'but I've got a natural taste.'

'You like music?'

'I love it,' Anthony said.

'Tonight,' Krogh said, 'we have to go to the opera. You will enjoy that then?'

'I always like a good tune,' Anthony said. He hummed a bar or two of 'Picking Daisies by Daylight', paused, and to the anxious man who watched him, he waved an airy salute. I'm employed again. Yours truly on the up-grade. Here's pickings. 'I bet you are busy,' he said. He paused at the door: 'I shall need some money for glad rags.'

'Glad rags?'

'White tie and the rest of it.'

'Miss Farrant – your sister – will see about that.'

'Well,' Anthony said, 'I'll be seeing you.'

[3]

Ex for All, thought Minty. The school phrases stung his lips, but they were always first to his tongue. It gave him a bitter tormented pleasure to say, not an afternoon free, but Ex for All. He hated and he loved. The school and he were joined by a painful reluctant coition, a passionless coition that leaves everything to regret, nothing to love, everything to hate, but cannot destroy the idea: we are one body.

And he imagines he can sport a Harrow tie and get away with it. No Captain of Games, no member of the Philathletic Club with a bow tie and a braided waistcoat, would have been capable of a more honest indignation. It was only that Minty had more self-control. The twisting of his arm had taught him it, the steel nibs dug into his calf, the spilt incense and the broken sacred pictures. It had indeed been a long and hard coition for Minty; and when the carefully chosen malicious moment had come for requital, after the correspondence with the chemist in Charing Cross Road, the receipt of the plain packets, it had not been Minty who had flinched, but his accomplice. His accomplice stayed, failed to reach the sixth, became something in the City; it was Minty who left, after long hours with the housemaster, not expelled but taken away by his mother. Everything was very quiet, very discreet: his mother subscribed for him to the Old Boys' Society.

99

Ex for All. There was no need to watch Krogh's now that Farrant was safely inside. Farrant needed money. Farrant sported a false tie. Farrant was safe. But the day, which had begun so well with a letter from the family, must be passed to the best advantage. Tomorrow he would have to remember to keep his mind free from malice and uncharitableness in honour of St Zephyrinus; today he could give full rein to every instinct. St Louis had never done anything to help him. Weak in bed he had prayed to him after he had been drained, but St Louis had not heard; the despised, the forgotten Zephyrinus had replied.

I will see the Minister. And Minty, he told himself with a sly twinkle, what a tease you are. Old enough to know better. A great big tease. He chuckled ingratiatingly to himself, coming out into Gustavus Adolphus's square, his black coat dripping rain; the grey monarch faced Russia, the rain running from his sword-hilt and the umbrellas clustered like mushrooms under the pillars of the Opera House. Minty and one random taxi had the square to themselves. There's no real harm in Minty, he thought, planning how he might get to the Minister past the so-efficient Calloway, the army of young diplomats with broadcasting voices.

Calloway nearly shut the door in his face, but Minty was too quick for him. 'I've got to see Captain Gullie,' he said. He knew the geography of the Legation well, slipped past Calloway, down a white-panelled passage, into the military attaché's room. The military attaché looked up with a scowl. 'Oh, it's you, Minty, is it? What the hell do you want now?' Self-consciously he twisted his ginger moustache, shifted his monocle. On the desk in front of him lay the bound volume of a magazine.

'I'm seeing the Minister,' Minty said, 'but he's busy for the moment. I thought I'd just pass the time of day. Busy?'

'Very busy,' Gullie said.

'I thought you'd be interested to hear that there's another Scotsman come to town. Name of Farrant. Says he's a MacDonald.'

The back of Gullie's neck flushed. 'Are you sure? Farrant. I don't know the name. You might hand me my clan-book. There it is. Just by your elbow.' Minty handed the little red book of clans and tartans to Gullie.

'Of course,' Gullie said, 'we Camerons can't bear a MacDonald. It's as impossible for a Cameron to be friends with a MacDonald as for a Frenchman——'

'I had the pleasure of meeting your mother the other day,' Minty said, rambling round the room with an air of secret amusement. Gullie flushed again. 'What a marvellous accent. Really one would never know she was German. But tell me, Gullie, you Camerons – what's your quarrel with the MacDonalds?'

'Glencoe,' Gullie said.

'Well, well,' Minty said. 'What are you reading, Gullie?' He looked over the other's shoulder at the bound volume of a German nudist magazine. 'Quite a little pornographic library you have here.'

'You know very well,' Gullie said, 'that my interest's artistic. I paint ships and the –' he twisted his monocle – 'the human figure. Damn it all, Minty, there's no Farrant here. The fellow must be an impostor.'

'I may have got the clan wrong. It may have been Mac something else. All those ships yours?' He waved at the little pictures which hung two deep round the white walls: small ships of every kind, barques, brigantines,

frigates, schooners, dancing on bright blue formal waves.
'Where do you keep the human figure?'

'I have them at home,' Gullie said. 'Look here, Minty.
The fellow's not a MacPherson, nor a MacFarlane, nor
a – is he a straight fellow?'

'No, I shouldn't think so,' Minty said.

'He shouldn't go about saying he's a MacDonald.'

'It may have been Mac something else.'

'We'll catch him out at the Caledonian dinner. I'll
spot his tartan.'

'I've come to see the Minister,' Minty said, 'about a
Harrow dinner. I'd better be getting along. He'll be
impatient. You don't mind if I use your door, do you?'
He left a little pool of water where he had been standing.
'So long, Gullie. Stick to ships. Cut out the human
figure.' His teasing tone altered to admit a touch of
venom, a scrap of sincerity. 'It's so ugly, Gullie, all those
protuberances.' Before Gullie could stop him, he was
through the door behind the desk.

Yes, it was ugly, the human figure. Man or woman, it
made no difference to Minty. The body's shape, the
running nose, excrement, the stupid postures of passion,
these beat like a bird's heart in Minty's brain. Nothing
could have more stirred his malice than the sight of
Gullie poring over the photographs of naked breasts and
thighs. A gang of schoolboys raced through Minty's
mind, breaking up his pictures of Madonna and Child,
jeering, belching, breaking wind.

The Minister sat writing among his bric-a-brac at the
other end of the deep carpet; Minty closed the door very
softly. His eyes were a little dilated. The Minister's
sedate white hair, the pink cheeks lightly powdered after
their shave, the grey expensive suit, Minty took them

in. He was a little afraid of the force of hatred that Gullie had released. To use powder, to take such care with one's clothes, to be so carefully brushed, the hypocrisy of it sickened Minty. The body still remained, its functions were not hidden by Savile Row. To think that God Himself had become man. Minty could not enter a church without the thought, which sickened him, which was more to him than the agony in the garden, the despair upon the cross. Pain was an easy thing to bear beside the humiliation which rose with one in the morning and lay down with one at night. He stood and dripped at the carpet's edge and thought that at least one need not be so coarse as to love the body like Gullie or hide it under powder and pin-striped elegant suits like the Minister. Hating the hypocrites he waited for the Minister to look up, exposing his shabbiness with a mournful malicious pride. At last he said: 'Sir Ronald.'

'Good heavens, my dear fellow,' the Minister said, 'you gave me a start. How did you get here?'

'I was calling on Gullie,' Minty said, 'and as he told me you were not busy at the moment, I thought I'd look in and see you about a Harrow dinner.'

'What an extraordinary thing for Gullie to say.'

'Of course you'll take the chair, Sir Ronald?'

'Why, my dear fellow, it seems such a short time since we had one, and frankly I'm horribly busy.'

'It was two years ago.'

'But you can't pretend,' the Minister said, 'that it was a success. Really, it almost developed into a brawl. And some horrid fellow spilt cigar ash into my port.'

'It would be a good way of putting over this new appeal they've sent out to old Harrovians.'

'My dear Minty, there's no one recognises more than

myself your really quite admirable work for the school, but one must draw the line somewhere, Minty. The trouble is there are too many soldiers here. Why can't they learn Russian at home – or in Tallinn?'

'There's another Harrovian come to live in Stockholm. At least, he wears the tie. Brother of Krogh's woman.'

'That's interesting,' the Minister said.

'He's in the business.'

'Remind him to write his name in the book.'

'I don't believe he was at Harrow at all.'

'I thought you said he was?'

'I said he wore the tie.'

'What a suspicious fellow you are, Minty. If he wasn't straight he wouldn't be in Krogh's. I'd trust Krogh with my last penny.'

'Why don't you?' Minty said. 'They pay ten per cent.'

'Well, I've had one or two little flutters in that direction,' the Minister said. He leant back and smiled with a certain complacency. 'It'll pay for my holiday this winter.'

'But the dinner?' Minty said. He began to plead quite seriously; he made his wet way across the carpet. 'It's a good thing. It keeps us in touch. One evening in the year when one's not a foreigner.'

'Damn it all, Minty, this isn't the Sahara. We're only thirty-six hours from Piccadilly. You don't have to be homesick. You can always trot across for a week-end. Look at Gullie. He's always going over. I prefer to wait and go over for a month at Christmas. It's the best time of year in England. Though I may take a few days' shooting. No, you can't pretend we're cut off here.'

It was true. He was not cut off in the white-panelled

room, behind the vase of autumn roses; his prosperity was like a studied insult. He has not asked me to sit down, he is afraid for his tapestry chairs because my coat's a little wet. 'A dinner's a good thing,' Minty repeated, filling up time while he thought of some story, some joke, some rumour to leave the Minister less happy than he found him.

He said: 'I saw your book was reviewed in the *Manchester Guardian.*'

'No?' the Minister said, 'no? Really? What did they say? I never read reviews.'

'I don't read poetry,' Minty said. 'I only saw the headline – "A Long Way After Dowson". Did you say,' he went on quickly, 'that you'd been buying some of the new Krogh stock? You ought to be careful. There are rumours about.'

'What do you mean? Rumours. . . .'

'Ah, Minty gets to hear a thing or two. They say there was nearly a strike at the factory.'

'Nonsense,' the Minister said. 'Krogh was here at tea. He advised me to buy.'

'Yes, but where did he go afterwards? That's what everyone's asking. Did he have a telephone call?'

'He had two.'

'I thought so,' Minty said.

'I bought a good deal of the last issue,' the Minister said.

'Well, well,' Minty said, 'there are rumours. Nothing that you can get hold of. They may send the price down a little, of course, but you can't expect every flutter to turn out well. Besides, you're a poet. You don't understand these things.' Minty chuckled.

'What are you laughing at?'

'"A long way after Dowson",' Minty said. 'You can't deny that's neat. Trust me always to tell you things. A diplomat can't be expected to know what's happening in the streets. But trust Minty.' He dripped his way towards the door. 'I'm always ready to help a fellow from the old school.'

In the long white passage he paused under the portraits of Sir Ronald's predecessors; in their ruffs, in their full-bottomed wigs, painted by local artists, they had a touch of un-English barbarity, a slant about the eyes purely Scandinavian, their breastplates obscured by furs. Behind a Stuart courtier could be seen a pair of reindeer and a landscape of mountain and ice. It was only the later portraits which bore no national mark at all. Wearing official dress, knee-breeches and medals and ribbons, these models represented an art international-ised at the level of Sargent and De Laszlo. They were much admired, Minty knew, by Sir Ronald who would soon join them on the wall, and an unusual tenderness mingled in Minty's brain with the more usual bitterness, a tenderness for the framed men in wigs who had indeed been cut off, though not so completely cut off as he was cut off, a tenderness for the paintings which Sir Ronald called 'curious'. He walked gently to the door, leaving a trail of damp footmarks down the silver grey carpet, and let himself out.

The rain had stopped, an east wind drove the clouds in grey flocks above Lake Mälaren, and darts of sunlight flicked the wet stones of the palace, the Opera House, the House of Parliament. The motor-boats passing under the North Bridge scattered spray which the wind caught and flung like fine rain against the glass shelters of the deserted restaurant. The naked man on his wet gleaming pedestal stared out over the tumble of small waves towards the Grand Hotel, his buttocks turned to the bridge and passers-by.

Minty went into a telephone-box and rang up Krogh's. He said to the porter: 'Is Herr Krogh still at the office? It's Minty speaking.'

'Yes, Herr Minty. He hasn't gone out.'

'Is he going to the opera tonight?'

'He hasn't ordered his car yet.'

'Get me Herr Farrant on the 'phone if you can.'

He waited a long while, but he was not impatient. On the dusty glass of the box he drew little pictures with his finger, several crosses, a head wearing a biretta.

'Hullo. Is that Farrant? This is Minty speaking.'

'I've just been out buying glad rags,' Anthony said. 'Shoes, socks, ties. We're for the opera tonight.'

'You and Krogh?'

'Me and Krogh.'

'You seem to be as thick as thieves. Listen. Could you get me a line on this strike they've been talking about?'

'He's not what you'd call a ready talker.'

'I can get you a good price for a story.'

'Do we go fifty-fifty?'

Minty smudged out with his thumb the face, the biretta; he drew another cross, a crown of thorns, a halo. 'Listen, Farrant. This is my livelihood, it's my bread and butter, why, Farrant, it's even my cigarettes. You've got a good job; you don't need fifty-fifty. I'll give you a third. Honestly I will.' Almost automatically he crossed his fingers and relieved himself of the responsibility for a broken promise. 'You'll take a third, won't you?' He prepared to plead further, his voice took on the tone of a small boy hanging round a tuck-shop door who begs his seniors to treat him to a piece of penny bun, a section of chocolate. 'Really, you know, Farrant' – but Anthony took him completely by surprise, granted him every-thing. 'Why, I'll only take a quarter, Minty, if it's like that. Good-bye. I'll be seeing you.'

Minty stood with the receiver in his hand, wondering. What does he mean by that? Isn't he going to play square? Is one of the others after him? And he felt a harassed jealousy of the horde of shabby men who waited like himself outside Krogh's, bribing the porter, watching doorways when Krogh dined out, going home themselves late and hungry to their fourth-floor lodgings on the further bank. Has Pihlström got hold of him? Beyer? Has Hammarsten bought him? He saw Pihlström in his mud-splashed suit trying to work an automatic with foreign coins. He saw Beyer shifting the mats from under his beer-glass to his neighbour. He saw Hammar-sten. . . . You can't trust them, he thought, you can't trust them. He hung up the receiver, drew the flat of his hand over the halos and crosses, and stepped out into the grey autumn afternoon.

A spot of lunch, Minty? It's the first day of the financial month: a letter from the family; a new reference at the top of the solicitor's note; I've teased the editor and I've teased Gullie and I've teased the Minister; surely a small extravagance would be timely, a spot of lunch. But duty first, Minty, always duty first.

He rang up the newspaper and told them to have a photographer outside the Opera House.

And then lunch.

But again he was detained. A church claimed him. The darkness, the glow of the sanctuary lamp drew him more than food. It was Lutheran, of course, but it had the genuine air of plaster images, of ever-burning light, of sins forgiven. He looked this way and that, he bent his head and dived for the open door, with the caution and the dry-mouthed excitement of a secret debauchee.

[4]

Anthony felt conspicuous until the lights went out, but he didn't care a hang. He knew he looked well in evening dress, even when it had been bought ready-made. There were two empty seats on his left-hand and two empty seats beyond Krogh. They were deliberately isolated in the fourth row; the two seats immediately behind them were also empty. Anthony began to calculate how much it cost Krogh to go to the theatre.

'Do you often come here, Mr Krogh?' he asked, glancing upwards at the glittering and tiaraed boxes, the curiously out-dated atmosphere of the house: shoulders and diamonds and grey hair; a woman studied them with a lorgnette. It was as if they were taking part in some traditional ceremony reserved to age.

'Every first night,' Krogh said.

'You must be musical,' Anthony said.

The Royal Box was occupied; the King was not present (he was abroad playing tennis), but the Crown Prince sat there with his wife and patiently exposed himself to Stockholm society; it was his duty so long as the lights were up to be seen. The interest of the theatre was divided between the box and the stalls where Krogh sat, between rank and money; Anthony got the impression that money won.

'Do you know each other?' he asked. 'I mean do you know the Crown Prince?'

'No,' Krogh said, 'I've been once to the Palace, to a reception. I know his brother.'

The dowagers watched them greedily when they spoke, a bowing of tiaras, a flashing of opera-glasses; a grey little withered man with a bright ribbon across his shirt-front bowed and smiled and tried to catch Krogh's eye. Anthony, looking up at the Royal Box, saw that even the Prince was watching them. It was curious to think that Krogh was probably the only stranger whom the Prince knew by sight. The square intellectual face was bent towards them with patient interest.

Both men were tired, but Krogh's tiredness gave an impression of physical exhaustion. His evening dress fitted him badly about the shoulders; there was a touch of vulgarity in the diamond studs which did not seem to belong to him; it was as if he were wearing another man's clothes, another man's vulgarity. 'Listen, Farrant,' he said, 'if I fall asleep you must wake me before the end of the act. I mustn't be seen asleep.' He added, 'Tuesday is always a tiring day for me.'

The lights of the great central chandelier went out; darkness ran quickly along the edge of the circle, descended on the stalls. *Tuesday*. The violins began tentatively to search for something and could not find it, wavered and despaired. *Tuesday*. A woman sneezed. The light on the conductor's baton-tip darted like a firefly downwards. *Tuesday night*. I promised, Anthony thought, that's tough on her, and the violins caught and held the emotion of regret: for loss, for the pain one gives, for what one forgets. She's dumb; she may have sat round all day. Wavering, lamenting, the cry of a bird over grey commonland, a poisoned draught, irreparable love, death that ends everything, a woman's sneeze again; it's tough on her, stone stairs, 'no milk today'. She's dumb. Davidge the name, and death the black sail.

The curtain rose; long robes of poison green and purple picked up the dust from the boards; an elderly woman sang shaking blonde pigtails; the footlights glittered on tin breastplates; a draught of wine was taken and a boat set sail. It was meaningless. *Tuesday*. I'll telephone in the first interval. It makes one feel guilty (returning, false friend, to face King Mark) when they are so dumb, when they fall for one. A kind of innocence; she ought to learn to make herself up properly: the lipstick the wrong shade for that sunburn lotion; she drank the schnaps that day in Gothenburg as if she had never drunk anything stronger than sherry before.

The coloured water in the beaker, the actress with tipped glass, the doped drink, soprano sorceries, this fuss over irreparable love.

It's not a question of love; only when someone falls for one so easily one likes – oh, hell, what, to let them down gently, to do as one would be done by (the remembered sudden pain of Annette's disappearance dwarfed the music, the agony in a sound superficial compared with the agony in a sight, the pencilled wall, the soapy stairs). If she were less dumb, if she had not fallen quite so easily to all those damned silly stories, I shouldn't mind. He looked at Krogh. 'Mr Krogh.' He shook him by the elbow and Krogh woke.

'It's getting so noisy,' Anthony whispered, 'I expect it's close to the end.'

He was right; great gusts of music billowed the purple velvets; stout Vikings strode singing to the footlights; betrayal; the panting breasts of a weeping soprano; my friend; the falling curtain.

III

'Do you mind,' Anthony asked, 'if I slip away and telephone?'

'No, no,' Krogh said, 'you can't do that. People will come and talk to me. They'll ask me if I like the thing.'

'Say that you were too tired to listen.'

'If only things were as easy as that,' Krogh said, 'but you don't understand. This is Art. Great Art.' He dropped his voice. 'I read about it somewhere. It's one of the great love-stories of the world.'

'No, no.' Anthony said. 'You've got it wrong. You're mixing it up with *Carmen*.'

'Are you sure?'

'Of course I'm sure. After all, I was awake, Mr Krogh. Besides, I know the story. This is just about a fellow who sends his friend to bring him back a wife. And there's a mix-up about a drink which is supposed to give people a letch for each other; the fellow's friend and the girl drink it and they get a letch for each other. But she's still got to go back and marry the other fellow. You can't call that a great love-story. It's all too fantastic. Why did they need to put in all that about the drink for? You don't need to drink anything to fall in love.'

'You may be right,' Krogh said.

'Then can I go and telephone?'

Krogh said with sudden suspicion, 'Is it the Press? I won't keep you a day if you get in touch with the Press.'

'No, no, Mr Krogh,' Anthony said, 'this is just a girl.' He began to explain. 'We had a date together and I forgot about it.'

'You mean,' Krogh said, 'you were going out to-gether?'

'Yes. We'd have gone to a movie or to a park. Is there a park here where you can sit about?'

'And you'd have enjoyed that?' Krogh asked. He turned in his chair and said in a low voice, 'You'd take her to the park and – what is it you say?'

'Neck,' Anthony said.

'That's the word. I remember friends of mine – oh, years ago – in Chicago.' He said in a tone of joyful surprise, 'Murphy. O'Connor. Williamson. How odd it is. I thought I'd quite forgotten their names. We were working on a bridge there. That was before I invented the cutter. I don't think Hall was there. Aronstein. That was another name.'

'Look here, Mr Krogh,' Anthony said, 'do you like this place?' Everyone had waited for the Prince to stop applauding; now they were streaming out, the women in their jewels, the men in their orders, winking like traffic signals, to the great stairs and the promenade.

'Of course,' Krogh said.

'But it's dull. What you want after a hard day's work is a bit of song and dance. Something light. Aren't there any cabarets here?'

'I don't know,' Krogh said. He added slowly, 'I've always been able to trust your sister. I've never kept things from her. After all, you're her brother.' He seemed to be working himself up towards a confession of the deepest importance. 'Yes, it seems dull to me, too. And that statue – but Kate likes it.'

'Mr Krogh,' Anthony said, 'you are coming out with me now. We're going to go and have a quiet drink somewhere where there's a bit of music and then I'm going to see you home to bed.' He added, 'I can telephone from the restaurant.'

'It's impossible,' Krogh said, 'people would notice.'

'They'll never notice. They are all going out to the promenade.'

'They'll see our empty seats when the next act begins. They'll think I'm ill. You can't imagine the rumours that might start. Just before a new issue too. And the reporters will be outside.'

'Then I'll be the one who's ill. You are taking me home. No one knows who I am. They'll think I'm a friend of yours.'

Krogh said, 'Farrant, if only I could. But you'd never convince them. And there are two more hours of this. Can you act?'

'Can I act?' Anthony said. 'I should just think I can act. You should have seen me in *The Private Secretary*. The whole school laughed, even the masters. The headmaster's wife – we called her Fuzzy Wuzzy – gave me a box of chocolates. Of course, I'm a bit rusty now, but I can act all right.'

But no, Krogh said, it wouldn't do. He was grateful, but Farrant didn't know the intensity of the Press publicity which surrounded him. There was one little shabby fellow in particular. . . . He said, 'It's gone on now for years.' He said, 'Of course in a way it's a tribute – I daresay I should feel lost without it. Go and telephone and come back.' He opened the programme for the first time and began to read it, page by page, from the large advertisement of Krogh's, methodically, through to the list of the cast.

Along the promenade a space had been cleared, up and down which the Prince walked accompanied by his wife, by an elderly man with a little pointed grey moustache, and an old-young woman, with long hair, an unpowdered face and a spotty complexion, back and forth, back and forth, like animals behind bars watched at feeding-time. There was a surge of whispers when the four backs receded, a scurry of disinterested conversation when they approached.

On the pad in the telephone-box someone had drawn a heart, an awkward lop-sided heart. The man at the exchange for a long while did not understand what Anthony wanted; over and over again Anthony said, 'Hotel York'. Inside the heart was a telephone number, and the artist had begun to draw an arrow. Up and down the promenade the Prince walked, and the women watched the Princess's dress and the men whispered. The pencilled heart seemed for a moment rather simple, rather touching, until one noticed in the corner of the page a little French rhyme such as one might find in a cracker at Christmas and the whole picture, while Anthony listened and waited, became clever, became pastiche, became a sophisticated joke.

'Is Miss Davidge in?' The porter at the York could speak English. 'I am not sure. I will go and find out. Who is that, please?' and Anthony could hear the tiny tap of his footsteps walking away. He looked at his watch. It was a quarter to ten. He thought: What is her name? She told me her name, but he could not remember it. It occurred to him that he could not properly remember even her appearance, only the faults he had found with it, the wrong shade of lipstick, the wrong powder. The idea of her complete anonymity momentarily touched his imagination. He felt responsibility as if an animal had been left in his charge and he had lost it. It will always answer if you call—— Yes, but if one has forgotten the name?

'This is Anthony,' he said. The voice was familiar: even the hopeless lack of concealment was familiar, the quick slight sigh of excitement, or hope, or possibly relief, which made itself heard across a lake, a bridge, a quay, running recklessly along the wires.

He said, 'Who's that?'

'It's Lucia.' How could he have forgotten the absurd pretentious name? She had confided to him in the corner of a warehouse that she had a brother called Roderick. Her father was responsible. He was a great reader of the obscurer classics, classics which if they had ever lived were by now dead and buried under the dust which gathers on the shelves of public libraries. Round and round Gothenburg he carried his favourite book; he had never for long been parted from it; it was responsible for Roderick – Lockhart's *Spanish Ballads*. She could not remember what book had given him the idea of Lucia. Over the *smörgåsbord* Mr Davidge had offered to lend him Lockhart. 'Scott's Lockhart,' he explained. He had gone on to say that he was a great reader of poetry. He lowered his voice and spoke with awe of Horne and Alexander Smith. 'I like something I can get my teeth into,' he had said, 'not lyrics. Epics.' His reading had been conditioned, his daughter said with sudden bright malice because he was usurping the conversation, by what he could buy from the sixpenny boxes at the second-hand booksellers. 'Look at it. Just look at it,' she said with scorn, pointing at Lockhart where it lay beside the salted herrings, in a black scratched binding with an old circulating library label covering the back.

'Lucia,' Anthony said. 'Of course. I'd know your voice anywhere. Only I thought it might be a family

116

voice, you see. I didn't want to spill the old heart out to your mother.'

'I suppose' the voice said hopelessly, 'you forgot.'

'Of course I didn't forget,' Anthony said. 'But I've just been given a rather important post by Krogh. I haven't had time to get to a telephone till now. I've been rushed off my feet. You wouldn't believe the things I've been doing. Listen, do you like tigers?'

'Tigers?'

'Toy tigers. I bought you one today. That just shows I didn't forget you. Can I bring it round to the hotel?'

'But when?'

'I could be round by midnight.'

'Oh, Anthony, I wish you had come. It's no good now. I'm half-way to bed.'

'But it's not ten yet.'

'We always go to bed at ten at home.'

'Tomorrow night, if I can get away' – My God, poor kid, he thought, going to bed at ten; it's stiff. I'd like to give her a good time. My good turn for the month. He thought with painful gratitude: she thinks I'm swell. She believes what I tell her. It's dumb of her, but it's sweet.

'It's no good. Mother's got tickets for something.'

'The next night. . . .'

'A friend of Father's . . . Anthony, it's no good. We'll be gone next week.'

'Have lunch with me.'

The small despairing voice worried him. 'It's no good, Anthony. You should see Father's list of engagements. The city hall, the museums, lunch here and lunch there. We're doing the place. How we're doing it!'

'Well then,' Anthony said, 'you can have breakfast

with me.' He said airily: 'We'll take a car to some place. When can you manage it?'

'Tomorrow?' the voice failed up the wire with excitement. 'Here's Mother. I don't want her to know. She'd put her foot on it. Will you be at the North Bridge at eight?'

'O.K.,' Anthony said. He hung up the receiver. Eight was damnably early. It would mean that he had to get up at seven-thirty; it was very cold most mornings at that hour; and he had a sudden cheerless vision of his room: the toothbrush in the glass, the noisy coil of pipes, the window opening on the narrow street and the dustbins, the hot-water tap which ran cold, the pictures still stuck up with soap; he had forgotten to buy any drawing-pins. My good turn for the month. Somebody tapped on the door.

One day something has got to happen. They'll drive me desperate. He had no idea who 'they' might be.

He turned and saw Krogh waiting for him outside the box, and immediately without effort he was smiling, he was full of bonhomie, he was a good fellow. 'Have I been long?'

'I've come away,' Krogh said, 'after all.' He said with astonishment as if he could hardly believe that it was as easy as all that, 'They've all gone back and here we are.' He stared up the broad empty staircase. 'And now what next?'

'That's fine,' Anthony said. 'Now we just walk out. We won't bother about our things or your car.'

Krogh smiled. 'As easy as all that,' he said, 'I've never thought of it before.' Side by side they went down the empty stairs. They could hear someone singing, the sound fainter than a voice over the telephone. 'This is quite an adventure for me, Farrant. It's a long while since I had an adventure like this.'

'But as your bodyguard,' Anthony said, 'I feel responsible. I haven't even got a gun.'

'That was nerves. I don't need a bodyguard.'

'You need a drink.'

'That's right.' He slipped his arm through Anthony's and they came out past the astonished door-keepers into the square. A man ran up carrying something like a picture-frame on a handle, a white light blinded them, made them see everything for a moment distorted in a cruel glare, a wavering retreating world of black and white.'

'A taxi. Quick. Get a taxi,' Krogh said. Two men came forward and said something to Krogh in Swedish, a taxi drew to the kerb, and Krogh pushed his way to the door. A crowd collected with extraordinary rapidity in the square. Through the windscreen Anthony could see six or seven people hurrying across the bridge. A woman under the Gustavus statue cried, 'Herr Krogh. Hurrah,' and everyone began to cheer in a weak questioning way as the taxi drove off. 'Fools,' Krogh said. He leant far back where he could not be seen, and the lights of the Grand Hotel slid across the windows. A blast of dance music shook them and receded.

'Shall we stop here?' Anthony asked.

'No, no,' Krogh said, 'somewhere quieter. We'll go up to the Hasselbacken opposite Tivoli. I haven't been there for twenty years.'

'Is it a good show, Tivoli?'

'I've never been there,' Krogh said.

'We'll go one night,' Anthony said.

The moon-drenched stonework of the Northern

Museum receded below them as they climbed above the lake. The music from Tivoli crept into the cold air which caught, enclosed it, as a block of ice might preserve two human bodies from corruption: a frozen riot, an iced abandon.

'What could I do in Tivoli?' Krogh said. 'You're a desperate fellow, Farrant. I'm not safe with you. To have left the opera like that. It will be in all the papers tomorrow. You heard them talk to me. They wanted to know if I disapproved of the production, if I felt ill, if I'd had bad news.'

'Someone's following us now,' Anthony said, looking back, watching a wide yellow broom sweep round the curve by Skansen. 'They'll catch us for certain in the restaurant. Tell the man to go to Tivoli. It's the only way; they'll lose us in the crowd.' He tapped on the glass himself. 'Tivoli,' he said, 'Tivoli.'

'No, no,' Krogh said, 'we can't do that. What will the papers say? To have left the opera to go to Tivoli. They'll think I'm mad. What will happen to the market?'

'Forget it,' Anthony said.

'Forget the market,' Krogh said with astonishment; he began to laugh uneasily, guiltily. 'What a desperate fellow you are,' he repeated. 'That scar – were you forgetting the market then?'

'Ah, that scar,' Anthony said, 'that's a long story. Do you remember the *Neptune* which sank in the Indian Ocean a few years ago? You wouldn't have read about it in your papers, of course. There was a panic; the passengers tried to rush the boats; I was helping the first officer keep them out and someone clubbed me.'

Krogh laughed. Anthony said with startled incredulity, 'You don't believe me?'

'Not a word,' Krogh said. The taxi drew up, but Anthony sat back and stared.

'Why don't you believe me? What have I said wrong?' He began to repeat the story softly over to himself – '*Neptune* . . . panic . . . rush for the boats.'

'Get out,' Krogh said. 'Here's the other taxi.' He put his hand on Anthony's arm, when they were past the ticket barrier, and stopped him. 'I want to see who it is.'

The second taxi drew up behind the first. A man in a thin grey summer suit got out; while he paid the driver he looked this way and that: every movement was slow and timed; thin though the skin of his face was, it sagged and hung in pouches under the chin, below the eyes. 'It's Pihlström.' But the taxi did not drive away. A pair of legs in black tight trousers felt for the step, dangled earthwards in a long disjointed tenuous way, like a leather-jacket's. 'Two of them,' Krogh exclaimed. 'I've never known Pihlström hunt in couples. Why, it's – how important they must think it is——' a long-tailed coat, a black tie as thin as a bootlace tied in a bow below the old chin, the white bristles, the high humourless face, 'it's – it's Professor Hammarsten,' the black soft hat, the steel spectacles, the pale-grey skin.

'Quick,' Krogh said, 'before they see us.' He led the way; he saw an avenue of astonished faces open and close again; he remembered that he was in evening dress and hatless, but a curious irresponsibility touched his brain; he thought of Hall sitting in his false nose while the *festa* churned around them saying: 'But what about the friction?' He said, suddenly out of breath, pausing behind a shooting booth, 'What would poor Hall think of this.' Poor faithful Hall. He could trust Hall to do anything, but not for Hall this sudden absence of reserve, this laughter. One kept that for someone who could not even tell a convincing lie. He said gently, panting between the words, 'It was not the Indian Ocean.'

Anthony said, 'Damn'. He smiled anxiously, blinked in the glare of the flood lamps. 'I've never tried that story before. It's generally a bomb.' He said, 'I'll tell you. Only Kate knows. I was skinning a rabbit and the knife slipped.'

'Pihlström,' Krogh said. Cautiously, round the corner from the main avenue, came the man in the grey suit, treading softly like a cat circumnavigating a dustbin. Krogh said wearily: 'The game's over.' He added with the same qualm of conscience he might have felt if he were betraying someone dear to him, selling him stock which he knew not only to be worthless in the long run, but worthless now, immediately, indisposable, 'We've been silly.'

'Leave him to me,' Anthony said.

He advanced on Pihlström, seized an arm, turned him round and pushed him round the corner of the booth. Pihlström made a succession of quick yapping cries: 'Hammarsten. Hammarsten.' Professor Hammarsten was standing with two or three other men in front of a betting booth lined with little brass handles. 'Hammarsten.' There seemed to be an argument going on about a coin which Hammarsten had presented. 'Hammarsten.' He turned round quickly and his spectacles fell off. 'Pihlström.' He groped blindly on the gravel with his foot, drawing an irregular circle round the spectacles. 'Pihlström,' he called appealingly. Anthony ran Pihlström forward. 'Hammarsten.' Professor Hammarsten began to stoop for his spectacles, then leapt straight again with a cry of anguish, his hand on the small of his back. 'Pihlström.' Three men began to explain to him something about a coin which the booth-keeper held. Anthony let go of Pihlström and pushed him into the Professor's arms. 'Hammarsten.' They held each other for a moment; then Pihlström stooped and picked up Hammarsten's glasses; Anthony and Krogh watched them from a distance. Presently they divided: one walked one way, one the other, and disappeared. They were not hurrying; there was a lack of enthusiasm in their movements.

'Have you ever been a chucker-out?' Krogh said. Anthony sighed. 'No,' he said, 'I'm not in the mood for stories; not after that mistake of mine. I could have sworn it was the Indian Ocean.'

'It was,' Krogh said.

'My God,' Anthony said. 'You mean there was nothing wrong? Never ask me to play poker with you; it'll have to be rummy; something where it's just honest luck and there's no room for bluff. What a poker face!'

'Can you really shoot?'

'Can I shoot?' Anthony said. He put his arm in Krogh's and hurried him down two avenues. Occasion-ally they stopped at a booth, but 'too easy', Anthony said. At last he found what he wanted. The prizes were numbered. 'Would you like a cigarette-case?' Anthony said.

'I have this one.' Krogh took from his pocket a case of thin inlaid wood. It had been designed by the same sculptor as the statue, as the ash-trays; it bore the monogram E.K. He was proud of it. He said: 'There's no other like it in the world.' It lay, almost as light as a powder-puff, in his palm.

'Yes, it's pretty,' Anthony said, 'but you want

something for formal occasions, something in pigskin. That one there: it would look well with a gold monogram. I'll get it for you.'

Afterwards he said, 'We'll have a drink.'

He didn't know a word of Swedish, but he had taken control. They had their beers. 'Weak stuff,' Anthony said, 'you come to England and I'll show you. Could I put down a Younger now? I'd say I could. Or a couple of Stone's special. You don't need more than a couple.'

He held Krogh entranced with his ease of manner, his air of knowing a thing or two of the very things which Krogh knew least. He watched Anthony as a middle-aged woman who had been brought up under another dispensation might watch a young girl who knew all the right cosmetics, the best ingredients for cocktails, the right doctor to go to if one started something one didn't want to finish. He felt a little envy, a little affection, even a little amusement, but chiefly a sense of how quickly time had passed for him and how slowly it must have passed for the other who knew so much, so early.

'What about shaking a leg?'

'I don't understand.'

'Dancing a bit.'

The loudspeaker played what were probably the latest tunes, a ring of arc lamps flooded the wooden boards; the small fair faces followed the intricate music with pinched attention, the girls stepping slowly on their delicate small feet, solemn, receiving like a sacrament the communication from their partners of a foot to the side, a foot between, a foot backward, thinking of the shop, of the office, of the dress they couldn't afford – 'in the silence of my lonely room' – of summer over – 'day and night' – of the winter fashions.

'No. I won't dance. But you go and dance. I'll watch you.' No good to assure himself, I am Krogh, to remember his initials in electric lamps, the factories working day and night; one shift going off at seven; the next at three in the morning; he was afraid to ask one of the girls who stood around the floor to dance with him. He saw Anthony tour the floor, taking a look at a girl here and a girl there; he did not speak a word of the language, but he was no more of an expatriate than Krogh, the Swede, born in the hut on Vätten, who learned arithmetic at the village school. Perhaps, he thought, I have unlearned too much, seeing Anthony take a girl by the arm and lead her on to the floor; when I was young——

But he would not deceive himself. The quality of truth was in the air of Tivoli; one could not be a hypocrite in a place where no one was present for mixed motives, where pleasure was the only, the undisguised inducement. Even when I was young, he thought, I was the same. They told stories in Stockholm of his schooldays, his early proficiency as a business man and as an inventor; how he had constructed a periscope which could be used through the window to disclose when the master was coming round the corner of the building, of how he had traded postage stamps for fruit and held them, packed in straw, till the height of the summer when his fellows would give all the stamps they possessed for a bite of something juicy. He knew the stories; he knew they were untrue, he knew the dullness of the truth – the plodding industry, the certificates gained one by one; he had hardly begun to live with any vividness before the idea of the new cutter had come to him one day of a Chicago spring. He could remember the exact pattern which the great dredger had made, swinging across the sky. He had seen it through the window of the foreman's hut. He had leant out and called to the driver, 'Five feet more to the left'. The long hard North American winter was over, he had smelt spring through the liquid asphalt, the smoke, the rain-wet metal; the macadamised road-ways were splitting under the gentle persistent pressure of the grasses. But he had no love for nature, he remembered that spring day not because it was more beautiful than others, but because, looking down at the plan of the bridge pinned out on the drawing-board, while the dredger swayed and flopped and sank through the pale-blue air, he thought: if I arranged the knife just so, the sliding tray, the brake detaching the cog, would the friction be too great? He had never been aware of having thought deeply on the subject of those small, absurdly cheap, absurdly necessary goods, which were now known as Krogh's. Once when he was a boy his father had said that So-and-So must be worth a million; for a week he had worked in the shops at Nyköping and seen the old type of cutter in action and given notice because he saw no future in so old-fashioned a firm for even the most stubborn diligence. Now, suddenly, the idea for a new cutter had come with no apparent effort and impressed on his mind for ever the spring day, the smell of shrubs and asphalt, the dredger dipping and swaying.

Something in the new ease he felt with Anthony recalled that period. It was no coincidence that he had remembered the names of Murphy, O'Connor, Williamson and Aronstein (O'Connor had been killed in Panama, buried under forty tons of mud when a dredger broke; Aronstein had gone into oil; Williamson and Murphy were probably dead in France). He had never known them well, though he had worked with them for eighteen months, but he had not been shy with them, as he had been shy with Andersson, as he was shy of the sunburned shopgirls solemnly dancing. Deliberately he made an effort to go back, to peel off the years and their inhumanities as one peels the leaves off a neglected calendar, glancing at the mottoes, the verses, the trite sayings of dead rhetoricians, occasionally pausing at some unexpectedly vivid line: 1912 when he went into partnership, 1915 when he bought out his partner, 1920 when he first began to aim at the world monopoly, 1927 the peak year when he bought the German interests, made his loan to the French Government, established himself in Italy; but it only brought him to the present, the short-term loans, the threatened strike, Laurin's silly voice from the microphone advising caution.

He thought: what am I doing here? This is absurd. The gentle creaking of the wooden boards under the dancers' feet; the orderly crowd moving in two lines up the shooting booths, down past the fortune-tellers, the switchback, the scenic railways; the sudden cool courts at either end with the coloured fountains rustling between the black sky and the white concrete; the seats by the lake side; the light of a ferry boat moving away like a bicycle lamp over the dark polished lake. These were Sweden as much as the silver birch woods round Vätten, the brightly-painted wooden hut, the duck staggering in mid-air, his mother waiting on the tiny quay; but the images had no longer any meaning for him, he was like a man without a passport, without a nationality, like a man who could only speak Esperanto.

The table rocked and righted itself; he looked round to see tall weedy old Hammarsten pull up a chair.

'Good evening, Herr Krogh.' He rubbed his finger across the white bristles on his chin, and leaning closer confided to Krogh, 'I've sent Pihlström home.' He said, 'I could see at once that you didn't want to be bothered by a man like Pihlström. I told him I'd seen you leave in a taxi.'

'And he believed you?'

'Oh, but Herr Krogh, I put it rather more subtly. I asked him to lend me a taxi fare to follow you.'

'Very clever, Professor, but really——'

'Of course he got into the taxi and drove away.' The old man made a sound as if he were drinking hot tea. He said with immense satisfaction, 'He'll be on the other side of the lake by now.'

'How are your language classes, Professor?'

'Not too good, not too good, Herr Krogh. One is compelled to drive the quill. It leads one into strange company. Pihlström, the Englishman Minty, Beyer – do you know Beyer?'

'I haven't that honour,' Krogh said.

'It is quite impossible to trust Beyer,' Hammarsten said. 'He was responsible for that article the other day on your career.'

'It was complimentary.'

'But so inaccurate. It is only we older men who pursue Truth amid the distractions – I confess it, Herr Krogh – of a not very *distingué* profession.' He said with extraordinary venom, under his breath, as if he were talking to himself, 'Mud-slingers.'

'It seemed reasonably accurate.'

'But 1911, Herr Krogh, for the date when you went into partnership. 1912 you must confess would have been – let me say, nearer to the truth.'

'Yes, it was 1912.'

'I know it. I know it. I have followed year by year, driving the industrious if humble quill, the career of Sweden's greatest——' The old man was horribly sincere. His steel glasses were misted with emotion. He was rapidly becoming inarticulate. 'I picture the day when beside Gustavus Adolphus——'

'A glass of beer, Professor?' Krogh asked with a weariness and an impatience he took no trouble to conceal. He thought of all the interviews he had been forced through the years to give to this decayed teacher of languages, not from pity but from necessity, because he represented the most respected of Swedish papers, because there was some justification in his boast: he did at least try to be accurate. He repeated sharply when Hammarsten failed to answer: 'A glass of beer?'

'Thank you, Herr Krogh,' Hammarsten said sadly (as if he had been woken from some dramatic dream to the thirsts of the body). He fell silent nursing the glass with his palm, watching with complete inattention the dancers.

'You wanted to speak to me?' Krogh said.

'I only thought,' the old man said, 'that you might wish to make some statement. Your leaving the opera after the first act will have been noticed. There will be rumours.' He paused and said into his beer which he lifted as far as his chin, 'Believe me, Herr Krogh, I know what you think of us. We pester you; you cannot get away from us.' His steel glasses slipped a little way down the bridge of his nose. 'You must remember, it is our living.'

'I have no statement to make,' Krogh said. 'Is it impossible sometimes to do what I want to do, spontaneously, without being questioned afterwards?'

'Quite impossible,' the Professor said.

'How one ought to envy you others.'

'It's just as impossible for us,' Hammarsten said, 'but we haven't your compensations.' He dipped into his beer and withdrew with some white foam on his nose. He had mislaid his handkerchief. He used the corner of his sleeve, blushing and looking this way and that way to see whether he had been observed. 'For example, Herr Krogh, it has always been my ambition – you will laugh at me – to have a little, just a little and in the purest sense, "flutter" with the theatre. I should like – but what an inadequate word "like" is – to produce in Stockholm——' he hesitated.

'Well?'

'The great *Pericles*.'

'What is that?'

'Shakespeare's *Pericles*. In my own translation.'

'Is it a good play?'

'Oh, Herr Krogh, it is a great, a daring play. It anticipated *Mrs Warren's Profession*. For years I have urged my pupils if they wished to understand the very spirit . . . It is Shakespeare's finest, most poetic . . . Of course it has difficulties. There's the question of Gower. Who is Gower?'

'You must ask my English friend. Here he is. Who is Gower, Farrant?'

'You don't mind if this girl joins us, do you, Mr Krogh? She's thirsty, you can see that, but she doesn't understand a word I say.'

The dark sunburn beneath the ash blonde hair was beautiful: a few drops of sweat lay on her upper lip. She watched the men with a complete lack of intelligence; she sat down, she took her drink, she said nothing; she was perfectly willing to be ignored. Krogh had quite forgotten that such women existed. He said, 'Professor Hammarsten talks English, Farrant.'

'In William Shakespeare's *Pericles*, the old man Gower. Who is the old man Gower, Mr Fecund?'

'I'm afraid I've never read the play, Professor.'

'No, no. But you must have seen the play acted often in London. The old man Gower. "From ashes ancient Gower is come."'

'I've seen *Hamlet* and *Macbeth*.'

'No, no, they do not interest me. *Pericles*, that is the greatest play. I have a theory about it. "From ashes": that is not from burnt coal but from trees. From ash trees. Ash, oak, and thorn, the sacred trees. Ancient Gower is a British Druid, he is an ancient in the sense of Methuselah, a priest and king. That is how I have translated it. "From ashes ancient Gower is come." Literally, it is "from the sacred ash trees the Druidic priest, Gower, has arrived" – not old man Gower. Do you agree?'

'It sounds good.'

Perhaps the girl realised Krogh's lack of interest in the conversation. Without a word she took his right hand and spread it palm upwards on the table in front of her; there was no coquetry in the act; she was just 'doing her piece'. Men liked to have their hands held and studied; it gave them a sense of importance; they liked to hear a girl saying 'you're going a long journey', they liked the touch of hands, as legitimate as in a dance, they liked to be warned, 'be careful of two women, one dark and one fair', they felt no end of dogs.

'Of course you will make this objection. The scenes

131

are Tyre, Antioch, Ephesus. You will say – why a British Druid?'

'Yes, I quite see that, Professor. It does seem odd.'

'But that is an objection I reply to in the following manner. Shakespeare is your national poet. He lived in the high old times of good Queen Bess, at a period of nationalistic expansion.'

'You are very successful,' the girl said. 'You ought to stick to the work you are doing now.'

'Where do you come from?' Krogh asked, astonished that she didn't know his face.

'From Lund,' she said, and ran her finger down the line of life. 'You are very healthy: you have a long life.'

He could not help listening with satisfaction. 'No break in it?'

'No break.'

She said, 'You don't make friends easily. You should beware of a man and a woman. You are very generous.'

The Professor said, 'I shall dress Gower in a sym-bolistic costume representing imperialism or nationalistic expansion.'

'You don't care much for girls. You like work best.'

'What is my work?'

'Something with your head.' She let his hand go and immediately seemed to lose all interest in him; she drank her beer and stared at the dance floor through large pale marble eyes. Presently a young man passed and bowed and she left the table and walked with him to the floor and danced with him. She was quite uninterested and very pretty and completely stupid; she left behind her in Krogh's brain a sense of ease and happiness which vanished almost as soon as it became conscious. It was like an unexpected scent in a mean street, a breath of mint between the tenements: one turns back, one picks one's way across the pavement, old fag packets and potato peelings and the runnings of a conduit (she didn't know me . . . a long life . . . generous), but the smell has gone. The music had stopped, at another table the girl was laying the boy's hand palm upwards on the table.

'When are you going to produce the play then, Mr Hammarsten?'

'Never. These are only idle ideas, dreams – I have no money, Mr Fecund.'

'Farrant.'

'Ferrett. I have no connections with the theatre, the managers won't look at my work, I am only a school-teacher with a great love for William Shakespeare.'

(A long life . . . generous . . .)

'I will let you have twenty-five thousand crowns, Professor Hammarsten.' The old man said nothing, he turned away from Anthony and stared at Krogh with his mouth a little open; he looked too terrified to speak. Yet, Krogh thought, he's always imagined this: for years he's day-dreamed that a rich man will hear him speak of this play – what name? I can't remember – and be convinced, give him the money. The old fool's angled for this and now he can't believe it, he's afraid that I'm joking. 'Ring up my secretary tomorrow,' he said.

Professor Hammarsten said, 'I can't speak . . . I don't know . . .' Some foam still clung to the tip of his nose, he tried to shake it off. He said, '*Pericles*? In my own translation?'

'Of course.'

Professor Hammarsten said suddenly, 'But my translation. I don't know, perhaps it's bad. I've never shown it to anyone.' He said, 'If people should not

133

understand. The Druid Gower.' He said: 'For years and years . . .' He wanted, it was obvious, to explain that one could not suddenly reach the end of a very long journey without fear of one's reception. Friends are older; one may not even be recognised. The white stubble on his chin, the steel spectacles told plainly enough just how long the journey had been. 'I wrote it twenty years ago.'

'Choose your theatre and your cast,' Krogh said. Already he was bored by his generosity. He had done this sort of thing so often before. It was expected of one. A hundred-crown note for a paper flower, a new wing to a hospital, a pension more than equal to his wages to the first employee who lost his hand in the new improved cutter. It was reported in the Press, it looked well. The more eccentric the gift the greater the publicity, and there were occasions when such publicity was useful, before a new issue, at such a time as this of short-term loans, of selling at Amsterdam, of throwing good money into a worthless company. It was curious that it should be old shabby Hammarsten who benefited, who had got himself involved in the anxieties of Laurin and Hall. He felt a deep contempt for the old language-teacher and half-time journalist who sat there in terror at his good fortune, doubting himself, letting his spectacles slip, giving the impression that some final disaster had befallen him.

'Excuse me, Herr Krogh,' a voice said, a hot husky voice, and cap in hand between the pool and the dance floor, grey and skinny and pouched under the jaw, appeared Pihlström. The great floodlights bleached his thin indeterminate coloured hair. Before either Anthony or Krogh could move, the Professor had risen to his feet.

134

He trembled with indignation, the spectacles shook, he thrust his hands behind his black coat-tails. 'Pihlström.'

'Hammarsten,' Pihlström exclaimed. He moved tentatively closer. 'You old liar,' he said suddenly. 'You ought to be ashamed of yourself.'

'We want nothing to do with you, Pihlström,' the Professor said. 'I will not have Herr Krogh troubled like this. If you want to know, Pihlström, Herr Krogh is here in order to discuss with me a little project, a little flutter in which we require each other's help. It has nothing to do with you, Pihlström, or the paper you represent.'

'But Hammarsten——'

'Be off now, Pihlström,' the Professor said, and turning with a rusted magnificence, his hand shaking in his pocket among his loose coins, 'Gentlemen,' he said, 'will you crack a bottle of wine with me?'

[5]

Up the long flight of stairs to the fourth floor, treading upwards from Purgatory (left behind on the other bank the public lavatories with the smutty jokes, envy, and the editor's dislike, mistrust, the nudist magazines) to Paradise (the house groups, the familiar face flannel, the hard ascetic bed), mounting unscathed, I, Minty.

He knew the number of steps, fifty-six: fourteen to the first floor where lived the Ekmans in a two-roomed flat with a telephone and an electric cooker; he was a dust-man, but he always seemed to have money to spend. Often he would come home as late as Minty; he would be a little drunk and would shout good-bye to a friend all the way up the fourteen stairs, and Fru Ekman would come out of the flat at the sound of his voice and shout good-bye too. She never seemed to mind that he was drunk; sometimes she would be flushed herself and the doorway would be full of friends saying good-bye, and the smell of cheap cigars would follow him up fourteen stairs to the second landing, burning his eyes.

Twenty-eight stairs and one came to the empty flat. It was the largest in the building and it stood furnished, tenanted, always empty. The owners were abroad; for the last two years they had not been home, but the rent was paid. Minty had never seen them; his curiosity prowled the landing; he tormented himself with his lack of knowledge; but he was afraid to be without it, to dispel it with direct questions; it was an interest. Once, when the landlady had opened the flat to dust it, he had seen into the hall, seen a steel engraving of Gustavus Adolphus and an umbrella-stand with one tired umbrella. Climbing, he left the flat behind, the Ekmans dropped further, by fourteen steps, down the wall of the long stair. On the third floor an Italian woman lived who gave lessons; she reminded him of his colleague Hammarsten, for they worked in the same school; he hurried upward, fourteen more stairs, to the fourth landing, to security, to home – the brown woollen dressing-gown hanging on the door, the cocoa and water-biscuits in the cupboard, the little Madonna on the mantelpiece, the spider under the tooth-glass.

He was tired; it was early; but there was nothing to do but sleep.

When he put on the light, he went at once to the window to close it; he was afraid of moths. The flats below made little rungs of light between him and the street: everyone was at home: the Ekmans had turned on their wireless set. His monthly account lay on the washstand beside the spider. Minty went on his knees and routed in his cupboard; he poured some condensed milk into a saucepan and added two spoonfuls of cocoa; he lit a gas-burner which stood beside a polished mahogany commode, and while the mixture heated, he searched for his tea-cup. He found the saucer, but there was no sign of the cup. Presently he saw a note which his landlady had left on his pillow: 'Herr Minty, I regret your tea-cup has been broken,' signed with a flourish, no further apology. I shall have to use my tooth-glass.

The spider was obviously dead; it had shrivelled; the landlady might just as well have cleared it away. He took the glass and drank his tepid cocoa, but looking round for the soap-dish where he kept his cigarette-ends, Minty found that the spider had moved. It was cunning, not death, which had withered it; now blown out to twice the size, it was dropping to the floor on its invisible thread.

The hunting teasing instinct woke in Minty's brain; it had been a good day's sport. He took the glass and caught the spider, broke the thread when it began to climb, and deftly, with quick wrist, had it imprisoned again on the marble beside the washbasin. The spider had lost a second leg; it sat in a small puddle of cocoa. Patience, Minty thought, watching it, patience; you may outlive me. He drummed his nail on the glass. Twenty years in Stockholm, I'm not as young as I was. I'll write a note tomorrow: 'Do not touch.' I shall have to buy another tooth glass as well as a tea-cup: a shopping day it will have to be for Minty; and feeling quite excited he forgot to say his prayers before he got into bed. Once there, it seemed unnecessary to climb out again on to the cold linoleum. God was no more a respecter of positions than of persons. All that mattered was prayer should come from the heart; and joining his hands under the harsh blanket he fervently prayed: that God would cast down the mighty from their seats and exalt the humble and meek, that he would give Minty his daily bread and guard him from temptation, and growing more particular, that Anthony would be preserved from Pihlström and the others, that the Minister would consent to a Harrow dinner, that he would find a match for the broken tea-cup, and last of all he thanked God for His great mercies, for a happy and successful day. In the opposite house the lights went out one by one; soon he could not see the moth which persistently pushed its way up the windowpane; he turned out his own lamp and lay in darkness, like the spider patient behind his glass.

And like the spider he withered, blown out no longer to meet contempt; his body stretched doggo in the attitude of death, he lay there humbly tempting God to lift the glass.

# PART IV

## [1]

Anthony was punctual. The bells were striking eight on either side the water when he came up on to the North Bridge. It was not his usual policy. He didn't care to be kept waiting by a woman; it put any relationship at once on the wrong footing. The woman should arrive first and he should be a little late, even if it meant hanging round a windy corner just out of sight, breezy and apologetic and incurably vague. But the case had altered. He had a job, and walking briskly through the early mist from Mälaren, which lay like dew on his new overcoat, he carefully considered his new technique: efficiency, punctuality, not too much time to spend with women, a man's man, must be at the office soon after nine, can spare you an hour, a weight of responsibility.

But already at the other end of the bridge she was waiting, and his manner weakened. Her absurd name was Lucia: poor kid, how tough. She'd dressed herself, without disguise, to kill: the small, the saucy hat which went so badly with the serious face. He thought: she might be meeting her lover and not a pick-up in Gothenburg, and again, as always, he found himself betrayed into tenderness by his astonishment that any woman should take the trouble to please him (even if it meant, as in Lucia Davidge's case, the putting on of too much powder). You might say what you would, even the toughest of them had a silly innocence which charmed; even Mabel had had that.

As he came close, she almost ran. They had the bridge to themselves. Her much-too-high heels skidded on the

misted pavement and her head butted him in the chest,
setting the small hat further awry. They kissed like old
friends, without premeditation. He drew out from under
his coat the tiger, but he had not thought of sheltering it
when he first left his room, and its fur was dripping wet.

'You dear,' she said. 'How wet it is. You're both wet.
You're nearly drowned.' Indeed the heavy mist lay on
his coat and hat like heavy rain. He thought, one could
hardly be more wet if one had been fished up from the
lake, and because a thought of that kind was apt to weigh
like a cold compress too long on his brain, he laughed it
away, 'I'm a good swimmer.' But it was not true. He
had always feared the water: he had been flung into a
baths to sink or swim by his father when he was six and
he had sunk. For years afterwards he dreamed of death
by drowning. But he had outwitted whatever providence
it was that plotted always to fit a man with the death he
most dreaded. It was the good swimmer who took risks:
Anthony, the bad swimmer, was safe. He took none.
Even now, reminded of his wet coat, he took none. He
was as careful of his own health as a mother of her
child's. 'What we both want,' he said, 'is a cup of good
hot coffee.'

'And some toast and marmalade.'

'And some eggs and bacon.'

'If only this was London.'

They laughed and sighed and felt English and
wistful and exiled. But there's no time to be lost,
Anthony thought. He knew how easily he caught cold;
his chest was an imposing façade hiding a congenital
weakness. He ran for a taxi and they flung themselves
into it anyhow, out of breath and laughing and not
knowing where to go and with the uneasiness that always

comes to two people who take a journey together for the first time alone.

'Where shall we go?' Anthony said, while the taxi-man waited at the door and the heavy mist fell and gathered on the bridge, dripping gently to the pavement, and somewhere near the city hall a ship's siren blew, the sound shrilling and catching in the pipe and shrilling again like a plover feigning a damaged wing. 'I don't know this place at all. You choose. Where shall we go?' He began to take off his wet coat and surreptitiously he felt his shirt: it was dry. That was the kind of pleasure trip's end he never felt certain of avoiding: bed and a bad cold, perhaps pneumonia.

She said: 'Drottningholm. I haven't been there. There's a palace.'

'But is there breakfast?'

'There must be breakfast.'

The mist slid across the windows, and she cleared a pane with her hand. Anthony kissed the back of her neck. She said, 'If only poor Father knew the life I led.'

'You mean me?' Anthony said.

She turned to face him with a look which was meant to be bold to the point of recklessness, but was more like that of a scared animal. 'You don't think you're the only one?' He thought: heavens, what is she after? He wanted to make some formal declaration of the purity of his motives, that he wanted nothing at the moment but his breakfast. She said airily, 'Even in Coventry, you know, there are one or two men one can look at.' Her eyebrows had been thinned unevenly, there was an amateurish touch about her whole face, the too-pronounced lipstick, the dry flakes of powder on her neck. Her manner had the unconvincing swagger of a new boy at a boarding school who has something to hide, some physical defect or perhaps only an absurd name. Lucia, he thought, Lucia.

But as if, having once established the fact that she was the devil of a creature, she were happy to leave the rest to him, she asked, 'How's work?'

'Fine,' Anthony said. 'Krogh and I are getting along like a house on fire.' He put his arm round her and absent-mindedly stroked her left breast.

'And what – what exactly are you?'

'I'm his bodyguard. You know these big men in industry are all afraid that someone will take a pot shot at them. Well, my job,' he said, swaggering in his turn, 'is to be first on the draw.'

She leant back against him, her saucy hat pushed askew, her mouth dry, and said in an uneasy voice, 'It doesn't sound right.' Her excitement reminded him of his position; he squeezed her breast in a friendly formal way and said, 'It's right as rain. He's made of money.'

'What I mean is,' she said, 'it's not a job for a gentleman.'

'I'm not a gentleman,' Anthony said and kissed her.

'Oh, but you are,' she protested. The mist began to peel away from the flowery suburban streets, leaving white tatters in odd places, round chimneys, broken columns, tall pots of flowers and fountains. 'I liked you for it from the first. That tie – I believe it's Eton.'

'Harrow,' Anthony admitted.

'I'm a snob,' she said. Her confessions were oddly mixed: they varied from the dare-devil to the humble. 'I'm a beastly snob.' There was nothing she was not ready to say about herself, Anthony thought, except that she was scared, that she didn't know how to behave next. 'It's nice seeing you after all these foreign men.'

'But you haven't been in Sweden a week.'

'Does it take a week, ' she boasted, 'to know a few men?' Then again she confessed quite humbly, 'I've never been out of England before.' He was confused; he couldn't keep up with her hinted experiences and her self-exposed innocence. When in doubt, he told himself, make love, say nothing. He kissed her again, played with her breast, stroked her thigh, but her response startled him. He was like an expert poker player who has picked too ignorant an opponent: coveting the jackpot, one has an extra ace concealed, one has expertly cut the pack, but at the same time one expects a certain primitive reserve, an attempt to play, from an opponent; there are formalities which even a swindler likes to see observed. One is irritated, watching the revealing face, hearing the too guileless bids, by the thought that one might have won as easily without all this preparation, without a doctored pack; one might really have played square.

She put her hands to his head and held his mouth to hers; he could feel her legs shift and strain. She was hungry, she wanted satisfaction, all Coventry was in her gesture; why trouble to plot and lie and charm? He wondered with dismay whether he was not simply being used, whether this affair was his defeat rather than his victory. He thought, while he embraced her, of bicycles, of how one changed trains at Rugby.

But it was impossible to pretend that one felt guilty. Nowadays, he thought, with a rather shocked puritanism, seduction is really too easy; it lacked the glamour of locked doors, the bottle of champagne, 'a man's rooms' at midnight; he wondered whether he could cope with this excitement. He was immeasurably relieved when she withdrew to her corner of the taxi and began to make-up again, but he longed to advise her, 'Throw away that lipstick. It's the wrong shade.' He thought of Krogh's suits, the good material wasted, the appalling choice of ties. I must take these people in hand. When I'm through with them, they'll have learnt a thing or two. The idea of a visit to Krogh's tailors, of a shopping expedition with Lucia, lent his face an air of responsibility. He said, 'I can't call you Lucia. It will have to be Loo.' He said, 'I suppose the shops in Coventry are rather dreadful.'

Loo said from behind her compact, blowing little scented grains of powder all over the taxi, 'Oh, we've got some good shops in Coventry. You'd be surprised. And then, you know, it's not two hours to London. Cheap tickets every day.'

He said, 'I suppose you manage to get a lot of fun.'

'Oh,' Loo said, 'I'm not promiscuous. Besides, it's not safe at home. Father screams if I'm not back by twelve. You can't imagine the ructions. Why, he sits up for me.'

'He's quite right,' Anthony said crossly. 'You've got no business at your age——'

'But don't you believe in freedom?' Loo said. 'You aren't going to go all stuffy, are you? What's the use of travelling all over the world, being in revolutions and things like that, if you don't believe in freedom?'

'It's different for a man,' Anthony said.

'Not now it isn't,' Loo said. 'Not now with birth control.'

'I don't believe in birth control.'

'How on earth do you expect a girl to go out with you——'

'Damn it all,' Anthony said, 'we are only going out to breakfast.'

She said with disappointment, 'Don't you love me a bit, Tony? Oh, I don't mean of course emotionally. I hate people getting sentimental about quite simple things. Before you know where you are they become all possessive and want you only and expect you to want them only, as if man was a molygamous, I mean monogamous, animal. But physically aren't I a bit attractive to you?'

'You don't know what you are talking about,' Anthony said.

'Oh,' she said, 'I don't pretend to have had all your experience. A girl in every port and any port in a storm.'

'I don't believe you've ever had a man,' Anthony said. 'I believe you're a virgin.'

She slapped his face hard.

'I'm sorry,' Anthony said. He was hurt and angry.

'It was a beastly thing to say.'

'I'm sorry – I said I was sorry.'

The taxi stopped. They were at Drottningholm. They sparred all the time they were drinking coffee and eating rolls. They were both hungry, but they didn't know the Swedish for eggs.

'How can you work in Sweden without knowing any Swedish?' Loo asked.

'You don't need any language at my job,' Anthony said.

'It's not respectable.'

'You oughtn't to mind whether it's respectable or not.'

Immediately she began to explain to him, quite gently, because she was no longer hungry, that respectability had got nothing to do with freedom. He lost his irritation and listened with a good deal of interest. You couldn't deny that she had brains. She used the word freedom several times; he was no longer shocked now that she was not practising it with him; she was, after all, as old-fashioned as himself. In Coventry, it seemed, they still found theories to excuse a 'good time'. She belonged to the age when latch-keys were a major problem. He couldn't help comparing her favourably with Kate. Kate was a bit cold-blooded; she didn't make excuses; he still felt ashamed and angry when he thought of that moment in Krogh's flat – 'that's my bedroom'. He had known, of course, long before he came to Stockholm that she was Krogh's mistress, but he had never learnt it before in so many words and she had never excused herself. He had an uneasy feeling that Kate, if taxed with it, would be more likely to speak of money and a job than freedom.

Dear Loo, he thought, she's old-fashioned, she's got principles. They walked up the road to the palace. The mist had gone; under a bright-coloured umbrella on a grey bridge a man was setting out his mineral water bottles, cherry fizz and lemonade. 'I want some cherry fizz,' Loo said.

'You've only just had coffee.'

'But I like cherry fizz.'

A family of ducks came downstream, one behind the other. They had an air of serious, if rather infantile, purpose, like a squad of Boy Scouts. One expected them to begin chalking messages on the bank or to gather around and light a fire with two matches.

'People make such a fuss about sex,' Loo said. The bright pink cherry fizz bubbled in her glass. The ducks one after the other stood on their heads. 'Just because one sleeps with a man——'

Anthony looked away over an acre or two of parched August grass to the low white palace, like a dead sea-bird, stuffed, with spread wings. 'Tell me, how many men——'

'Only two,' she said. 'I'm not promiscuous.'

'In Coventry?'

'Once in Coventry,' she said, 'and once at Wotton-under-Edge.'

'And you are ready for a third?'

'Barkis is willing,' she said.

'But you'll be gone in a few days.' They came out on to the terrace at the back of the cold northern Versailles. Anthony had never felt more of an exile. It was windy on the terrace: a few trees with yellowing leaves, an attempt at topiary, outside a door in one of the wings a bottle of milk. They stood side by side, with hands clasped, above the bitten grass. A man with a broom came to tell them in English that the palace was not yet open to visitors.

Lyons in Coventry Street would be open, Anthony thought, and after breakfast it was always possible to find somewhere; there was an hotel off Wardour Street, innumerable rooms above the foreign cafés to be hired by the hour, not romantic, not very clean, but one could always be happy given the girl, given the bed; some people would count themselves lucky without a flat on the North Strand. He dug his nails into his palm in a spasm of longing for the tea-urn, the slattern with the clean towels, the stacks of English cigarettes. He thought: I was a fool to leave; if I had waited I could have found a job; no one could down me there: I knew the ropes.

'They won't let us in?'

'No, they won't let us in.'

'There's nothing to do, I suppose, but go back.'

'Wait here,' he said, 'I'll try a tip.' He followed the

man with the broom and presently found him outside a small detached building at the end of the terrace. No, the man said, he couldn't show him the palace; he hadn't the keys. If he came back in an hour . . . but he had the keys of the theatre if they cared to see that.

The small theatre had been left exactly as it was in the eighteenth century. The royal seats were still surmounted by their crowns, the long claret benches were labelled and reserved for the dead, for the ladies-in-waiting, the gentlemen of the bedchamber, the barber and the perruquier. Anthony and Loo sat down, and in the wings of the small deep stage their guide began to pull the ropes which worked the old elaborate scenery. Blue and white clouds puffed out like Cupids' bottoms descended round the worn armchair used by Venus or Jupiter in masques and operas. He turned out the lights and made the thunder roll. Dust rose and fell.

Anthony said, 'We've got to find some place to go to. If we were in London——'

'Or Coventry.'

'What did you do in Wotton-under-Edge?'

'We had a car.'

All the scenery began to move sideways, and a faded elegant flower garden appeared in jerks from the wings. Sitting side by side on a bench once occupied by the royal barber and the court chaplain, they felt their legs touch and press; they strained towards each other through their clothes; they felt physically ill with the want of a bed. A trap shot up on the stage and the guide appeared suddenly from below. Everything, he said, was in working order as on the day when it was made, then vanished again. They heard him stumbling about under the stage.

148

'I've got it,' Anthony said, 'we'll go and see Minty.'

'Who's Minty?'

'He's a journalist. A lonely devil. We'll pretend we've come to breakfast. He'll know of somewhere we can go to.'

'You do want to go with me?' she asked with an absurd air of formality. 'I don't want to drive you into it.'

'There's nothing I want more. It'll be just like home.'

'It's good for one.'

'Oh,' he said with a sudden sense of coldness, of unfamiliarity, of the stone buildings round the lakes, water, water everywhere, and the stiff men bowing to each other over schnaps, with a nostalgia for easy friendships, for a language he understood, for the guardsmen in the Park, the cars waiting for pick-ups, the shopgirls and the saloon bars, 'I wish you were staying or I was going. Kate's a careerist. She doesn't understand. I can be happy with so little' – whisky with a splash, a copy of *Razzle*, the Paddington hotels and the club under Lisle Street, not this: the millionaire, the steel and glass, the incomprehensible statue. 'If only I could come with you.'

'It's not respectable what you are doing. I do wish it was something respectable.'

'After you've gone I shan't know a soul.'

'I daresay it's better like this. We don't want to start a relationship.'

'Why not?' Anthony said. 'What's wrong with a relationship? Don't be a snob. I like you and you like me. Why shouldn't we go on seeing each other till we are tired of it?'

'A relationship's so limiting,' Loo said. They kissed,

149

and into their kiss crept the desperation, the hunger of departure, the sadness of railway stations; one was going and one was staying; a holiday was over; the fireworks were dead on the grass, other people were watching the pierrots and curling of an evening in their glass shelter on the front, and one had done nothing more complete than this kiss. You have my address, the slamming of doors, write to me, the waving of a flag, we'll meet again, and the smoke blowing between. She took her mouth away. 'So limiting,' she said again uncertainly. He looked for her mouth and missed it; her cheek tasted salt. 'Oh, damn it bloody all,' she said, and 'Excuse my language,' with an attempt at flippancy.

What an odd thing, he thought, what the hell of an odd thing to happen to me. He asked hopelessly, 'Will you be back next year?'

'Not a chance,' she said. 'This is the holiday of a lifetime for the old people. Unless Krogh makes their fortune. They've put a little money into Krogh's since they've been here.'

'He pays ten per cent.'

'It'll have to be fifty per cent before they come here again.'

Their guide rolled the thunder a second time. Then he began to pull up Venus's chair; it dangled for a while on frayed ropes over the boards, then shot above the clouds and disappeared. 'Time's short,' Anthony said, 'and we are wasting it.'

'I know what that means,' Loo said.

'Well, you don't mind, do you?'

'Of course I don't. It's healthy, isn't it?' She became unreasonably bitter. 'It's a whole six months since Wotton-under-Edge.'

'For God's sake,' Anthony said, 'forget Wotton-under-Edge.'

The road unwound the other way; it seemed a long distance to have come for so little reason. They had each had a coffee and Loo had drunk a cherry fizz; nothing had happened. 'We've wasted two hours,' Anthony said.

'Well, we're both young,' she said. She sat in a corner well away from him, with her knees drawn up; they jolted her chin as the car shook. 'This time next year——'

'Where will you be?'

'I expect we'll go to Bournemouth.'

They stopped at a shop and bought some sandwiches. Loo carried the parcel. Anthony hated to be seen with one.

They were tired before they reached the third landing in Minty's tenement, and they paused and panted beside a window. They could see all the way down the street to the water's edge; they could hear the tram-bells ringing across the lake from near the central station, the slapping of the water against the quays. Then they climbed up another floor. Minty's card was nailed on his door with a drawing-pin. Mr F. Minty. They looked for a bell and couldn't find one, so Anthony banged on the door with his hand.

'I wonder what F. stands for,' Loo said.

Minty opened the door and Anthony explained, 'We've come to breakfast.'

'Really,' Minty said, 'this is a great pleasure. Excuse Minty a moment while he nips in and tidies the bed.' They could hear him pulling at blankets, emptying a washbasin, padding here and there in his bedroom slippers, shutting a wardrobe door, shifting a chair. Then he rejoined them. 'Come in, come in,' he said.

'Let me introduce Miss Davidge.'

'Good morning,' Minty said. 'I'm so pleased, so embarrassed. Do you mind sitting on the bed? Will you have some cocoa?'

'We've brought some sandwiches.'

'Quite a picnic,' Minty said. He knelt down and rummaged in his cupboard, and then suddenly remembered. 'Oh dear, oh dear, the landlady's broken my only cup. I'll have to go down and borrow from the Ekmans.' But he remained on his knees with a tin of condensed milk in his hand. 'Unless we just drink this. I don't see much of the Ekmans. They mightn't want to lend.' He said brightly, 'It'll be just like the old days, Farrant.'

'The old days?'

'One always had condensed milk in one's tuck-box at prep school, don't you remember? One sucked it through a hole in the lid.' He said suspiciously, 'I suppose you've never sucked condensed milk, Miss Davidge?'

'Call her Loo,' Anthony said. 'We're all friends here. Have a sandwich?' Minty took a knife out of his pocket. It had two blades, a curved instrument for taking stones out of horses' hoofs, and a corkscrew. Its size explained the curious hang of his pocket. He began to jab at the tin.

'Wouldn't it be easier,' Loo asked, 'to take off the whole lid with a tin-opener?'

'It wouldn't be the right way,' Minty said sharply, 'and besides, I haven't a tin-opener.' He handed her the tin and eyed her balefully when refusing to suck she handed it to Anthony. 'Why, really,' he said, 'are you visiting Minty?'

'Just for friendship's sake,' Anthony said. He sucked with an air. 'I wanted to catch you before you began work.'

'No news?'

'Not a scrap,' Anthony said, 'I thought we'd just get together.'

'Hammarsten's got news. And Pihlström.'

'We saw them yesterday up at Tivoli.'

'That's what I meant,' Minty said. He knelt on the floor beside the washstand and said sadly, 'I knew they'd get hold of you – I suppose you've come here to break it gently. You're going to work for them not for me. They've offered you fifty-fifty.' He took another tin out of the cupboard and shook it close to his ear, then put it back. 'I finished this one yesterday.'

'What have they written?'

'Pihlström says that he left the opera before the end and took a car to Tivoli. Hammarsten says that he went to Tivoli to discuss a theatrical venture, which will be exclusively announced in his paper tomorrow.'

'Do you call that news?'

'Everything he does is news.'

'If that's all you want to know,' Anthony said, 'it's *Pericles*. He's putting up the money for Hammarsten.'

'What?' Minty said. 'For Hammarsten?' He laid down his tin of milk. 'He's mad. They're all mad, these men with money. They get an idea, and that's that. It might have been you, it might have been me. But it happened to be Hammarsten.'

'After all, he can do what he likes with his own money,' Loo said.

'If only it had been me,' Minty said. 'I've been with him often enough these last ten years.' He went to the door and searched the pockets of his dressing-gown for cigarettes; there were none there, only the fluff you find under beds and a scrap of paper. He read what was

153

pencilled on it aloud: 'Mem: Canary, cake, gooseberry jam (?).'

'Have you got a canary?' Loo asked.

Minty said, 'That must have been five years ago. It sang too much and died. But I wonder why the gooseberry jam. I never liked gooseberry jam.' He crumpled up the piece of paper as if he would throw it away; then he changed his mind and put it back. 'If I'd had what Hammarsten's got ten years ago——'

'Me too,' Anthony said. 'I patented a Winter Hand-warming Umbrella. I only needed capital. It was a sure thing.'

'Oh, for God's sake,' Loo said, 'talk about the present. Don't talk about the past all the time. That's what's wrong with you both. Haven't you got futures?'

'Frankly,' Minty said, 'no. We wouldn't be here if we had a future.'

'Why not? What's wrong with Stockholm?'

'It's not London,' Anthony said.

'No, it's not London.'

'It's a damned sight better than Coventry,' Loo said.

'Dear child,' Minty said, poking with his finger in the soap-dish. Behind his back they whispered; Anthony bounced the bed. Loo said, 'I admire a man like that. It's all his own money.'

Minty turned on her; his eyes were damp and burning. 'It's not his own money. He's a borrower, nothing more than a borrower. We can't borrow because we are not trusted. If they trusted us, we should be Kroghs ourselves. He's only one of us. He has no more roots than we have. But we, we have to live within our means; the banks won't trust us; we count our cigarettes, live where it's cheap, save on the laundry, pick up pocket-money by

154

our wits. You're too young, my dear,' he said, with open malice, 'to understand these things.' He didn't like girls, he couldn't have said it in words more plainly; tawdry little creatures, other people's sisters, their hats blocking the view at Lord's.

'I'm not,' Loo said. She fidgeted; got off the bed, moved here and there, measuring the dust on chairs and window-sills and curtain-rods with her finger-tip.

'Why haven't I got a job?' Minty asked her rhetorically. 'Why does he have to depend on his sister? Krogh's the answer. Buy Krogh's. It's cheaper, less labour, nearly a monopoly, costs cut down, ten per cent dividends. All the money goes to Krogh and he doesn't employ half the men who were employed in the old cut-throat days. It's Krogh who swells the labour exchanges. Put that down, please,' he said as Loo moved a glass. 'Please don't touch my spider.'

'You're just jealous,' Loo said, 'because you can't make money.'

'Trust Minty, he won't go on for ever. When he begins to take short-term loans——'

'Oh, he's not a bad sort,' Anthony said. 'Loo's right. He's got more guts than we have.'

Minty hiccuped. 'You've made me all excited,' he said. 'My stomach. Ever since I was drained.' He hiccuped again.

'Try drinking out of a glass backwards,' Loo said.

'Please don't touch my spider,' Minty whispered breathlessly. He counted up to twenty aloud. 'This isn't much of a party,' he said. 'I'm not used – if my cup had not been broken – you took me by surprise, and then this about Hammarsten.' He followed Loo with his eyes, maliciously observing every unfortunate point in her

155

appearance. 'It was good of you to come.' But in his scorched eyes he expressed quite clearly his disapproval of the bad make-up, the cheap pretentious dress, the saucy hat. There were people these days one could not avoid meeting, but one retained standards.

'I ought to be going,' Loo said.

'I'll come with you,' Anthony said. 'I've got to talk to you. We'll find somewhere to sit. Skansen. Is it far to Skansen?'

'Please, please,' Minty said, 'make yourself quite at home.' He twisted himself this way and that in the convulsion of hiccups. 'Treat my room as your hotel. Stay here and talk. You won't be interrupted. No one comes to see Minty.'

'That's what I wanted to ask,' Anthony said.

He laughed at them gently, patted them on the shoulder, the perfect Pandarus. 'And I thought it was the pleasure of Minty's company. False, false Farrant. And the sandwiches were no more than a bribe, you only pretended to like my condensed milk.' But his expression disconcerted them: it was hopeless, but not quite resigned. Like a third-class berth in a boat going abroad he seemed to have known only strangers, he carried about him the smell of oil and misery. He said, 'I must be off and get this news to the paper. Make yourselves at home.' He put on his black coat and had trouble with the sleeves; one arm stuck in a torn lining and for a moment he was like a small black splintered pillar set in the open space the room provided. He was so lonely, so isolated that he drove the others back into the companionship they had lost; even a shared uneasiness, a shared bickering, had a friendly air compared with his extreme friendlessness. He said, 'Good-bye,' but pointedly to

Anthony; he couldn't bring himself to look at Loo. He said, 'Could you by any chance lend me a few crowns? I have my month's cheque but no change.'

He wouldn't look at them, he wouldn't look at the bed, while he waited for payment. His gaze got no further than the ewer and basin, the spider under the glass.

'Of course,' Anthony said.

'I'll pay you back when I've been to the office, and pay you for the story as well. You said a quarter, didn't you?'

'You can have this one for nothing.'

'You are too kind. Minty couldn't possibly – Well, perhaps, this time. There's so much shopping I have to do.' At last he left them. He wore boots and they could hear him going slowly down until he had passed the third floor.

'Oh,' Loo said, 'I knew it wasn't respectable.'

'What?'

'Your job, of course. Mixing with people like that.'

'It's not my real job.'

'Your real job's no better. If *he* can say that about Krogh. . . .'

'You can't believe him.'

'There's a lot in what he says.' She picked her way gingerly round the room; from everything she touched and saw she seemed to catch a little of Minty's misery. It was contagious. It lay like a germ in the brown dressing-gown, it was a dusty scum on the water in the ewer; when she opened the cupboard (she was innately inquisitive) it was concealed in the litter there. She said, 'A saucer, an empty tin of condensed milk, a knife, a spoon, a fork, a plate – it doesn't match the saucer——'

'Leave him alone,' Anthony said. It had been decent of him to lend his flat when (it was obvious) he didn't like girls. There was no need for indictment, but she wouldn't stop. She said, 'A box of matches – they've all been struck – why does he keep them? An old memo-pad. He doesn't seem able to throw away anything. A magazine. A school magazine. An address list. A prayer-book – no, it's a missal. What are these funny little things? Some game?'

Anthony knelt beside her. 'They are incense-cones,' he said. He juggled them in his hands, and the thin smell attached itself to his fingers like misery. 'Poor devil,' he said. Their bodies touched and suddenly they were together again in their hunger, their sense of time passing. 'It's a dreary world.'

'No,' Loo said, 'no. It's good. There's always this.' 'This' was their kiss, the closer embrace, the half-reluctant effort which took them to the bed. But his passion wore itself out in his hands, it was vanity only which he experienced in the final act, it had never been anything else but vanity. One liked to make them helpless, to cry out, one was satisfied because one gave satisfaction, but there was no pleasure to match theirs, which was deep enough to make them surrender momentarily every mental conviction, so that Loo now used all the terms she scouted. She said, 'I love you'; she said, 'Darling'; she said, 'It was never so good'. But his mind remained apart, working a trick, conscious of the house-group over her head, the Madonna on the mantelpiece, peacocking himself when she cried, 'I don't want you to go. I don't want you to go,' deceiving himself that it was his victory, that he remained untouched, that he had only added a scalp, when already as he dropped beside her, vanity was doing its work, exaggerating her charm and her naïvety, branding his brain with half-fictitious memories. He looked at her, he put his arm round her, vanity worked his defeat more completely than passion could do: already she was recovering. One could never feel the same again about a girl one had laid: one couldn't avoid a certain tenderness.

'Yes,' Loo said, 'there's a lot in what he says. I did economics at school. He's quite right about short-term loans. I do wish you had a respectable job.'

[2]

At last Amsterdam spoke in the slightly Cockney tones of Fred Hall. Krogh stood at the window and let the voice silt into the room through the loudspeaker. The early mist had nearly cleared, but the bowl of the courtyard still held it like a milky fluid. The statue was obscured.

One had to have a sense of proportion. The statue was not of such importance.

'I tried to get you last night,' the voice said reproachfully. 'They put me through to the opera but you'd gone. I tried your flat, but you weren't in. I've been up all night, Mr Krogh.'

He knew a thing or two, Farrant, and he didn't like it. It was no use saying that it was unimportant. Everything was important just now when money was scarce and he had got to keep things steady until the American company was launched. A joke might ruin him at the wrong moment. 'Go on, Hall,' he said. 'Tell me what's worrying you,' but the line that morning was bad. He had to come to the desk to speak. After this is over, he thought, I'll go upstairs for an hour away from people.

'They are still selling.'

'Then we must go on buying.'

'There's a limit, Mr Krogh.'

'No limit.'

'Where's the money to come from?'

'I've arranged that. The A.C.U. will lend the money.'

'We shall need every penny they've got.'

'You can have it.'

'But the A.C.U. They'll have to pass their dividend. It'll start a panic. This won't be a single break. It'll be like a sieve. You'll have holes sprung in Berlin, Warsaw, Paris, everywhere.'

'No, no,' Krogh said, 'you exaggerate. You live too much in the centre of things, Hall. I'm right out of it here. When once we've started the American company next week, we can do what we like with the market.'

'But the A.C.U.?'

'We're selling it. Batterson's are buying. A million pounds down. That will fill any holes for a week, Hall. You've just got to go on buying.'

'But the A.C.U. won't have a farthing.' He could hear the thin whistle of Hall's breath far away in his room in Amsterdam.

'They'll be worth exactly what they are worth now. Only it'll be in the form of shares in the Amsterdam company.'

'But you know we aren't worth the money we're spending.' Krogh had no need of television when he spoke to Hall; they had been together so long that he could associate every inflection with its accompanying action: the reproachful swinging leg, the doubting dangle of watch-chain.

'Yes, you are, Fred,' Krogh said. He was quite happy

again because he was dealing with figures; there was nothing he didn't know about figures, there was nothing he couldn't do with them, there was nothing human about them. 'You are worth everything. Our credit's bound up with you. The A.C.U. is nothing. It has nothing to do with the main business. It's an investment we are willing to sell. But if you go, the I.G.S. goes.'

'Yes, but in actual value . . .'

'Three minutes up,' a voice said in German.

'There's no such thing,' Krogh said, 'as actual value.' He took up an ash-tray and put it down again: E.K. 'There's only the price people are willing to pay. We've got to clear up every one of your shares on the market in Amsterdam. The price has got to be maintained.'

'They're unloading a packet. There are rumours——'

'You've got the money. You can keep the price steady. The selling won't go on.'

'So I've got to go on buying all today?'

'Your ghosts may give out. The money won't.'

'But Batterson's will never buy.'

'I've given them my personal assurance of the value of the A.C.U. holdings. They are dealing with Krogh's, Hall.'

'But when they do examine the books——'

'They'll find the holdings are all in the form of shares in our Amsterdam company, and the Amsterdam company is a daughter company of the I.G.S. You can't have a better investment than Krogh's.'

'We can't get the money any other way, Mr Krogh?' The voice was not really very troubled; what Krogh said went with Hall, went a great deal further than a little fraud. He was obedient to the letter; there was something medieval in his devotion: like the knights who attended on Henry the Second he hung on Krogh's wishes, would have anticipated them if he had had the brains. 'Will no one rid me?' and Hall was at his elbow, arranging what he understood better than Krogh did, a little frame-up, a spot of blackmail.

'You know as well as I do, Hall, how close money is. We can't take any more short-term loans. Too many are falling due as it is.'

'I suppose they'll raise hell when they find out.'

'Not when the purchase is over. They'll be responsible to their shareholders. They won't dare to press us. They'll have to give us time. When America has gone through, I'll buy the company back from them if they want it. We can do what we like then. And I've taken precautions. I've pre-dated the purchase of the shares.'

'Six minutes up.'

'Did the directors agree to that?' Hall asked with respectful admiration.

'Yes, yes,' Krogh said. It was not worth while explaining to Hall that one did not trouble to consult Stefenson, Asplund, Bergsten about such small routine matters as signing cheques. He had their signatures on a rubber stamp. He had not approached Laurin in the matter; that could wait awhile. The purchase of the Amsterdam shares was pre-dated too far back for Laurin to have had any say. He said gently over the telephone, 'Everything is all right now, Hall.'

'What you say goes.'

'A few days ago I was nervous, a little nervous. I didn't feel prepared. There are methods these Americans use. They worked a strike here and Laurin was ill. But I settled that. It never even got into the papers, and I gave no written promises. Things are going very well now, Hall.'

'And I'm to go on buying?'

'This morning should finish it. You can count on the money from Batterson's. When you are finished in Amsterdam, come to me here. I may want you. Someone's causing trouble at the works.'

'I'll come at once, Mr Krogh.'

'Good-bye, Hall.'

'Good-bye, Mr Krogh.' But the voice came back, broke across the announcement 'nine minutes'. 'Don't think it's a little fraud I object to. You know I wouldn't stick at a little fraud. If the value's there.'

'There are values *and* values,' Krogh said gently. Value isn't a thing you can measure. Value is confidence. As long as we receive money, we're valuable. As long as we're trusted.' He disconnected Hall.

Hall was the right man in the right place. A clever man would have been more frightened. He felt a little drained of strength after reassuring Hall, but not the less confident: a pleasant physical weariness. Hall had said, 'The friction'll be too great,' and Hall had been wrong. Hall had always been wrong, but never obstinately wrong. Arguing with him, one marshalled one's facts, one cleared one's mind; now, one could have tackled the less trusting, the more cowardly Laurin. He rang up Kate and asked her, 'Where's Laurin?'

'He's still ill – at Saltsjöbaden. Listen, Erik, I want to speak to you.'

'Not now. In five minutes. I'm going up to the silent room. Where's your brother?'

'He hasn't come in yet.'

He laid some papers straight upon his desk; there

were a few letters he would take upstairs with him. He noticed an envelope containing the tickets for a series of concerts; he smiled and tore them up. Things are going very well now. It seemed incredible to him that a few days ago he had been worried to the point of hallucination. I've been thinking too much about the past. He had always despised people who thought about the past. To live was to leave behind; to be as free as a shipwrecked man who has lost everything. Chicago, Barcelona, the school in Stockholm, the apprenticeship at Nyköping, the hut beside Vätten dropped away like the figures on a platform when the train moves out; they dropped back against the waiting-rooms, the buffet, the lavatories; they were left behind, they hadn't caught that train. He thought: I enjoyed last night. I've never felt so rested. I can look ahead now.

Passing the window to reach the door, he was caught again by the fountain. But this time, suddenly, he saw it, the great handled block of green stone, with delight. It wasn't the past, it wasn't something finished to the nipple, to the dimple, to the flexed knee, it was something in the present tense, something working its way out of the stone. His delight was momentary, but it enabled him to forget the fountain. He thought: Next week America, and then we can go ahead, no depression can hurt us then and he thought with pity: They call it fraud, this clarity, this long intricate equation of which at last I can see the solution. He was possessed all the way up the glass lift-shaft to the silent room next the roof with a pure inhuman joy.

[3]

Kate read the memorandum over carefully. At first it meant nothing to her. She knew nothing about the A.C.U. except that it was the most prosperous combine of paper-mills in Sweden. It had been one of the best investments that Krogh had made and he had made it on his own responsibility without consulting his directors. It had been an investment pure and simple, a use for surplus money, and its sale to Batterson's meant nothing at all. He was selling his control at a profit to be used elsewhere. Why worry?

But she worried none the less. The short-term loans worried her. It was untidy, the continual shifting of small blocks of capital; it offended her in the same way as dust on a mirror. One wanted a clear image. Somebody knocked on the door. She thought: There can't be anything wrong, this is solid – these offices of glass and steel, the rare woods, the eighteenth-century wall-paper in the directors' dining-room, the works at Nyköping, this bowl of expensive flowers. She thought of the A.C.U. The figures were set out on the memorandum: production 350,000 tons annually, of which 200,000 tons are for export; associated pulp-mills: production of mechanical pulp 300,000 tons, of chemical pulp 1,000,300 tons; the associated saw-mills, 15,000 miles of logging channels, 50,000,000 logs floated annually. This was real, nothing was more real.

'Welcome your erring brother,' Anthony said.

Kate looked up. This is more real, she thought: those are figures, I've seen what Krogh can do with figures, but this is myself. He grinned at her. 'I'm late. Is the great man angry?'

165

She said: 'What's up?' He was cocky, but he was sullen. He stood there pluming himself in her mirror, waiting for her to guess what he had been at. His was the weakness which should have been hers, the uncertainty, the vanity, the charm of something rash and unpremeditated. It was the nearest she could get to completeness, having him here in the same room, arguing, bullying, retreating. She bitterly envied lovers their more complete alliance.

'I've been seeing Loo,' Anthony said.

'Who's Loo?'

'The Davidge girl.'

'You needn't tell me that,' Kate said. 'She's left her powder on your coat.'

'She wants me to leave here.' He said uneasily, 'She doesn't think my job's respectable.' He wilted with grace against her desk; he was all the moral conscience, she thought, that they could summon up between them. She could see her own face in the mirror behind his back – the pale careful profile, the long lids which qualified the hardness of the eyes, so that it was possible to believe that perhaps in the last resort she hadn't the energy to be completely ruthless. Good Looks and Conscience, she thought, the fine flowers of our class. We're done, we're broke, we belong to the past, we haven't the character or the energy to do more than hang on to something new for what we can make out of it. Krogh is worth us both, but she watched the graceful curve of Anthony's attitude, the padded shoulders of his new overcoat: one can't help loving oneself.

'Well,' Anthony said, 'there's something in what she says. I don't know whether it's a job for – well, you know what I mean.'

'I wish I did.'

'Well, damn it all, if one must use the word, for a gentleman.'

'You don't understand,' Kate said. 'It's our only chance.'

'I don't mean your job. That's different.'

'It's our only chance,' Kate repeated. 'We haven't got a future away from here. This is the future.'

'Oh, come,' Anthony said, 'that's pitching it strong. After all, here we are foreigners.'

'We're national. We're national,' Kate said, 'from the soles of our feet. But nationality's finished. Krogh doesn't think in frontiers. He's beaten unless he has the world.'

'Minty was talking,' Anthony said, 'about short-term loans.'

'That's temporary.'

'You mean he's had to take them already?' Anthony asked. 'Is money so close? It looks bad. Do you think we are safe here? I'm all for rats. I don't believe in any Casabianca stuff.'

'You don't imagine,' Kate said, 'that Krogh could be beaten by us. That's all that nationality is – it's we, the hangers-on, the little dusty offices I've worked in, Hammond, your pubs, your Edgware Road, your pick-ups in Hyde Park.' Deliberately she turned away from the thought that there had been a straightness about the poor national past which the international present did without. It hadn't been very grand, but in their class at any rate there had been gentleness and kindness once.

'It's home,' Anthony said.

He raised his lonely small boy's face. 'You don't understand, Kate. You've always liked this modern stuff, that fountain.'

'You're wrong,' Kate said. 'It's home to me too.' She spread her hands hopelessly across the desk towards him. 'It's you. As long as I have you, I've kept it even there. You're my Ladies' Bar, Anthony, my beastly port.'

'And, of course,' he went on, following his own thoughts and paying her not the least attention, 'you're fond of Krogh.'

'I've never loved him. I'd have despised him if I'd loved him. Love's no good to anyone. You can't define it. We need things of which we can think, not things we only feel. He thinks in figures, he doesn't feel vague things about people.'

'He was human enough last night,' Anthony said. 'Leave him to me. I'll educate him.'

Kate said, 'For God's sake. Have I got to save him as well as you?'

'I'll make him human.' He was hopeless; he couldn't see her point.

'I don't believe,' Anthony said, 'he even knows his staff. I've been talking to a man here and there. A young chap in the publicity department. He's never even seen Krogh. They get dissatisfied, you know. The managers have too much power.'

'They seem to have been telling you a lot,' Kate said.

'Those that can talk English. Of course, they think I can help them. They know I've got on well with Krogh.'

'You've told them that, of course?'

'Well, one likes to be liked.'

Kate said, 'I've got to see Erik now. Shall we have lunch together? I can show you a place——'

'I'm sorry, old thing,' Anthony said, 'you know how it is. I've promised, if Krogh doesn't want me, to have lunch with Pa and Ma.'

'Pa and Ma?' She added quickly: 'Of course. I'm sorry. I've been working. I know whom you mean.' But she wasn't quick enough; she felt his irritation. He explained laboriously, 'They are leaving at the end of the week. I've got to do the polite. Show them where to eat.' She thought, with a sense of hopeless ennui: I had been looking forward to showing *him*. 'You know where to eat?'

'Oh yes,' he said, 'I've picked up a hint or two. I've been talking to the fellows here. I like them.'

'You must have made a lot of contacts.'

He said again apologetically, 'One likes to be liked. Has old Hammarsten rung up yet?'

'What about?'

'Krogh promised him money yesterday at Tivoli to produce a play by Shakespeare. The one about Gower.'

She stared at him. 'Money for a play? Now?' She accused him, 'Did you have a hand in this?' She laughed, 'How could you?' but she watched him covertly. He was weakness, but weakness could be very strong. She remembered his first post in an office at Wembley and the letter to their father she had intercepted, not to save her father anxiety but to protect Anthony's own story from harsh contradiction. He was clever, the managing director had written, he had a fine head for figures, there were no specific complaints, but he was corrupting the office. 'How could you?' she said, and touched his sleeve; his coat was damp. He stood away from the desk to let her by and she saw the mark he left on the polished surface of her desk; she rubbed it dry with her hand. It was like mildew.

'Have you been in the lake?' she said.

'The mist was heavy. I met Loo before breakfast.'

She said, 'You ought to take a cinnamon and quinine. Your chest's always been weak since that pleurisy.'

'Forget it,' Anthony said. 'You know too much, Kate. One might as well be married.'

'I'm sorry. It's a long time since we've been together. I expect you are stronger these days. There are plenty of things I don't know about you. I didn't know that you shot well.' She gave in; it was no good being proud; strength couldn't hold out against that sullen obstinate weakness. 'Have lunch with me tomorrow. There's a lot I want' – no, not to ask, I mustn't use the word 'ask' – 'you to tell me. Postcards and one night in Gothenburg. It's not much. We used to know each other well.' Standing at the corner of the class-room, she thought, listening to that cry; it wasn't a question of knowing each other well in those days; it was as if one were bearing a monstrous child who could scream or laugh or weep audibly in the womb. I would have welcomed an abortion in those days; but is this how one feels when the abortion has been successful? No more pain, no more movement, nothing to fear and nothing to hope for, a stillness indistinguishable from despair.

'Sorry, Kate. I'm afraid tomorrow – after all,' he said wryly, 'you've got me now for years. Give Loo a chance at me.'

'All right,' Kate said, 'keep me a day or two next week.'

'I'll take a cinnamon and quinine,' Anthony said. He was suddenly apologetic. He drew a flower from her vase and said, 'You ought to wear one. It just matches your dress. Have you got a pin?'

'I don't wear flowers in the office,' Kate said. As she went out of the door she looked back and saw him fit the flower into his own buttonhole. It was the culmination of all her plans, to have him there, making himself at home beside her desk, 'a home from home'. The sun was out, the mist had drained upwards from around the fountain, it was hot in the glass passage waiting for the lift. She tried to reassure herself with uneasy humour – 'a home from home'. But she was handicapped; she couldn't build up his London inside the glass walls of Krogh's as a seaside landlady can construct Birmingham with the beads, the mantel ornaments, the brass-work in the fender. She wouldn't if she could; she wanted security for him now; he had accused her – 'you've always liked this modern stuff' – and she had denied it, but with only partial truth. Her dusty righteous antecedents pulled at her heart, but with all her intellect she claimed alliance with the present, this crooked day, this inhumanity; she was like a dark tunnel connecting two landscapes, on one side the huddled houses, the backs with their washing and their splintered window-boxes, on the other——

She knocked at the door and went in. Erik lay on a sofa in the padded beige room.

'What is it, Kate?' he said. 'Sit down.'

There was no telephone in the room, no pictures, no table; only a chair for his secretary.

She said, 'I'm a little worried.'

'Why?'

'These short-term loans.' She was grateful to him because he didn't laugh at her; he considered her remark as seriously as if it had been made at a conference by someone with special knowledge. She was suddenly touched by the pity one is compelled to feel for anyone who has been mercilessly 'used'. She had used him from the start, from the first day in Hammond's office; she had recognised what he needed and she had supplied it with no other end in view than this: Anthony downstairs talking to 'the fellows', presenting her with her own flower, Anthony making himself at home.

'I know,' he said, 'these are not easy days. Everyone is suffering in the same way.'

'But are we safe?'

'Quite safe as long as we keep our heads – and our tongues.'

'But this help to Hammarsten. Is that keeping your head? Can you afford it at the moment?'

'Twenty thousand crowns is not very much to afford. The publicity is worth five times the amount. This is the moment to spend money. I've ordered two more cars. The others can be sold as soon as the new ones are delivered. Go shopping, Kate. Get yourself new things.'

'Publicity?'

'You don't realise how closely we are watched.'

'Why are people so interested? When I buy a tooth-brush——'

'You know better than I do. I don't know much about people.'

She believed she knew: men were conditioned by their insecurity. It was not that they envied him his money or were consciously opposed to his international purpose; it was that increasingly they needed sensations to take their minds off their personal danger: a murder, a war, a financial crash, even a financial success if it were sufficiently startling. She was disturbed when she thought of the immense impersonal pressure that was exercised on any man with power, to induce him to make a sensation at the cost of security: by ultimatums, telegrams, slogans, huge bonuses with nothing paid into the reserve. It was only a man completely out of touch with what people thought, without a private life, who could resist this pressure. And Anthony wanted to make him human.

'I was worried, too, about this sale to Batterson's. The A.C.U. has been useful. Why must we get rid of it now? It's sound, isn't it?' She was struck by the curious irresponsibility of his gaze; he was excited, he was heavily mischievous. She said, 'I know it's sound. I've been looking at the figures.'

'Even the A.C.U. needs capital,' Erik said.

'But it has the capital. The investments are sound.'

'The directors,' Erik said, 'have rationalised the investments. Its capital is now invested in our Amsterdam company.'

'I see,' Kate said.

'You are quicker than Hall.'

She thought: This is the moment I've always been expecting, the moment when we leave the law behind, push out for new shores. It seemed curiously unimportant. One had always expected the drawn-out business of good-byes, tears on wharfs, last sight of shipping. There was only one question to be asked: 'Is it safe?'

'Very nearly safe,' Erik said. She trusted him absolutely; if it was nearly safe, there was no more to be said. One couldn't afford to be squeamish or unadventurous when one was responsible for somebody one loved. He said, 'You'll find that some cheques, some entries in our books have been pre-dated.'

'Of course,' Kate said. 'Is there anything I can do?'

'No, everything's arranged.' He got up. 'You know, Kate, you were not wrong, after all, about the fountain.

173

I like the fountain.' He put his hand on her arm. 'You are quicker than Hall, Kate. Hall never liked the fountain.' She could feel uneasiness in his finger-tips.

She said, 'We are not safe.'

'We'll be safe when the American sales have gone through,' Erik said. 'We shall be safe in less than a week. We are all but safe. The strike's settled.'

'You mean something else may happen?'

'We've got to be very careful for a few days. You can see,' he said, 'how I trust you. We've known each other for a good many years now, Kate. Will you marry me?'

'A wife, you mean, doesn't have to give evidence? Is that true in Sweden as well as in England?'

'There's no danger in Sweden. I'm thinking of England.'

'It was good of you not to make love to me.'

'We are two business people,' Erik said.

'I shall want a settlement for myself.'

'Of course.'

'And something, too, for Anthony.'

'I like Anthony. He knows the way around. I'm fond of him, Kate.'

'But a settlement?'

'Yes.'

'It's a pity,' Kate said, 'that we can't pre-date the marriage like the cheques.' She smiled. 'Anthony will be pleased. There's nobody more respectable than Anthony. Anthony——' she dwelt on the name; she might have been marrying Anthony and not Erik at all; he stood at her side as stiffly as a best man in a vestry. Anthony's safe, she thought; I've undone the damage I did him when I sent him back, back from the barn to conform, to pick up the conventions, the manners of all

174

the rest. He tried to break away and I sent him back. Now I've discovered a way out for him. But the exhilaration was touched with regret; she couldn't help remembering the Bedford Palace, the apples they'd eaten to take the smell away. One believed in a new frontierless world, with Krogh's on every exchange; one believed in having no scruples while one got what one wanted most – security; but the old honesties and the old dusty poverties of Mornington Crescent spoke in one's voice when one said again: 'Anthony will be pleased. When shall it be?'

'We'll wait a day or two,' Erik said, 'and see how things go on. If the sale of the A.C.U. goes through all right,' he hardly hesitated, 'we'll be able to take our time.'

Kate nearly loved him. He was so clumsily honest with her even now when his books, she supposed, were already immaculately forged. She had often heard rumours of how much he had to pay in blackmail; for the first time she was in a position, if she wished, to blackmail him herself. But she didn't want to; she had used him, it was only fair that he should be allowed to use her. She said, 'You could have trusted me anyway.'

He nodded; he was always ready to accept what she said to him as truth; he would never have let a column of figures go by like that, he would have checked them every one, whatever accountant had been over them before him. She took his hand and kissed it; she pitied him as he stood there in his padded silenced room where nobody could trouble him. She said, 'Dear Erik, I'm going to tell Anthony,' and left the room. Going down in the lift she remembered, she didn't know why, a tram-car she had seen out of control on the North Bridge; glass and steel and the face of the driver with his hand pressed on a lever and the current running through and sparking behind the glass. It rocked by her in the dark and she could tell by the flicker of light that something was wrong. It went by her like something in the grip of a passion, bright and quick and unreliable.

'Congratulate me,' she said aloud in the lift, 'I'm going to be married. Anthony, I'm going to be married,' and she thought with sudden kindness: Perhaps this is what Erik feels, this sense of a sum solved, the square root taken, the logarithm correctly read. She said again in her own doorway, 'I'm going to be married, Anthony.'

'Who to, Kate?' he asked. He looked up quickly, he was sitting at her desk, and again she had a sense of dampness; her desk was marked with it where his elbows had rested.

'To Erik, of course. Who else?'

'No,' Anthony said, 'you can't.' She saw then that he had been reading the papers on her desk. He had even opened a telegram which had been delivered since she had left him.

'How dare you?' she said. 'You little cheat.'

'He can't get away with it,' Anthony said.

'I don't know what you mean.'

'Oh,' Anthony said, 'you can trust me about these things. I've got a head for figures. I can put two and two together.' He said with a schoolboy gravity, 'You know, Kate, there are limits to what you can do. Believe me, I've discovered them. He can't pass the buck like this. Batterson's weren't born yesterday.'

'Nor was Erik.'

'Loo was right. It's not respectable.'

'Give me the telegram.'

'Why,' Anthony said, 'you can see it all. He's

176

bolstering up Amsterdam with the A.C.U. It's as plain as a pikestaff.'

'You don't have to tell me,' Kate said. 'I know it all, too. Even to the pre-dated cheques.'

'The pre-dated cheques!' he whistled. His gravity broke. He said, 'To think that Krogh's ... and we know.'

'You've got to keep it to yourself.'

'He must make it worth our while, Kate.'

She thought: I've always believed there was this difference between us; that there was nothing I wouldn't do for him, but there were things he wouldn't do for me or for himself. She smiled with tenderness, she wasn't angry any more: I haven't discovered yet what they are. It gave her a deep pleasure to think there was something she didn't know about Anthony after all these years. She said, 'Anthony, I'm not going to blackmail him. I'm going to marry him.'

'But, Kate, you don't love him.' He was incorrigibly conventional, he was hopelessly innocent, the idea of blackmail lay as lightly on his spirits as a theft of plums. She was frightened by his superficiality; he didn't know where he was; he needed protection. She would do anything, she thought again, for him; she did not wish to deny him even blackmail. She felt that to deny him anything would mar the absurd happiness of his discovery. So she explained gently, 'It's a form of blackmail. He's going to make a settlement.'

But on this point he was stubborn. 'You don't love him.'

'I love you.'

'That's not the point.' He was worried; he was muddled; he said something under his breath about 'children' and blushed with self-consciousness.

Kate said, 'I'm sterile. You needn't be afraid,' and

177

seeing his embarrassment, added with an enraged despair, 'I don't want them. I've never wanted them,' and felt her body stretch to receive him. 'You're so conventional, Anthony,' and she thought: a child inside me would be no closer than we've been, and yet there he stands, and there it would stand, blushing, self-conscious, my God, how prim, forgetting what they don't want to remember.

'Such a waste,' he said, staring back at her, flushed, childish, inarticulate. She was prepared for him to say something about a good man's love. But they were at cross-purposes. He didn't mean that she was wasted; he meant the opportunity was wasted. 'The chance may never come again. We could lift a good sum from him and clear out. Why, we could catch the train tonight. Tomorrow Gothenburg. We'd be in London on Saturday in time to go to Twickenham. Kate,' he said, 'we could go to Stone's for a chop and a pint of special. I daresay my room hasn't been taken yet. The landlady would find a room somewhere for you. We shouldn't have to look for a job; he'd have paid us our price.'

She watched him fascinated. It almost seemed as if there was nothing he wouldn't do, but she knew that somewhere on that straight steel track down which his brain now so quickly drove there burned a permanent red light; somewhere he would stop, waver, make a hash of things. He wasn't unscrupulous enough to be successful. He was in a different class to Krogh.

'It's so easy, Kate. He'll just have to pay us our price. If he refuses I'll give the whole story to Minty; even that way we'd make our fares home, and I expect you've got a little saved.'

She asked curiously, 'You wouldn't mind living on

me?' She believed that she was reaching the end of what he was willing to do, but when without hesitation he agreed (after all, he said, they were brother and sister) she felt the weariness of a traveller who discovers that his maps again are faulty. Was it possible that she had over-estimated the simplicity of that bland loved conventional brain?

Anthony got up from her desk holding the telegram. 'I'll see him now.'

'What are you going to say?'

'Best be quite blunt.'

'No, no, Anthony,' Kate said. 'I've just been letting you run on. You can't really blackmail Erik.'

'Why not? Kate,' he said, 'you don't know a good thing when you see it.'

'You aren't clever enough, Anthony, that's why. You wouldn't be here now if you had the brains to blackmail Erik. Oh, Anthony,' she said, with a deep affection, 'what a pair we are. How I love you. If only you had the brains, if only you weren't so respectable——' She didn't finish: she was thinking of Saturday morning at Tilbury, the long ride home, the shilling in the meter and the small blue flame ready for their toast and tea. She thought: I've saved him from these, but he brought the memory with him wherever he entered, like a sandwich-man advertising some dear cheap tune: Anthony saved from Anthony, but herself incomplete without Anthony. A white bird blew up against the window, rattling its beak against the Vita glass, then drifted backwards on flat wings, like a bird seen from a plane, out-flown. This, she repeated to herself over and over again, is security, the future, this must be ours. No more past. We've lived too much in the past.

179

'Trust me,' Anthony said.

'Not with him,' Kate said sadly. 'Dear Anthony, you're newly hatched compared with him. You don't really think that you could hold up Krogh's. He'd break you before you could open your mouth. He'd have you in prison, he wouldn't stop at anything. You wouldn't be safe. Why do you want to, anyway, now that we are getting all we need, a settlement——'

'He's not good enough for you, Kate,' Anthony said stubbornly. He was still worried, it was obvious, about such problems as Marriage without Love, the Childless Wife. But he surrendered the chance, in a graceful friendly way he surrendered it, with no more than a backward look at her desk, at the thought of the pre-dated cheques, the telegram, the sale to Batterson's. 'Of course, Kate, what you say goes.' She could see the birth of a new idea in his rather flashing smile. ' At any rate we've got to celebrate tonight.'

'It's not public.'

'Never mind. He's got to have a party. Listen, Kate, ring up the manager of the hotel at Saltsjöbaden and book a table, tell him whom to expect.'

'Erik won't come.'

'If I got him to Tivoli, I'll get him to Saltsjöbaden. This is the point: we can get a big rake-off for this dinner. Ask for a hundred crowns.'

Kate went to the telephone. 'You think of everything, Anthony.'

'Wait a moment. He must make it a hundred and fifty or Krogh dines at the Opera.'

'Saltsjöbaden three-two,' Kate said.

# PART V

## [1]

Young Andersson, directly he heard what his neighbour said, dropped his hand from the lever and took his foot from the pedal of the Krogh cutter. The machine stopped with a flap, flap, flap of its leather belt; immediately the moving tray which fed it became cluttered. His neighbour shouted to him; young Andersson took no notice. He had few ideas and small power of expression. He turned his back on the cutter and walked down the aisle between the machines towards the cloak-room. On the floor above, one of the drying-chambers became congested, its tray stuck in its groove; in the room behind an electric saw piled a tray so deep with strips of wood that they overflowed on to the floor. The man who fed it with wood went on feeding it with wood; it was his job, he didn't know what else to do, so that news of the congestion did not reach back to the room where the logs were being unloaded. The men there continued to take them one by one from the hook which drew them from the lorries waiting in a long queue in the courtyard.

Young Andersson stepped out of his dungarees. The failure of one machine made little difference to the racket in the hall he had left, but long familiarity with his particular cutter had made him familiar with a slight recurring cough in its whine. He couldn't hear the cough. His pale thin face became momentarily troubled; he had never before failed to hear that cough every six seconds. He couldn't visualise the trouble he had caused; he had seen the drying-room; a friend of his worked one of the

181

saws; but he knew nothing of the further depths, nothing of the hall where the trunks were unloaded, nothing of the lorries and where they came from. A man from his shift passed through the cloakroom to the lavatory. Young Andersson watched him; he walked quickly with his head bent; he had raised his hand, and his place at the machine had been taken; he would be allowed four minutes; if he was longer than four minutes he would be fined. Young Andersson took off his jacket from his peg and left the cloakroom. He had to cut across the end of the machine-room; a man came down the room carrying an oil-can; he dripped the heavy black oil into the well of each machine on the left-hand side; a man carrying a similar can walked up the other side. They knew so exactly the position of the wells that they had no need to look; they walked and turned the wrist and walked and turned the wrist.

The man carrying the can down the room stared at Andersson; he was astonished, he hesitated with his can and left a little dropping of oil like an animal's pad on the polished steel floor; he watched Andersson out of the door. Andersson climbed down the curving steel stair of the emergency exit into the courtyard; he was afraid to wait for a lift in sight of the machine-room. He carried the man's face with him in his mind, tiredness, astonishment, envy. Andersson walked across the court-yard to the gateway where he clocked in and out. The porter was unwilling to open the gate. 'Sick,' young Andersson said, 'sick.' It was unnecessary to act sick-ness; his pallor, his habitual slight stoop, the new worry which sat his face uneasily like a recruit at a riding-school, were his bona fides. The gate of the factory was opened for him.

He had a sense of strangeness, seeing the long asphalted road between the high wooden walls quite empty. One side lay in shadow; a long way off the walls ended and a few silver birches stood in a pool of afternoon sun. Young Andersson began to run along the two-foot strip of shadow. It's not right, he thought with astonishment, it's not right. The idea had never occurred to him before.

Young Andersson was conservative. He read the papers, he believed in the greatness of Krogh's. His father's socialism was something old, tiresome, didactic; it smelt of night-schools; like the morality of old people it was a substitute for experience. 'A fair share for the worker', 'proletarian unity', like a long Lutheran Sunday his father's phrases went droning on. They had no more meaning to young Andersson than 'three in one', 'the persons of the blessed Trinity'.

'Do you believe in nothing?' his father asked.

'Stick to my job,' young Andersson said. 'Things all right. Good wages. Save a bit. Well off myself one day.'

Now he ran gasping up the shadowed wall.

'Krogh one of us once. Chance for us all.'

The smell of tar, of oil, very far away the trees, the man with the oil-can envying him. It's not right, young Andersson thought, it's not right. Father wrote that he came himself, joked, gave him a cigar, why he even asked after me, promised that everything was all right. That was only a few days ago. Of course he doesn't know; he's got to be told. He's a just man. Young Andersson believed in justice. He had seen it working, the idle man dismissed, the industrious rewarded. His own wages had been raised two years ago.

He couldn't run any more; he was out of training; the oil man's job was the healthiest, walking up and down;

he must cover a good many miles in a day. The end of the wooden walls seemed as far away as ever; they were nearly a mile and a half in length. When a man left work it took him twenty minutes quick walking to get clear of the factory. Some men complained that they should be paid for that time. They couldn't live nearer than they did. The wooden bungalows began where the wooden walls left off.

He passed them, walking fast; they were good bungalows painted in bright colours. They all had a small piece of garden; some of the men's wives kept chickens. Young Andersson was unmarried; he lodged with a man on the night-shift. The man's wife was digging in the garden as he passed. She stopped digging and called to him, 'What's the matter? Where are you going?' He was embarrassed, he stood in the middle of the road and kicked the surface.

'I shan't be in to supper.'

'Is anything wrong at the works? Where are you off to?'

Young Andersson blushed and kicked the road. He looked at her sideways. He always blushed when he spoke to her and he never looked straight at her. He slept in the next room and the thin matchboard wall kept out no sounds. He could hear her clean her teeth, wash, he could hear her when she lay with her husband; he wouldn't have minded if she had been old and plain, but she was young and pretty. It made him shy and furtive to know so much about her.

'Nothing wrong. I've got to go up to Stockholm. I'll be late tonight.'

She wasn't inquisitive. Nothing which he did, he knew, really interested her. She thought him a poor sort of a fellow; she was passionately in love with her husband. He knew only too well how passionately. He blushed and kicked the road and said, 'I'd better be getting on.'

'Don't get into mischief,' she said without interest and began to dig again.

At the station he found he had only just enough money to reach Stockholm. There was half an hour to wait. He need not have hurried. Now he had to walk again, up and down the platform; there was nothing else to do. He tried shaking a slot machine; sometimes a coin had stuck. He tried another. He shook every slot machine he could find. At last he was successful. A coin tinkled into place and young Andersson drew out the drawer; it contained a paper handkerchief. Well, he thought, it's something for nothing, and put it in his pocket. A long goods-train laden with timber for the factory drew up at a siding. She's pretty, he thought, it's not right hearing everything like that, and then he thought of his father. A faint premonition of injustice touched his brain. He told himself, Herr Krogh just doesn't know, he'll put it right. A joke, cigar, he asked after me.

One of the work's managers came on to the platform; he was seeing off his wife and daughter. Young Andersson knew him by sight, but he didn't know Andersson. He carried a big box of chocolates for his wife and a bunch of flowers for his daughter. Young Andersson came near; he was curious to know what these people talked about when they were not at work. He knew what he talked about: money, drink, the factory.

'Yes,' the manager said, 'yes. It will be quite all right. I'll be up for the week-end. Make up the four.'

'Count me out,' the girl said. 'I'm going dancing.'

She was very fair with very small ears; her lobes were prettily painted. Young Andersson thought of the matchboard wall again and blushed. It just wasn't right. When she walked along the platform, she was like an athlete entering a stadium. Her legs moved so freely that she might have been wearing nothing under her fur coat; she seemed quite unconscious of her sex, but there was in her manner a dash of desperation, of nerves, she looked over-trained.

'You're spending too much time dancing,' the manager said. He was hurried and irritated; he kept on looking at the clock. It was obvious that the flowers and the chocolates meant nothing, he had no affection for either of them, it was simply an act that he always performed.

When the train drew in, young Andersson had to pass the group to reach the third-class carriages. The manager kissed his wife on the cheek, but his daughter shook hands with him. Young Andersson touched his cap. The manager never noticed. He said to his wife, 'You'll have to order some more drink. Ask them for eight o'clock. I shan't get home earlier.' The girl saw Andersson touch his cap and nodded to him; there was no condescension in her nod; she might have been recognising a fellow competitor on the running track.

Young Andersson sat back in the bare-boarded carriage and saw the station, the manager, the factory, the bunga-lows drawn back and out of sight. Between a narrow hem of silver birch-trees a lake spread under the flat late sunlight. He sat with his hands pressed between his knees, jolting with every movement of the slow country train. He thought: what should I say to her? . . . dancing . . . spending too much time, tobogganing in winter, the scream of the runners cutting the snow at the bend under the fairy lights, talking in a friendly way on an inn bench, cold and happy and having fun; he nodded in a sleepy way, seeing great possibilities in the life before him.

The trees became dark against a lower greyer sky; the lake lay like lead between the gaps; somebody looked to see if the heating handle were turned; a long whistle before a tunnel and on the other side an abruptly darker world; a few sparks tingled against the window-pane. Young Andersson opened his eyes and saw a group of men bicycling home from work; the lights on their machines had been lit; outdistanced they carried their small burning globes backward. The train whirled away from the lake and the trees, and darkness fell over a long wide waste of grass.

'You're going up to the city?' an elderly woman asked and she opened a basket to find a buttered roll. The light in the carriage roof burned suddenly brighter; darkness was like the drawing of blinds before the evening meal. Those in the carriage began to feel towards each other a companionship, a sense of trust; they were all happy together with the night outside. 'Yes,' young Andersson said.

'Aren't you in work?' she asked, slipping a piece of ham between the two halves of her roll.

'Oh, yes,' he said with pride, 'I'm in Krogh's,' and they both stared out of the window with a momentary sense of well-being, he because he was in Krogh's and she because of her roll. The train stopped at every village and the warmth and friendliness of their carriage were duplicated by the lights outside, by a woman cooking, by a child sitting up in bed to see the train.

'You're lucky to be in Krogh's,' the woman said. 'There's a future in a job like that.'

'There's a future,' young Andersson said and then was silent. He had remembered how he had left his job in the middle of his shift. His pale unintelligent face grew stubborn; he had done the right thing. All the stubbornness which had kept him for years reliably by his machine, earning a little more money every few years, had conditioned him to leave it the moment he heard the news about his father. Stubbornness had made him a conservative; stubbornness made him believe in justice; stubbornness had checked his machine, cluttered the tray, congested the drying-chamber. It will be all right, he thought, when I tell them. If I'd stayed to argue I might have missed the train.

'Don't get up to mischief,' the woman said, shaking crumbs from her skirt on to his knees. Everyone was telling him not to get up to mischief. He said sadly in explanation, 'I'm going up on business.'

'We all know that sort of business,' the woman said and rummaged for a bottle of milk in her basket, and the word 'mischief' and the word 'business' in her large friendly voice took on an unusual meaning to young Andersson, something not to be blushed at or hidden, something cheerful, common, careless, come today and gone tomorrow. He said, 'There might be time when this is over. . . . It won't take long.'

'You're only young once,' the woman said, shaking her grey ribald head.

When the train drew up in the Central Station it was nearly seven o'clock. Young Andersson had no idea how late they worked at Krogh's. He had never seen Krogh's. He had to ask the way of a policeman, and the man watched him suspiciously out of sight, curious at his workman's clothes, his collarless shirt and heavy boots and air of determination. But the porter at Krogh's wouldn't let him in. 'What do you think you are?' he said, talking through the wrought-iron gate. 'He wouldn't see you even if he was here.'

'I work down at the factory.'

'What difference does that make?' the porter asked.

'It's about my father,' young Andersson said. 'Herr Krogh knows my father.'

'Your mother, you mean,' the porter shrieked through the gate, laughing and holding on to the iron-work with long simian arms. Then he grew serious. 'You've no business here. This place isn't for the likes of you. You ought to be down at the factory.'

'I've got to see Herr Krogh.'

'Even the Prime Minister doesn't see Herr Krogh except by appointment.'

'I'd make an appointment.'

'Ah,' the porter said, 'but first you have to see the secretary.'

'I'll see the secretary.'

'But nobody,' the porter said, cackling through the iron flowers, 'can see the secretary without an appoint-ment.'

'I'll make an appointment,' young Andersson said.

'Why, at this place,' the porter said, 'you are lucky to see me without an appointment.'

'But Herr Krogh knows about me. My father wrote to me. He said Herr Krogh asked after me.'

'Your father's a liar.'

Young Andersson lowered his head. He came nearer to the gate with his fingers crooked. He had not lost his air of stubbornness, of determination.

'Why, look about you,' the porter said. 'This is Herr

Krogh's. What do you think he'd have to do with you or your precious father? Look about you,' the porter repeated, and Andersson looked, at the initials burning against the sky, the glass walls, the water splashing down the side of the green block of stone.

'That fountain,' the porter said, 'was made by Sweden's greatest sculptor. You wouldn't believe me if I told you what this place cost. They dine off plate which would cost you a year's wages; he has diamond studs in his shirts.'

'Diamond studs?'

'In every shirt.'

Old Andersson had often spoken about wages; his son never listened; it was an old dull story. But now he became aware of an uneasiness; he looked from his oily hands to the porter cackling behind the gate. He thought of the man in the night-shift who had gone off his head and killed his wife and himself because she was going to bear another child. 'That's a fine uniform you have,' he said. *Dear Anna,* the man had written on a piece of toilet paper, *forgive me. I can't bear the anxiety. I've got to do it. We've been happy. Love to your sister; she always was a help.* He must have killed his wife as an after-thought to spare her pain. There's sure to be some explanation, young Andersson thought, staring upwards at the highest glass floor.

'You see, mine's brain work,' the porter said. 'I have to know what to say to visitors. They give me a new pair of shoes every six months. One's got to be smart up here.'

'I've got a new suit at home,' young Andersson said. 'But I left work in a hurry. I've got to tell Herr Krogh about my father.'

'You'll have to go to Saltsjöbaden then,' the porter

said. 'They've all gone out to dinner at the hotel.' It was as if he had a grievance against young Andersson which had to be washed off his brain in mockery. 'You'll need evening dress.'

'Is it far?' Andersson asked.

'It'll be twenty kilometres.'

'I'd better be going,' young Andersson said.

'No hurry. No hurry,' said the porter. 'Plenty of time to change. There's a train every half-hour.'

'I haven't any money for trains,' young Andersson said, 'I'll have to walk.'

'But you won't get there before midnight.'

'I'll get a lift,' he said uneasily, turning away, hearing the porter laughing behind the iron flowers, not quite as confident as he had been in the comradeship of other men.

[2]

They left the chauffeur behind and Anthony drove. It was his idea. He said that the chauffeur made the car conspicuous. Krogh offered no objection; he had offered no objection from the start of the drive. When Anthony stopped and ordered a drink, Krogh drank too. Kate watched him with anxiety. He sat solidly over his drink, saying nothing.

At the restaurant where they stopped for the third time, Krogh broke a glass. Anthony had said, 'Tomorrow Erik and I are going shopping. I'm going to choose him some clothes. After all, we're almost brothers now.'

She had not realised till then how much Krogh had drunk; he had had no lunch; he had been busy all the afternoon with long-distance calls. 'We are going shopping, aren't we, Erik?' Anthony said and Krogh began to explain carefully that he wanted the party to be a success. He had every reason to be grateful to Anthony.

'Have another drink?' Anthony said. But Krogh was still intent on finishing his speech. 'All this morning,' he said, 'I was able to work very clearly, because I hadn't to worry about tonight. I tore up the concert tickets. I thought – tonight we'll have a good time like we had in Tivoli.' He said suddenly, '*Skål*,' raising his glass, but his glass slipped, his hand followed it and it splintered between the table and his hand. He said, 'I thought we won't care a damn.'

'Let's move on,' Anthony said, and they got into the car again. It was quite dark now, but the huge headlamps of the car made the air in front of them a pale-green daylight. It was as if time were visible; day with night on either side. A rabbit rushed from night into day and up the hillside into night again. They left the little restaurant with its bright beady lights under an awning in night and carried day with them at increasing speed down the blue level metallic way.

'You've cut yourself,' Kate said, but Krogh was asleep beside Anthony, his hand bleeding on to the cushion between them.

'My God,' Anthony said, 'I've never had a chance to drive a car like this.' He accelerated, but one had no sense of speed; one was stationary; it was the rocky corner which whipped behind, the lighted cottage which flashed down the road, drenched for one moment in the green under-water daylight, so that one wondered at the extravagance of its small dimmed illumination as the head-lamps washed through the curtains and swept the garden.

'Erik's cut himself.'

'It's nothing,' Anthony said. 'The bleeding's stopped. Why wake him, Kate? It's just as good as if we were alone.' The dial trembled on 170. Anthony began to sing: 'As I to you, As you to me'; they were alone in the great grey car.

'We might leave him at a cottage,' Anthony said. 'Let him have his sleep out.' He whistled a plaintive moony tune; the thin sound was spilt along the road out of the car's belly like the silk thread of a spider.

'You wouldn't get your rake-off.'

'That's true.'

They ran for a while beside the railway line; an electric train rushed noiselessly towards them and swerved away with a flicker of blue lightning along the rails; a small red light dodged and rocked before them. The sky was lit up behind a bluff out of range of the headlamps and when the road curved they came in sight of two cranes, steaming on either side the line, and a great treble arch of iron girder spanning the rails. A circle of arc lamps gave the workmen light; they sat astride the cross-girders, thirty feet in the air and tightened the bolts. The ground beneath them was littered with crowbars, screws and rusty brackets. Anthony braked the car and Krogh woke. 'Stop here,' he said. 'It's the new bridge. I want to see——'

A small man in a shabby brown suit and a broken nose picked his way among the iron strands.

'Brackets 145, 141, and 137,' he called, and a man threw a rope to him and came down it, hand over fist.

One of the cranes swung and dipped a hook through a cloud of steam, and a man loaded it with squares of brown rusty metal like giant grid-irons. They dangled over Krogh's car.

Krogh said, 'They still use English brackets. Do you see the name? Chepstow.'

The men worked quietly, without hurry, talking gently to each other while they worked. They were joined by ropes, by the iron girders, by a common interest; the lamps of the grey car burned weakly outside the ring of arc lights. Anthony had shut off the engine and it grew cold in the car. No one took any notice of them, no one resented their presence. 'Here a moment, Erik,' the foreman said, and a man in torn trousers followed him into the shadows behind the light and they turned over the bolts, looking for something in the confusion of iron.

'What brackets did you say?' a man called from the farthest girder. '145, 141, and 137,' the foreman said. 'It's painted just where you are sitting,' and they laughed good-humouredly, allied together against the cold and dark, against death in the falling bolt, in faulty metal, in the frayed rope.

Krogh said, 'I worked on a bridge myself once.' He pulled at the door of the car, 'I want to talk to the foreman,' and stood awkwardly beside the car in his evening dress, his fur coat over his arm. He said, 'It was a bigger bridge than this.'

'Give me a hand here, Erik,' the foreman said, passing in front of them, the pockets of his waistcoat stuffed with scraps of paper. He pushed his soft hat away from his smudged forehead and wiped his nose with his fingers. 'What have you done with the fifty-seven bolts?'

'You don't mean fifty-seven. You mean forty-three,' a man said.

The foreman took a piece of paper out of his breast-pocket. 'You're wrong. It's fifty-seven.'

'Then they are over there.'

The foreman limped straight towards Krogh down the sleepers. He put a cigarette in his mouth. He looked small and thin, peering this way, peering that way in the glare of the arc lights. The man in the torn grey trousers followed him and the men on the girders shouted that the bolts were here, there, beyond.

'Give me a match, chum.'

Krogh shifted his fur coat to his other arm and felt in the pockets of his white waistcoat. 'I'm sorry,' he said, 'I don't seem——'

'Here you are,' the other man said, 'catch.' The foreman caught the box and struck a match; he had to shield it with his hands from the wind. The arc lights showed up his hands against the night like close-ups on a screen; the fingers blunted, twisted with rheumatism, the stump on the left hand. His face was hidden by them; judging by the hands one would have expected something tougher, older, less friendly than the youngish smudged face with the broken nose.

'Good evening,' Krogh said.

'Evening,' the foreman said, passing him, going down the line with his companion, looking for a fifty-seven bolt.

Krogh came back to the car. He got in and sat down. 'Scratched my hand,' he said. 'Let's go on. It's only a small bridge.' He sat deep in the seat beside Anthony, his white tie a little crooked. 'They have to work at night because of the trains,' he said. 'They still get their brackets from Chepstow. Things don't alter much.' But he was altered, Kate thought. The sight of him standing on the track, interested in spite of himself, without matches when he was asked for them, without words to explain what he wanted, disquieted her. They moved slowly past the gang and he did not look out again; they had stayed the same, but he had altered.

'On with the family party,' Anthony said.

Kate began to laugh. 'Yes,' she said, 'a family party. A damned dull family party.' She thought: He's one of us, fighting for his own security like one of us, he's not the future, he's not self-sufficient, just one of us, out of his proper place.

'Oh boy,' Anthony said, driving down the accelerator, making the grey wings buck from the road, 'this is going to be a night. Dull? Wait till you see the dinner I've ordered.'

'It must have been the glass I broke,' Krogh said and nursed his hand.

Kate leant over his shoulder – we're a family party, one of us, I've used him and he's used me, but he's one of us, only a damned climber after all, as we are – 'Show me your hand, darling,' she said. She tore up her handker-chief and spread it with cold cream. She took his hand with tenderness and touched the cut – poor devil, what a long and tiring way he's come, and they wouldn't take any notice of him, wouldn't recognise that he was once of their own kind, they humiliated him. She bound his hand firmly and put her arm round his shoulder: a family party, one might as well be kind: three of us now climbing together, honour among thieves.

[3]

The Royal Dutch plane swung off the ground, treading air; the great rubber tyre below the window bounded twice from the rough grass and then stood

196

poised above the bright clean air station, the white roofs, near the sea the oil containers like rows of buttons on a grey-green suit. Fred Hall stuck the cotton-wool in his ears and the pilot took off his gold-laced cap and put on a little black skull-cap. One had the impression of settling to some important business. The cockpit of the Dutch plane was open to the cabin; one could see the legs of the pilot on the level of one's eyes, and above a great arc of blue cloudless sky. The wind eddies lifted the plane fifty feet at a time, as if a giant fist were exerting a personal pressure.

Fred Hall opened *Bagatelle*. The Zuyder Zee crawled backward as slowly as a worm; there was no sense of speed; it lay the colour of mud with inky patches, one island white buttressed against the low depressing swell. The plane climbed, tilted. As it climbed the air grew warmer, the sun beat more directly upon the windows. Fred Hall took off his overcoat and folded it carefully, brown with velvet lapels. With his narrow tanned face, his watch-chain with a dangling nickel disc, the silver armlets which kept his cuffs in place, he had the appearance of a prosperous bookmaker.

The plane pierced through the clouds; the sea was no longer visible, except occasionally like a small land-locked lake surrounded by Alpine peaks. '*Pilules Orientales*', Fred Hall read, going through the advertisements. At 1,200 metres a storm drove towards them, the rain flying like arrows parallel with the plane; in half a minute the storm was behind them, the clouds had broken, and a rainbow lay flat across the ground, moved slowly with them across country and hid a whole village under its pale colourings. '*La Timidité est vaincue en quelques jours*', Fred Hall read with astonished interest.

It seemed odd to him that so extensive an industry, art photos and Oriental pills and invigorating medicines should be built up about a lot of skirts.

Again the clouds gathered; they lay round the plane like a heavy fall of snow. For a while they lit the page of *Bagatelle* with a brilliant rimy light, but at 1,800 metres the plane flattened out, all the clouds in the world were below; they lay, blindingly white to the horizon, and one had no sense of movement; the great rubber tyre, the heavy wing, trembled above the limitless frozen plain. Fred Hall undid his waistcoat; there was no protection from the sun; he wore a striped shirt. '*L'Amour au Zoo*', '*L'Amour au Djebel-Druse*', '*Amours et hantises d'Edgar Poë*', '*La Dame de Cœur*'. Fuss about a skirt, Fred Hall thought, letting the paper fall with melancholy morality upon his knee. 2,700 metres he noticed automatically and felt his right pocket and was only reassured when he remembered that he had them in his overcoat; you never knew when you might need them. All was settled in Amsterdam, he had nothing to do but report, but all the same he'd never yet been without a pair of knuckle-dusters. If you weren't a particularly good boxer, you had to look out for yourself in other ways.

The plane slanted, his knees pressed the seat in front, they passed through bumpy air, working down through the clouds until the land appeared, square fields lying out flat to the horizon like a many-windowed skyscraper, photographed horizontally. They drove straight towards a thin mast upright in the air, but it sank away, it was a road two thousand metres down. They seemed to move so slowly that it took a minute for a farm, an exact square of white thatched buildings, to shift from the centre of the window out of sight; their shadow on the ground was the size of a thumb. The pilot's bearings taken, they rose again into the waste of cloud.

Fred Hall fell asleep. With his mouth open showing a blackened broken tooth, the nickel club medallion swaying as the headwind struck the plane, he carried with him the atmosphere of third-class Pullmans to Brighton, the week-end jaunt, the whisky and splash, peroxide blonde. His soft brown hat with a turned-up rim slipped over his forehead, and the movement registered itself in his sleeping brain as the touch of a hand. He cleared his throat and said 'Elsie' aloud. In his dream Krogh was trying to tell him something, but Elsie interrupted, drew his attention away, wanted him to take a bath. Krogh stood outside in the road calling up to his window. 'You haven't got your loofah,' Elsie said and told him that Lifebuoy soap was indigestible. She couldn't understand that he didn't want a bath, he wanted to speak to Krogh. He shouted loudly, rocking backwards and forwards as a storm came up over Denmark: 'I don't like bath salts.' The Scandinavian Air Express climbed and climbed to get above the storm: 3,200 metres. 'Skirts,' Fred Hall exclaimed and woke up. He was momentarily startled in the rocking roaring machine, rain streamed behind them like smoke, and then again they were in clear air, and the heavy grey clouds tumbled between them and the earth.

He closed his eyes again; he was no longer interested by the flight from Amsterdam; he knew the airports of Europe as well as he had once known the stations on the Brighton line – shabby Le Bourget; the great scarlet rectangle of the Tempelhof as one came in from London in the dark, the headlamp lighting up the asphalt way; the white sand blowing up round the shed at Tallinn;

Riga, where the Berlin to Leningrad plane came down and bright pink mineral waters were sold in a tin-roofed shed; the huge aerodrome at Moscow with machines parked half a dozen deep, the pilots taxi-ing casually here and there, trying to find room, bouncing back and forth, beckoned by one official with his cap askew. It was a comfortable dull way of travelling; sometimes Fred Hall missed the racing tips from strangers in the Brighton Pullman.

When he woke for the second time he scrambled back to the lavatory and smoked a cigarette; he sat uncomfortably on the seat, blowing acrid rings. There was about him in his ridiculous posture an air of complete recklessness; his flat narrow skull had no room for anything but obedience to the man who paid him, fidelity to the man he admired, and the satisfaction of certain physical needs: cigarettes, a monthly drunk, and what he always called 'blowing off steam'. He wanted to blow off steam now; the amount of money he had been spending in Amsterdam frightened him. Krogh had begun where he had begun; he was perhaps the only living person in a position to measure Krogh's achievement – from the bed-sitting-room in Barcelona to the palace in Stockholm. But it did not seem strange to Fred Hall sitting on the lavatory seat; he thought with love, a love which expressed itself in gaudy presents (the jewelled cuff-links he carried in his hip-pocket), 'I always knew the bugger had brains.' He swung his legs and spat out small perfect rings, endangering the lives of twelve passengers, a pilot, a wireless operator, and several thousand pounds of property. A little thing like that did not worry Fred Hall.

What had worried him was Laurin's directorship. He had met Laurin; he had no opinion of Laurin; unconsciously he judged men by their physique (it was doubtful whether he would have recognised Krogh's brains if they had been housed in a fragile body); Laurin was always falling sick. For a while he had been recklessly jealous; he was Krogh's oldest friend; he had never let him down, but he was not a director, he was only the man Krogh could always trust to do exactly as he was told. It was not that he was paid less than Laurin or the other directors, but sometimes ambition stirred in Fred Hall to see his name in print. He was not unreasonable, he didn't expect to be a director of the I.G.S., but sometimes it seemed to him that he might at least be on the board of some small subsidiary company like the Amsterdam one.

He stubbed out the butt of his cigarette between his legs and stood up. He didn't trust Laurin, he didn't trust anyone near Krogh except himself, he wanted to blow off steam, there was nothing he would like so much at the moment as to beat someone up. Suddenly with a fierce possessive affection he remembered Krogh's voice that morning over the telephone. 'Fred,' he had said, as in the old days before they were employer and employed; he had told him to come directly everything was settled, he might be needed. Fred Hall stood with his legs apart in the swaying lavatory; under his feet he could feel the framework of the plane weighing on the wind currents, trembling with the engines' tremendous forward drive. My God, Fred Hall thought, if anyone's played the dirty on Mr Krogh, I'll just blow off steam. He didn't trust Laurin, he didn't even trust Kate. She's not our class, he thought. She was a skirt, she only lived with

Krogh, he was convinced, for what she could get out of him. He didn't count his own three thousand pounds a year; he counted it so little that he had spent already more than a fortnight's earnings on a present for Krogh, which he would present with embarrassment, obstinate if it were refused, saying he had bought it for someone else who had no use for it and must find it a good home somewhere; they were smart cuff-links, you couldn't just throw them in the dustbin.

He staggered back to his seat; he was a little bow-legged, and that increased the turfy air he carried with him. He was anxious and impatient; he had left Amsterdam at 12.30, the selling of the shares had been quite checked, the price had even a little appreciated, he had his private information that there would be no more abnormal dealings; he had intended to catch the night train from Malmö to Stockholm. But now nothing would satisfy him but seeing Krogh before he went to bed. The plane was due at Copenhagen at 5.25, at Malmö at 5.40. He decided that Krogh's direction to come to Stockholm immediately the Amsterdam business was settled would cover the cost of an air taxi in his expenses sheet.

The wireless operator hung up his earphones; the pilot put on his gold-laced cap; the engines were shut off, and the sudden silence pressed on the ears through the wads of cotton-wool. They sank through deep cloud towards a dark-green sea, towards evening sparkling on the ripples, flat, yellow, luminous. Denmark was like the jagged pieces of a jig-saw puzzle. Nosing down, they swung in a wide arc over the sea, the wings were flattened out to lose the wind's resistance, they soared up again in a burst of the engines, then drove down, touched and sprang from the pale

202

grass, bounced and beat it down. To Fred Hall the ten minutes' wait at Copenhagen seemed like an hour; he was fussed and aggravated, but he showed it only in his restless bow-legged walk.

And then at Malmö there was more delay, no taxi in the seaplane port; he had to wait until they fetched him one from Stockholm. He went into the refreshment-room and had a plate of creamy pastries and a cup of strong tea with a dash of brandy in it. Outside the water darkened and the masthead lights came out. With nothing better to do he began to write a letter to his mother at Dorking. He used an indelible pencil and a tear-off memo pad.

*Dear Ma,* he wrote, *I'm going back to Stockholm for a day or two. I saw Jack in Amsterdam but not to speak to. Has the cat kittened yet? It's no good going on showing it that drawer; if she wants to kitten in the lavatory she will. I expect I shall be over for a few days at Christmas. Business is pretty lively. If I were you I'd lay off those shares for a week or two. Wait till I send you a wire. Did you put a fiver on Grey Lady as I told you to do? Don't you mind what the Vicar says, I'll have a chat with him at Christmas, we'll show him where he gets off. A man like that makes me cross. If I'd a day to spare, I'd just like to come across and blow off steam.* He looked out anxiously above his pile of crumbled pastry (he never had the patience to finish the dull parts of a cake) at the blue empty sky; he looked at his watch; he went on writing in a suppressed fury at time wasted; aware of the lights turned on, glittering in the glasses at the buffet, cracking in the mirrors. *I don't know what's come over the Vicar, talking to you like that. There's no harm in a little flutter.*

He put down his pencil; a light dropped out of the dark sky; a shadow brushed the water. He picked up his suitcase and dived for the door. 'What do you mean,' he asked the braided official at the head of the steps (the water of the harbour slapped and sucked), 'by saying there was no seaplane in the port? What about that seaplane?' and he pointed at the green light which bobbed and ducked towards them over the swell.

'Your taxi is on the way,' the official said. He turned away from Fred Hall and shouted, but Hall caught his elbow and swung him round.

'I'll take this one,' Hall said, 'see. This one. I'm in a hurry.'

'Impossible. This has been chartered for Krogh's. One of the directors,' and Fred Hall saw a staid procession advance towards the stairs: two black-coated valets with suitcases, and a thin middle-aged woman, her pinched face heavily painted, who shivered in furs, an officer from the seaplane station, who kept on saying: 'Herr Bergsten . . . Herr Bergsten,' and the director himself, with his old bored eyes, a silk muffler twined round his scrawny neck. 'Thank you, thank you,' he repeated, taking the officer's hand, feeling for the stairs with polished patent-leather shoes, while the official saluted and Hall stood back and thought with jealous rage: The old figurehead, treated like royalty, director Bergsten, he's never even heard of me, the nights in Barcelona when I paid for the drink: with pained possessive love: Erik can't depend on any of them, he pays them, he makes them famous, but when he wants something done he trusts Fred Hall.

'Your taxi will be here in half an hour,' the official said, and when there was no reply he looked round, astonished at the speed with which the thin furious figure had faded into the dark.

[4]

Through the wide hotel windows the sea was present as a band of darkness, slipping and gleaming under the light of a small private boat bringing some business men home to dinner.

'But this is supposed to be his celebration, not yours,' Kate said, dancing with Anthony. It was years since they had danced together. All their mutual childhood went into the perfect precision of their movements; they carried with them Mornington Crescent and their father's disapproval and the little stained-glass hall.

'Never mind, he's marrying you, isn't he?' and the years they had been apart were pressed out between their bodies stepping to the obscure voluptuous muted tune.

She protested: 'It'll make no difference,' and leant her cheek against his to hear 'He's not good enough for you', to catch some sign of jealousy: he couldn't really care for Loo.

He said: 'By God, there's the Professor,' and the music stopped. She clapped and clapped for an encore, his breath was winy, his hand damp, he was free as she could never be free; he had no responsibilities, other people would always do the fighting for him. They returned to the table, he was a little drunk and whistled some war-time tune, picked up in what club, on what old creaking horned gramophone, in the company of ex-officers, about an only girl; his melodies, like his slang, never contemporary; he lived the life of a generation before him, snatching a girl between leave trains. 'When I'm in love and you're in love.' He said: 'Now, if Loo were here——'

'Is that really Hammarsten?' Erik said.

Past three mirrors, past a bank of flowers, the Professor sat in state with a small neat platinum blonde girl on his knee; he had lost his glasses down her dress and now he looked for them, while she wriggled and laughed. A tall handsome black-haired woman with a white tragedy face beat her glass up and down on the table and told him she was disgusted, that she wouldn't take the part; a pale withered man lay across the table with his head in a plate. He hadn't got beyond the soup.

'He's choosing his cast,' Kate said.

Erik Krogh began to laugh. Everyone looked at him. The manager came out from behind the bank of flowers and clapped his hands to the orchestra with blithe relief; he had been spying for half an hour between the leaves and the petals to see whether the party would be a success; all the waiters began to run about filling up glasses; a weight was lifted. Hammarsten suddenly spied them; he had his glasses again and now, spilling the blonde girl in her primrose dress on to the floor like a glass of hock, he came towards them, slipping and sodden and the worse for wear, tight black trousers and tail-coat. The two women trailed after him, leaving the pale man in the soup.

'Sit down, Professor,' Kate said. 'Are you choosing your cast?'

The black tragic woman said, 'What an idea. There's

a brothel scene,' she said using the English word as if she wouldn't sully the Swedish language.

'Hot stuff,' Anthony said.

The little blonde said: 'Well, if you won't take the part, I will. Won't I, Professor?'

'Back row of the chorus.'

'Well, I've legs, haven't I? Much good you'd be in a brothel.'

'Ladies,' said the Professor, 'ladies,' and dropped his glasses on the dark woman's lap.

'But have you chosen,' Anthony asked, 'what's his name – the druid?'

'Gower,' the Professor said, 'where's Gower?'

'He's asleep in the soup,' the blonde said. 'Let him alone, dear.'

'I think you'd do fine,' Anthony said.

'What do you mean, fine?' the blonde girl said, speaking English with an American accent.

'In the brothel scene.'

For no reason at all the dark woman began to talk French; the party began to have the international and aggrieved character of a conference on disarmament.

Anthony said, 'Come for a walk. It's hot.'

'What do you mean, hot?' the blonde said, as if she'd been insulted. She began to talk Swedish again to the Professor, who answered in English out of politeness to his English friends. He began to extol Krogh's virtues. He spoke of a statue next to Gustavus's facing Russia. 'Facing Russia,' he repeated with overpowering significance and a knowing nod to Krogh. They were all amazed by Krogh's approachability; they gambolled round him excitedly; his presence lent to the party a background of peril; they were like children putting out

207

their fingers towards the cage of a fierce but drowsy bird. They had a delicious sense of daring; they wondered when he would snap.

But Krogh smiled at them with complete happiness. He thought: all these years the keeping up of appearances, the concerts, the operas, the receptions. He said to the waiter, 'Some brandy.'

'*Une bouteille*,' Anthony said vaguely, and the tragic woman turned on him at once with a flow of French. He caught the words '*Académie Française*' and '*Cochons*' several times repeated.

'Are you French?' he asked.

'She French?' the blonde said. 'You make me laugh.'

'Are you American?'

'American,' said the dark woman, 'she's never got further than Ellis Island.'

'It's hot in here. Come for a walk.'

'Have some more brandy.'

'We begin rehearsing to-morrow. Where's Gower?'

'You know they are going to be married.'

'Don't make me laugh.'

'The idea – a brothel scene.'

'Well, I don't mind taking the part.'

'A miserable little film actress.'

'It's hot in here.'

'What do you mean, it's hot?'

'You need someone from the legitimate stage, Professor dear.'

'It's the only legitimate thing about her.'

'Where are my glasses?'

'Where's Gower?'

'Where's the brandy?'

'Don't tickle, Professor dear.'

'There ought to be a statue. There will be a statue.'

'It's a secret. Don't tell anyone. They are going to be married.'

'Anthony, keep your mouth shut. You're drunk.'

'Facing Russia.'

'It's the greatest play of the greatest dramatist.'

'In the greatest translation, Professor dear.'

'She makes me laugh.'

'Here are your glasses.'

'From ashes ancient Gower is come.'

'Why not play the part yourself, Professor dear, instead of letting that drunken swine——?'

'Come for a walk.'

'Where's the brandy?'

'By many a dern and painful perch.'

'Ask *her* to go for a walk. She's hot. She's sweating.'

'I don't want her. I want you.'

'Thank you for nothing. Leave go of me. I want to talk to Herr Krogh.'

'Kate, tell me. Do you think my job's respectable?'

'Oh, Anthony, be careful.'

'Let me tell your fortune, Herr Krogh. Oooh, what a long, healthy life-line! You are going to be married and have three, four, five little kiddies.'

'You bet he's not.'

'Anthony, be careful.'

'Oh dear, I quite forgot. You ought to have crossed my hand with silver. Of course we don't have silver nowadays, do we? But I daresay nickel would do – or a note. Just for luck, you know. I'll give it back afterwards, if you like.'

'With whom the father liking took,
And her to incest did provoke.'

'Frankly, I can't think why the Professor's so pleased with this play. It seems vulgar to me.'

'Oh, see what Herr Krogh's given to me. Would you believe it?'

'Vulgar little thing. I'd act Marina if only to save the dear Professor's play from her. Oh, Professor, your glasses again. No, no, let *me* fish them out.'

'And she calls *me* vulgar.'

'Come for a walk. It's so hot.'

'Well, I certainly will after that. She's shameless.'

'The ground's the lowest, and we are half-way there.'

'By heart, the whole play.'

'Waiter, another bottle of brandy.'

'Shan't be long, Kate.'

'Don't talk, Anthony. Be careful what you say. Do be careful.'

'I'll be as mum as a fish, darling.'

'Must cast thee, scarcely coffin'd, in the ooze.'

'Somebody's being drowned now.'

'Or tie my treasure up in silken bags,
To please the fool and death.'

'He's so intellectual. It'll be a pleasure to work with him.'

'Do hurry. If there's one thing I hate it's drowning.'

'They say it's the nicest death.'

'How hot it is. Please come along.'

'You see the whole of your past life. In a flash.'

They came out among the flat flood-lit trees; high heels stumbling on the leaves, a thin metal complaint against the wind and dark; Anthony kissed her pinched prehensile lips; far below in the dark the tide broke along the jagged shore. 'For look how fresh she looks,' through the wide windows the Professor's voice drunk but deeply moved, 'They were too rough that threw her in the sea.'

'What a wet play it is,' Anthony said. 'The sea. And ooze.'

'I love the sea,' the blonde said with Garbo in her voice.

'I suppose we could find a boat,' he said, reluctantly: full fathom five: all your past life: the easiest death.

'Not in these shoes, darling. What's your name, darling?'

'Anthony.'

She was like a bundle of thin ropes when he kissed her; she pulled his hair with fingers which smelt of pear-drops; her mouth was sweet, synthetic, a laboratory fruit. She asked, 'Is that your sister?'

'Yes.'

'I don't believe you. You're in love with her.'

'Yes.'

'You naughty boy.' She licked his chin. 'You need a shave, darling,' lick, lick, mechanically, like a match against emery-paper. 'And her to incest did – did,' he thought, the Professor's voice telling of death at sea, Lloyd's list, his never-known mother's photograph face down in the suitcase in the attic, Kate. He put out his hand and felt in the darkness for the blonde; she stood a little way above him on the steep path; his hand touched silk and climbed to skin. Melancholy drunk or sober, he wondered, and said, 'There's someone behind you on the path.' The blonde jumped and screamed and Anthony slipped, held her and slipped, recovered with his heels deep in the path. 'It's steep here,' he said, 'you nearly sent me over.'

'But who is it on the path?'

'I don't know.'

They climbed back together to the lighted windows, the other side of the terrace with the tipped-up tables, the balustrade, the shifting sibilant leaves.

'There's no one there.'

'Walking in front of us. There.'

The blonde screamed again, this time for effect; she aped the legitimate stage – the tragic woman, with flung hands and tilted enamelled face; the air was full of pear-drops and sweet chemicals. Anthony said, 'I'll see what he wants.'

'*Farväl,*' the blonde said, dramatically Swedish, making-up her face beside the balustrade.

Anthony came round the hotel on to the drive. 'What do you want?' The man was in the light now. He turned his perplexed smudged face and waited for Anthony. He was the younger: no collar, heavy boots; shyness. Anthony said again: 'What do you want?' It had rained while they sat at dinner; Anthony came no nearer. The man was soaked; the loose sole of one of his boots clapped when he moved.

'*Förlåt mig,*' the young man said. The damp gleam of Anthony's pumps, the white tie caught his attention. It was as if he were losing a piece of confidence with everything he saw, the flood-lit drive, the kiss in the dark, the blonde against the balustrade, pumps and starched shirt: it was as if he expected something different, had come to the wrong party.

'Do you speak English?' He shook his head and began explaining in Swedish what he wanted. It was something reasonable and urgent. 'Nyköping', Anthony heard, and 'Herr Krogh'.

The pale primrose dress came out of the shadows. 'What does he want?' But the young man had stopped.

212

'Darling, have you got a car here?'

'Krogh's.'

'Let's find the car and sit in it awhile.'

The young man saw that they were leaving him and began to talk urgently.

'What's it all about?' Anthony said.

'He wants to see Herr Krogh. Something about his father. His father has been dismissed. His father knows Herr Krogh. Nothing to do with us.' Her accents went on and off like an electric road sign: American, English, now charmingly Swedish. 'He is yust a bore, Anthony darling.' She was gleamingly international under the floodlights, between the puddles; the minor theatrical companies of every capital had embellished her with innumerable accents, had worn away any trace of a national origin. 'He says his name is Andersson.'

'A hard-luck story?'

Andersson at any rate was national in his heaviness, his fairness, his inability to talk another language, and a thin spray of sympathy passed between the two of them, as if they recognised each other's limitations in a strange world.

'Might go in and tell him,' Anthony said.

'What are you thinking of?' the blonde said. 'Herr Krogh wouldn't see a fellow like that.'

'He looks all right to me.'

'Come and have a good time in the car, Anthony darling.' She had the high-class prostitute's contempt for working men; she was firmly conservative; she had risen and she wasn't going to look back.

The young man stood patiently, waiting for their decision.

'You go and wait for me,' Anthony said. 'I'll just pop in and see Krogh.'

'All this fuss about that dismal Yonnie.'

'Been down and out myself,' Anthony said.

'He's not down and out. He says he works for Krogh.'

'Well,' Anthony said angrily, 'it's just about time he met one of his workmen. The man's wet through. We can't leave him out here.' He flung himself petulantly at the glass door and beckoned to Andersson. The man followed him on tired dragging feet: a pillar of light glowed softly in the centre of the hall; the pale brown walls, the deep square seats, the music from the restaurant, these seemed to take his dust, his weariness, his heavy boots and hang them there like an odd exhibit, a scarecrow fetched in for a sophisticated joke.

'Now you tell us a story, Herr Krogh,' the tragic woman was saying. Everyone was eating cheese-biscuits out of a tin, everyone except Kate, who sat watching Krogh with apprehension.

Krogh laughed, smoothed his bald papery head. 'I – I haven't any stories.'

'Oh, but in the life, the romantic life you've led——'

'I'll tell you a story,' Hammarsten said.

The tragic woman oscillated wildly between them in the effort to keep them both. 'Dear Professor, in a moment . . . Your Marina would love it, but first . . .'

Krogh said, 'There's a story about the three men who went to a bawdy house in Chicago.' He said: 'Wait. I must get it right. So many years . . .'

'Listen,' Anthony said, 'there's someone wants to see you. A fellow called Andersson, Erik. Says he works for you.'

Krogh said, 'They'd no business to let the old man in. I won't be bothered. Send him away.'

'He's not an old man. He says you know his father. His father's been dismissed.'

'Erik,' Kate said, 'was that the man you saw the other day? The man you promised . . .'

'Get fire and meat for the poor man,' Hammarsten said fiercely, his glasses falling this time among the cheese-biscuits, ''T'has been a turbulent and stormy night.'

'I put nothing on paper,' Krogh said.

'You've had him dismissed?'

'It was the safest thing to do. We put something on him at the works. The union couldn't object. I couldn't risk a strike.'

'A frame-up?' Anthony said. 'His son doesn't realise. He thinks you'll be of help.'

'Send him off,' Krogh said. 'He has no business here.'

'I doubt if he'll go.'

'Then throw him out,' Krogh said. 'I pay you, don't I? Go and throw him out.'

'I'm damned if I will,' Anthony said.

'For God's sake,' Kate said, 'let's stop this party. It's no fun. We've finished the brandy. Why in hell's name did you bring these biscuits, Professor?'

'An old car,' the Professor said, 'I thought we mightn't get here. The girls couldn't be allowed to starve.'

'Let's go home,' Kate said. 'Go and send the man away, Anthony.'

'I'm damned if I will,' Anthony repeated.

Kate said, 'Then I'll go. You're crazy, Anthony.'

'Hall,' Krogh said suddenly. 'Hall.' He was the first to see him: under the chandeliers, down the long lit room, the bow-legged walk, the tweed suit, the brown waisted coat with the velvet collar ('Why,' he told them, 'it's Hall'), narrow stream-lined hat, the lean flat Cockney face.

'They told me at the office you were here, Mr Krogh.'

'Everything's all right, of course?'

Hall took them in, the Professor, the tragic woman, Anthony and Kate, with a deep obvious mistrust. 'Of course, Mr Krogh.'

'Sit down and have a glass, Hall. You've flown?'

'I got stuck at Malmö for a couple of hours.'

'Have a biscuit, Hall?' Kate said, but he would take nothing from her or anyone. Even the glass the waiter brought him he cleaned surreptitiously under the table with the edge of the cloth. He killed the conversation with his mistrust and his devotion.

'The sea works high, the wind is loud,' Hammarsten began to quote, then caught Hall's eye and cracked a cheese-biscuit instead.

'Take off your coat, Hall,' Kate said.

'I won't be staying. I just ran down in case there was anything . . .'

Anthony said: 'We can't leave the fellow out there all night. He's dripping wet.'

'Who's that?' Hall asked. He wouldn't even look at them; his shifty dog's eyes were for Krogh; the eyes not of a sentimental family dog, but of some brown tight-skinned terrier which lounges outside the doors of pubs, trots at a bookie's heels, a shifty dog which chases cats for bets and goes ratting in old cellars.

'It's young Andersson,' Krogh said. 'His father was behind the strike they threatened at the works. I talked him round. No written promise – a joke, a cigar. Some trouble about American wages.'

The blonde appeared trailing her primrose dress past

216

the orchestra, innocent pinched painted mouth, im-
ploring eyes, a picked bedraggled flower which had been
left out all night upon the tiles. 'You yust can't treat me
like that, Anthony.'

'Then I had him sacked. They planted something on
him. It was the best way. This boy's asking for trouble.'

'Sitting there in the car till I was frozen.'

'Get him a drink anyway,' Anthony said.

Kate said, 'Let's go home, Erik.'

'You'll have to see him then. I brought him inside.'

'You don't want to see him, Mr Krogh?' Hall asked.
'You want him to beat it?'

'I told you to send him away,' Krogh said to Anthony.

Hall said nothing. He didn't even look at Anthony;
there was no need to look at anyone to know that they
couldn't be trusted with Mr Krogh. He got up, hands
in his overcoat pockets, hat tilted a little forward, walked
bow-legged past the orchestra, the silvered palms,
through the glass door into the wide waste of the entrance
hall, looking neither to right nor left, past the reception
counter to the deep rug under the central light, where
young Andersson stood and stared about him.

In the restaurant the orchestra began to play again.
'I'm waiting dear'.

> 'I'm waiting, dear,
> Leave off hating, dear,
> Let's talk of mating, dear,
> I'm lonely.'

'You young Andersson?' Hall said. His Swedish
consisted mainly of nouns learned from a pocket
dictionary.

'Yes,' Andersson said, 'yes.' He came eagerly forward
to meet Hall. 'Yes, I'm Andersson.'

'Home,' Hall said, 'home.'

'You can't ration, dear,
This kind of passion, dear,
Though it's not the fashion, dear . . .'

'Home,' Hall said again, 'home.'

'I only want to see Mr Krogh,' Andersson said and smiled tentatively at Hall. Hall struck him on the point of the jaw, stood for a moment above him in case he needed a second blow, then slipped off his knuckle-dusters and said to the reception clerk, 'Outside.' He thought bitterly as he retraced his steps: There they all are, the bloody spongers, drinking his wine, not one of them would do a little thing for him when he wanted it.

In the mirror by the restaurant door he watched young Andersson heave himself on to his knees; he knelt with his face down, dripping blood on to the beige rug. Hall felt no anger against him, no sympathy; only a deep un-selfish love for Krogh which had no relation to the money he was paid. He remembered the cuff-links; they lay in his pocket beside the knuckle-dusters in a little brown leather case, which was now darkened and marred by blood. Hall sadly, angrily, examined it. He had chosen even the box with care, nothing gaudy, in the best of taste. He strode across the hall and shook it in Anders-son's face. 'You bastard,' he said in English, 'you bloody bastard.'

Young Andersson's mouth was full of blood; blood was in his eyes, he couldn't see clearly. 'I don't under-stand,' he said, his breath bubbling on his lips, 'under-stand, don't understand.'

Hall shook the box at him and raised his boot and kicked him in the stomach.

# PART VI

## [1]

There was half an hour before the train left for Gothenburg. Anthony and Loo walked all the way up the Vasagatan, past the post office, and then down again.

'We ought to go to the station now,' Loo said.

'I've bought you these chocolates.'

'Thanks.'

'Have you got plenty of cigarettes?'

'Yes,' Loo said.

The morning in Gothenburg, breakfast at Drottningholm, one lunch with the family: the scarcity of their meetings fell on the spirit like a famine. The English pleasure-cruiser which had lain opposite the Grand Hotel the night they came to Stockholm had raised its anchor; the chairs had been taken in outside Hasselbacken, Tivoli was closed; the whole world was turning over to winter; everyone was going home.

'Have you got magazines?'

'Lots of magazines.'

They turned away from the vibrating noisy square below the station and trod the same street again, up to the post office and back. Anthony waved his hand to Minty who sat in a restaurant opposite the station pouring his coffee into a saucer. There was nothing to say but 'Sorry you're going, meet again some day, I had a nice time, thank you, au revoir, auf Wiedersehen, if you are ever in Coventry,' nothing to do but kiss on the platform and watch the train go out.

'I've had a nice time.'

'So've I.'

'We ought to go to the station now.' One step more to the stamp machine, turn on the heel, back down the Vasagatan.

'I wish I was going too.'

'I wish you were.'

'Miss me a bit?'

'Yes.'

'Write.'

'What's the good?'

'There's your father. He's looking out for you. Wave, and he'll go away again. He's carrying Lockhart.'

This is one more coming-to-an-end, to be remembered like the landing and the messages on the walls and the milk which hadn't been taken in.

'Why come on to the platform? Ten minutes before the train goes.' The grey clouds, high and concave, spread thinly against the bright arched sky. 'It's going to rain.'

Anthony said, 'I'll come a little further.' It's not so bad, he thought, this ending as other endings, not so bad as ringing at the empty flat, waiting all the morning on the landing, trying to recognise a writing I'd never seen: 'No milk today'; 'Back at 12.30'; 'Called away. Home tomorrow'; among the stale messages, the errand-boys' crude drawings of women's torsos; not so bad this ending, slip away, there's good old Minty, have a cup of coffee, what next tourist season may bring one doesn't know, one hopes. 'I like your hat.'

'It's as old as the hills.'

Not so bad this ending because one is getting used to endings: life like Morse, a series of dots and dashes, never forming a paragraph.

'That must be my train. If you are ever in Coventry——'

'I might be after all.'

'Quick. Here's my card. We're on the telephone.'

Is it that one gives way too easily to this mood of departure, this hurry along carriages, no time for second thoughts, losing something——?

'Don't come any further.'

'I must. There's your carriage further down.' Just because a porter shouts and slams a door.

'Listen, Annette.'

'Loo to you.'

'I mean, Loo. Stop here. There are three more minutes. I've been thinking. You're right about my job. I'm going to throw it up. A few days ago at Saltsjö-baden. . . . I'll be back in England in a week, Loo.'

'You won't.'

'I will.'

'Oh, it'll be fun.'

'A relationship?'

'I don't care. Just for once.'

'A week today in Coventry. Where can we meet?'

At the end of the long train the Davidges waved, but there was no hurry: two minutes to go and the English Minister was going aboard. The station-master bowed, the porter ran, Sir Ronald padded on suède shoes to the bookstall: two suitcases, just home for a day or two. 'A week today.'

'Listen,' Loo said, 'there's a café in High Street. Moroccan. You can't miss it. It's on the same side as Woolworth's, but nearer the post office. I'll be there at tea-time a week today. If you can't come ring up.'

'I'll be there,' Anthony said.

'In the second room.'

They couldn't kiss each other: the presence of the

221

anxious Davidges restrained them; they shook hands, and feeling the small bones of her fingers grate in his, Anthony thought: A relationship, this is a relationship. She ran away from him down the train; he felt tired and torn as though she had ripped away her share of his brain – a breakfast, a lunch, a bed in Minty's flat. Sir Ronald climbed into his first-class compartment and opened *The Times*, and the carriages gathering speed went by, a glitter of glass, a flash of electricity, like a regiment of polished preened young soldiers, and like an ageing dug-out left behind he took their salute. Then he went to find Minty. He had to talk to someone.

Minty poured his coffee into the saucer and back into the cup and people passed. Anthony said: 'I'm throwing up this job. I'm going back to England, to Coventry.'

'A job's a job,' Minty said.

'Something will turn up.' But he was not as certain as he had once been; he had never starved, he had never for very long been out of pocket, there were always the vacuum cleaners.

'You're lucky then,' Minty said.

'You're the lucky one. You've got an income,' but he did not really envy Minty. Sitting there in the café opposite the station, watching the Swedes go by to their work, the small bustle by the station which meant that another train was sliding out for Gothenburg or the farm lands, he saw himself and Minty clearly as one person: the exile from his country and his class, the tramp whose workhouses were Shanghai, Aden, Singapore, the refuse of a changing world. If Minty were to be envied at all, it was that he had chosen his dump and stayed there. They hadn't the resources to hold their place, but the world had so conditioned them that they hadn't the vigour to resist. They were not fresh enough, optimistic enough, to believe in peace, co-operation, the dignity of labour, or if they believed in them, they were not young enough to work for them. They were neither one thing nor the other; they were really only happy when they were together: in the clubs in foreign capitals, in pensions, at old boys' dinners, momentarily convinced by the wine they couldn't afford that they believed in something: in the old country, in the king, in 'shoot the bloody Bolsheviks', in the comradeship of the trenches: 'My old batman,' 'I said, "Don't I know your face? I believe you were at Ypres in '15".'

'Why are you throwing it up?' Minty asked.

He thought: it's because I'm not young enough and not old enough: not young enough to believe in a juster world, not old enough for the country, the king, the trenches to mean anything to me at all. He said, 'There are things I won't do even for Kate.'

'If you could stay another month, there's the Harrow dinner. I got Sir Ronald to consent at last.'

'I never was at Harrow.'

'Of course you weren't.' Minty blew his coffee. 'Winter's here. I always feel it in my stomach where they drained me.'

'You should wear a cholera belt.'

'I do.'

'I had to wear one for years after they took my appendix out.' Wearily, without relish, they let themselves down into their common stream of interest. 'I was done at the Westminster.'

'I was done here.' Minty added with indignation, 'In the common ward.'

'When they took out the stitches on the sixth day——'

'They had to leave a tube in me. Even now I can't bear anything hot.'

'I get a pain sometimes. I wonder whether they left something inside, a sponge, or forceps.'

'Did you see the Minister,' Minty said, 'off for a few days in town?'

'He'll be there by the week-end.'

'I often wonder,' Minty said, 'whether I won't go back. Turn up suddenly. Surprise them all. I had a letter a few days ago from an aunt. One isn't quite forgotten. I'd like to be able to go to the Oratory again.' He tried to drink his coffee and put it quickly down and wiped his scalded lip.

'A week today I'll be in England,' Anthony said.

'I'll miss you,' Minty said, lifting his yellow hang-dog sorry-sullen face. 'Everyone goes. Only Minty stays.'

'Well,' Anthony said, 'I'll have to go and tell Kate, gather enough of the ready. Have another coffee before I go?'

'Thank you, thank you,' Minty said, very quickly in case the offer should be withdrawn. 'It's good of you. I'd like another. It can stay cooling while I drink this one. If I wait long enough Nils is sure to come by. But one doesn't like to wait too long on just a single coffee.'

Anthony ordered the coffee. What the hell, he thought, I'm going home. If I don't feel happy at this moment, everything decided, only to get some tin and pack my bag and say good-bye again to Kate (we've lived without each other all these years, why worry now?), if I don't feel happy, when will I ever feel happy? And his brain stirred with a good enough substitute for happiness, a dry bitter quite cheerful recklessness. To burn one's boats. He said, 'How about a farewell present, Minty?'

'I would, really I would,' Minty said, 'but really I haven't anything till next month.'

'I mean one for you, a piece of headline news. I'll give it you for nothing because I like you, because you're as damned hard-up as I shall be next week.'

'Too generous,' Minty said mechanically, anxiously watching for the waiter with the coffee.

'Krogh's going to marry my sister.'

Minty said, 'Oh, Holy Cnut. Is it true? Are you sure it's true? I daren't lead them up the garden over that. They'd have my blood.'

'Word of honour. Honest Injun.' He spread his fingers (a prep school memory) to show that none was deceitfully crossed.

'Holy Cnut.'

He left Minty, swung his umbrella recklessly up the clouded watery streets; a few drops of rain tingled on the tram-tops in Tegelbacken, colour faded out of the City Hall, a tall dark pillar above the metal lake; boats burned; one couldn't stay now. In the Fredsgatan people stood in the shop doorways waiting for taxis. Anthony prodded at the iron flowers outside Krogh's with his umbrella, until the porter opened the gate: the perfect taste, the shrewd modernity of the great glass building touched his mood with malice. Everywhere the lights were on, although it was not yet midday; the electric heaters glowed and hummed. I could have told Minty a great deal more than that: the frame-up on Andersson, the sale to Batterson's. He ran up the stairs; he wanted to exert himself; the lift overtook him, shooting silently upwards with a black-coated clerk, his arms full of

225

flowers. On a landing a girl in horn-rimmed glasses altered the position of a fleet of little metal ships creeping over a chart; she whispered aloud: '55' 43".' A telephone rang: a red light flashed above a door. Krogh's was at work. Like a great liner built on credit, dependent on blind trust in the officers' control, Krogh's was on its diurnal putting out to sea. '67' 25".'

He opened a door: a great desk in the shape of a horse-shoe under low shaded lights, twenty draughtsmen sketching their ideas for twenty posters. An automatic gramophone played soft seducing tunes; a voice from a microphone instructed them. Wrong door. He opened another. Here there were separate desks of black polished wood.

'Good morning, Lagerson.'

'Good morning, Farrant.'

Anthony leant across one of the desks, laid his mouth close to a large pink ear. 'I'm giving notice.'

'No?'

'Yes.'

The young man, Lagerson, with his mouth open had an underwater look; protuberant pink ears, a pale greenish face, he nuzzled gasping along the glass front of his tank. 'Why?'

'I'm tired of this place,' Anthony said. 'No room for push, initiative.' He lowered his voice and his eyes clouded at sight of the sedate severe room. 'What chance of making your fortune here? You ought to leave, see the world. What are you doing?'

'Just a publicity story.'

Anthony perched with a swagger on the desk edge. In the rapt stupid gaze of Lagerson he saw himself: the bold adventurer, the man with drive. He kicked his foot

viciously against the black wood. 'This day week I have
an appointment in Coventry.'

'What's Coventry?'

'A great industrial city,' Anthony explained. 'Stockholm is nothing to it. Room for enterprise.'

'Yes, it's dull here,' Lagerson whispered, mouth like
rubber pressed against the tank-side. 'One daren't say
what one thinks. The sneaks there are.' His immature
schoolboy face grew sullen.

'Never you mind,' Anthony said. 'Speak your mind.
You'll find supporters. Make yourself felt, that's the only
way.' He dropped his dangerous advice quite irres-
ponsibly; he didn't care for Lagerson one way or the
other; all he knew was that he was against Krogh,
because of Andersson, because Krogh was in authority,
because of Kate, and because he owed Krogh some
gratitude.

'Well, good-bye, Lagerson. Just got to get some tin.'

And so to the next floor.

'Good morning, Kate.'

'One second, Tony.'

He watched her hands move over the desk, arrange
the opened letters in two piles, leaving everything neat
before she spoke to him. Even her face was arranged
carefully, he thought, in terms of affection, the right
measure of affection: not yours sincerely, yours devotedly,
yours passionately, but simply 'Love from Kate'. He
loved her, he admired her, but her efficiency irritated
him as much as the fountain in the courtyard. He had
been away too long, had come back to find her marked by
Krogh's. He thought with gross self-pity: After all, I'm
a burden to her, better be off, let her be, we've grown
apart.

227

'I've just been talking to Lagerson.'

'One moment, Tony.'

They had grown apart and grown differently; life had pruned her, she had been developed by dangers along one line. He bore the knobs, excrescences, fungi of a dozen careers. He was conceited with failure and she puzzled him with the humility of success.

'I'm going home,' Anthony said.

'Home?'

He said with irritation, 'I mean London – I don't suppose my room's still free. I know we haven't a home. It's a manner of speaking.'

'Couldn't you have waited till after lunch to tell me?'

'After lunch?'

'I suppose you'd forgotten we were lunching together for the first time since we've been here. And you wouldn't have noticed, would you, that I'm wearing these?' she touched her flowers, 'and this?' she touched her mouth. 'Couldn't you have kept the cheery news until the coffee?'

'I'm no good to you here.'

'I suppose this is Loo's doing. What a bloody silly name it is.'

'I don't see anything wrong in it. Names are just sounds, anyway. Kate, Loo – one's no sillier than the other.'

'When are you going?'

'I'm meeting her a week today.'

'A week today.' Her engagement-pad, fourteen days at a glance, lay by her left hand. 'Six o'clock. Cocktails at the flat to the directors.'

'I'm meeting her for tea.'

'And what about a job?'

'One'll turn up. They always do.'

'You could have kept this one. Aren't you tired, Tony, of job after job? There's no end to it after this.'

For a week, imagining that he was settled, he had forgotten how tired he was: the new faces, the new desks, interviews. He beat them off with memories of Loo, the familiar faces of the whores in Wardour Street, the kind paid companionship in hired rooms. 'It's not respectable. The other night. What was wrong with Andersson? I won't do their dirty work. There are things I won't do.'

'Poor Tony,' Kate said. 'There's the difference between us. You ought never to have gone back.'

'Gone back where?'

'To school. I told you wrong that night you ran away.'

'You're talking gibberish, Kate.'

'You need money if you're going to have scruples.'

'That's what I've come about, some tin.' He tried to pass it all off lightly, pain and good-bye, the going back. 'I thought to myself when I got up this morning, Kate'll let me have a little ready. I'll pay it back.'

'You thought that?' Kate said. 'You were wrong. Don't be a fool, Tony. If you stay here a week, you'll have forgotten her.'

'I know,' Anthony said. 'That's why I'm going.' He was as obstinate as if his honour were involved in not forgetting, as if Loo were some message with which he had to pass the enemy lines, a verbal message, fading in his brain with every delay.

'I knew this was happening,' Kate said. 'I had my warning. Aren't I dressed to kill? But I expected it over the coffee. Your favourite lipstick, flowers.' She said with her first sign of weariness, 'A sister's handicapped, isn't

229

she? I can't appeal to you like Loo can; you'd think it indecent to say you loved me.'

'But I do love you, Kate. Honestly.'

'Like that. In that tone. This is how I love you, Anthony.' He had put his hand on her desk amiably, conciliatingly; she drove at his fingers with her penknife. He whipped them away. 'For heaven's sake, Kate. . . .'

'The lover's pinch, Tony, which hurts and——'

'You nearly cut me.'

'Poor Tony, give it here. I'll make it well.'

'I don't understand you, Kate.'

'You used to, Tony. Don't you remember how we played telepathy in the holidays? I'd lie in bed and think of something and next morning at breakfast. . . .'

'It was an old trick of ours, Kate. I don't think we could work it now.'

'I can. I knew this morning when I got up that this was going to happen. I heard you just as clearly as the time you screamed.'

Anthony laughed. 'Then you've got the money all ready for me?'

'No. No. You don't really believe that. Would you care for any girl who didn't think it worth her while to plot to keep you? I'm going to keep you, Tony.'

'Against my will?'

'Oh, I could say it was for your own good; it is for your own good; but what do I care? Because I love you, because you're the only damned man in the world I love.'

'Brother and sister,' he jeered, with a sense again of a great waste; because it was impossible, in the same room with her, aware of her candour, her firm familiar fingers still holding the knife, even her scent, her choice of

230

flowers, not to be disloyal to Loo. Loo was a recurring itch of the flesh; this was thirty years in common. But the itch when it was there, he knew, would always be stronger. Kate was for his satisfied moments; when you were satisfied you could turn to a sister, to family love. He said, 'I'll ask Krogh for money. He owes me a week's pay.'

'He'll give you nothing.'

'I'll go to Minty then, sell him a story; I gave him one for nothing as it is. I told him about your wedding.'

'You told him that? Tony, what a fool you are. Erik told you to have nothing to do with the Press.'

'I could sell the story about Andersson.'

'Tony, you're too innocent to live.'

'He doesn't want another strike till America's through.'

He was fighting with all his resources for the itch. He tapped them out on her desk with his finger: 'Andersson; the sale to Batterson's; dirty work at Amsterdam,' and he was aware with bitter self-pity that the itch had won: the common life, telepathy at daybreak, the scar above his eye had no power against the itch. He was as good as in Coventry already: the Moroccan café, the second room, between Woolworth's and the post office.

'Listen,' Kate said. 'When will the story be out? Tonight? Here's your money, and for God's sake keep out of the way.'

'Thanks, Kate. It's good of you. I'll be off tomorrow. I'm no good really here.'

'And Erik's ties must just go on – being Erik's ties.'

'I'll choose him some this afternoon.' He kissed her with sudden passionate jealousy; he didn't really want to leave her, one never really wanted the itch to win.

'What are you worrying about, Kate? You'll be coming across yourself soon. It's not as if I'm going East.'

'No,' Kate said.

'Don't worry, Kate.'

'I'm just thinking,' Kate said. 'Erik wants me.' The light was on above his door, but she waited; her face was momentarily open to him like a wide difficult plan of campaign. 'Have dinner with me tonight, your last night, won't you? Keep me that free.' But he couldn't follow the plan; he'd lost the knack of map-reading: out of practice, far away from her.

'Of course I will. At home?'

'No, not at home. Somewhere quiet where we can be alone, where nobody will know where we are.'

[2]

Hall bought a paper and carried it unread across the brown autumn square. He wondered whether he had made a mistake about the cuff-links; he might have bought a ring, or a cigar-case, or a paper-weight. No one seeing him scuffing up the dead leaves, with his small dead eyes fixed on his toe-caps, could have guessed the devotion which lay on him like a heavy responsibility. For it wasn't just a present, it was a pledge and an appeal. Hall as much as any young man in the idealistic stage of love wanted to be remembered.

A cigar-case? A silver bracelet? It wasn't too late.

He opened the paper to look for the jewellers' advertisements and saw Krogh's name written large across the sheet. He didn't read on because in an electrician's window he saw a green table-lamp shaped like a naked woman. That's pretty, he thought, and remembered with uneasiness the fountain in the courtyard. He strode on down the Fredsgatan muttering to himself: no taste, they have no taste. At a corner waiting for the traffic to pass he looked at the paper again: 'Erik Krogh to marry English Secretary.'

Hall grunted, took no notice of the traffic, stepped between the cars, moved like a marked bullet to his object. Through the gate, not looking at the fountain, saying nothing to the porter, the brown-gloved hands deep in his overcoat pockets, he moved in a bitter dream of his own making: no use any longer for Hall, skirts on the board, petticoat government. He went straight into Krogh's room without asking leave.

'I brought you a present,' he said.

Krogh said, 'I'm glad you've come. I wanted to talk to you. Will you go out to New York for us?'

'On the board?'

'Yes, on the board.'

It was what he had always wanted, but now his only thought was: They want to get rid of me, new ways here, I'm not respectable. He evaded answering. He said, 'I saw these cuff-links in a shop. I said to myself they'd do nicely with my new pin-point. But somehow they don't go. Bit too grand for me. Too many jewels. Thought I'd give them to you as a wedding present.'

'Wedding present?'

He laid the paper on the table and the cuff-links beside them.

Krogh said, 'I never authorised this.'

'Ah,' Hall said, 'then I know who's done that. He's been going round among the clerks talking.'

'Farrant?'

233

'Why did you have him here, Mr Krogh?' Hall said. 'Why did you have him here?'

'I needed a bodyguard.'

Hall's terrier face twitched. 'There's me. You could have sent someone else to Amsterdam. That fellow gave me the willies the moment I saw him. Like passing under a ladder. What good was he the other night?' He took up the stained little leather case and laid it down again.

'He doesn't mean any harm,' Krogh said sadly. 'I liked him. But I'll send him home.'

'Does Miss Farrant know about the sale to Batterson's?'

'You can trust her, Hall.'

But Hall trusted nobody. He stood by the window and filled the room with his suspicion, his jealousy and his devotion. Against his integrity everything had to be measured; the bright modernity, the chic perverted shapes were tarnished beside the genuineness of his brown Strand-made suit. He had never minded appearing vulgar (the wasp waist), sentimental (the trinket on the watch-chain), foolish (the paper nose at Barcelona). He didn't flicker like a fashion, he didn't change his standards like good taste, he was just Hall.

There was nobody who would not have been diminished by his devotion. Krogh hesitated, looked at the cuff-links, repeated sadly, 'We'll send him home.'

'Mr Krogh,' Hall said, 'you don't understand these fellows. Leave him to me. I'll fix him up.'

'We'll give him his ticket.'

'Listen, Mr Krogh,' Hall said. 'You can't do that. He's been poking around, talking to the clerks about short-term loans. How does he know anything about our loans?'

'It must be from his sister,' Krogh said.

234

'And how much more does he know? Suppose he goes home, can't get a job, goes to Batterson's. We've got to keep him here a week.'

'Well, he seems to know the Press here.'

'We can fix the Press here.'

'All right,' Krogh said, with sudden cheerfulness, 'we keep him. That's easy. He doesn't want to go. He won't make trouble while he's being paid.'

'Mr Krogh, you'd better say a word to Miss Farrant,' but Hall twisted away at the sight of her; he couldn't bear the thought that she was trusted: a skirt. He left it to Krogh to explain, 'Your brother's been talking to the Press.'

'You've found it out already,' Kate said.

'Hall has.'

'Ah, our Mr Hall.'

'It's got to stop.'

'Don't worry,' Kate said, 'he's going back to England tomorrow. I've given him the money.'

'To England? Why to England?'

Hall turned back to them. His hands came a little way out of the pockets in a movement of solicitude which remained unfinished. 'Don't *worry*, Mr Krogh.' He was like an old nurse whose charge has grown up, who wants to comfort in the old way of the clasped arms and the big breasts but knows her charge has outgrown it. 'You've no cause to worry. I can fix everything.'

'He's got a girl there,' Kate explained, but her anxiety to convince them that it was all right, that there was nothing to fear was too obvious. She said sadly, 'He's in love.' Her explanations demanded a hearing, they beat like a bird against the blank pane of Hall's inattention and fell at its base. There was something admirable, pathetic, vicious in his love: he had completely surrendered himself. He was as much Krogh's as the block of stone in the courtyard, the marked ash-tray, the monogrammed carpet (he said, 'We can frame him like we framed Andersson'), and Krogh's for that very reason was his. It was marked with his cheapness, his particular brand of caution, his irresponsible ferocity; it was Hall-marked.

'No,' Kate said, 'you can't do that.'

'We'll frame him,' Hall repeated.

'Then don't blame me,' Kate said, 'if he talks. He's not a fool.'

'You mean he knows about the sale?' Hall said. 'Does the whole office know about the sale?'

He watched her with fierce anger, dislike and suspicion, but he respected her too much to waste any time. They had the same ideas, neither had cared a hang what happened to Andersson; the only difference was that they did not work for the same man. He had no time to think, but there was one line along which his brain easily and rapidly ran. He said, 'Does he play poker?'

'Yes,' Kate said.

'Does he play it well?'

'He plays nothing well.'

'I've known a card debt before now,' Hall said, 'keep a man off a skirt. You'd better have a game tonight, Mr Krogh. He can't go back to England.'

'We're going out tonight, Tony and I,' Kate said.

'It's that or a frame-up,' Hall said, 'he can't leave Stockholm.'

He was like a little pillar of brown bitter smoke. His malevolence came out of his suède shoe-caps, lay like scurf over his overcoat. 'I'm not worrying,' he said, 'and I'll see that Mr Krogh doesn't worry.'

236

'So you'll have dinner with us tonight?' Kate asked, with irony.

'I'll be there,' he said. 'You can bet your boots I'll be there.' He stood there brown and bitter, narrow and ferocious, the self-appointed defender of the great glass buildings, the works at Nyköping, the log-mills in the north.

[3]

Hall got up and shut the windows, pulling down the great double panes to keep out the damp late air. Anthony pushed forward two crowns, Krogh four. Kate said, 'I'll put down. I haven't had a hand tonight.' Hall came back to the table. Innumerable poker hands had perfected the mechanism of his approach; it was hardly bluff he used; there was no acting in his performance, he merely withdrew his interest from his cards completely. He would bid quickly and then relapse into his patient suspicious silence. 'I double you,' and his eyes met Anthony's across the table with absolute indifference to the other's hand. He had other things to think about, and when his turn came to discard his cards, he discarded without relation to the cards he held (two tens of spades, a four, and two of diamonds, a six of clubs). 'One card,' he said, and threw away the six. He played with a complete disregard of the poker-player's table of chances, with indifference; he depended recklessly on the weakness of his opponents; he was careless of consequences. If he met a really strong hand he was beaten, but against an average hand or a weak hand he always won. He hardly troubled to look at the card he had taken, a three of hearts.

Gullie said, 'I'll have three.' He became jovial under the influence of cards; he was convinced that he could read anyone's bluff. 'The military attaché gets reckless,' he said, 'ha, ha,' and flashed his monocle like a small revolving light from face to face. 'The military art of camouflage, ha, ha,' and was momentarily disconcerted by Hall's lack of response.

'I'll double,' Hall said.

Kate went to the window, passing behind Anthony. She could see his hand, three nines, a knave, a two, a weak strong hand. He played as he believed judiciously, never bluffed to a high figure, but always supported his hand for a little more than it was worth; he was either called at once or laid down his cards before Hall's high bids. He had only won one hand.

'Well, well,' Gullie said, laying an elaborate smoke-screen about his intentions, 'this calls for thought.'

'Double again,' Hall said. She watched him from the window; one hand was flat on the table, one hand held his cards in a tight pack on his lap; he was staring at Krogh. Every time a bid was made Gullie looked at his hand.

A steamer went by outside, its lights lying thinly along the surface of the low grey mist; it slid by below the reflections of the card-players, driving into the night past Hall's face. The lit windows in the workers' flats lay in tiers, like a liner's portholes, on the opposite shore.

'The Minister's taking a holiday?' Kate asked.

'He always goes up to Scotland for the First,' Gullie said. 'This is where I drop out. Do you shoot, Farrant?'

'Oh,' Anthony said, avoiding Kate's eye, 'I hope to have a few days.'

'Going across?'

'Tomorrow.'

'You'll have a rough passage,' Gullie said. 'Good sailor?'

'Not very.'

'Give a man a horse he can ride,' Gullie said. 'I've never wanted a boat to sail, ha, ha. Puffin Travers invited me across the other day. He's taken a moor.'

'Double again,' Hall said. He took no notice of the conversation which wavered round him, he smoked cigarette after cigarette with the same concentration he had shown in the lavatory of the airliner, the yellow nicotinous smoke blew through his nostrils.

'I'll go down,' Anthony said.

Krogh said, 'I'll call you.' Hall laid down his cards, the two tens side by side, the rubbish in a pack beside them.

'I've got two queens,' Krogh said.

'And yours truly is stung again,' Anthony said, pushing his money over to Krogh. He lit a cigarette, beaming happily at nothing, or at everything: the thin spray of smoke, the cards Hall gathered from the table for a new deal.

This, Kate thought, is a tune to remember: Tony here, Tony happy, the boat going by outside, the lights turned off one by one over the lake in the workers' flats. The wind stirred the low mist, drove it up from the water till it stood a man's height round the lamp-posts; very faintly through the double panes the sound of hooting cars. This tune to remember. Sink it deep.

'Have the *smörgåsbord* before we deal again,' Kate said. She pushed the dumb-waiter over to the table and poured out the glasses of schnaps. They all helped themselves, except Hall, to the thin buttered slices laid with ham, sausage, smoked salmon. Hall lit another cigarette and shuffled the cards. '*Skål*,' '*Skål*,' '*Skål*.' This tune to remember.

'That's a fine wireless set,' Gullie said.

'Yes?' Krogh said. 'I never play it.'

'Half-past nine,' Anthony said. 'The last news in London.'

Kate turned the pointer. 'A depression advancing from Iceland,' a smooth anonymous voice said and was cut off.

'Good old London.'

'There's Moscow,' Kate said, swinging the pointer; 'there's Hilversum, Berlin, Paris. . . .'

> '*Aimer à loisir,*
> *Aimer et mourir,*
> *Au pays qui te ressemble.*'

'The Duke of York, opening the new premises of the Gas Light and Coke. . . .'

The voices went out one by one like candles on a Christmas cake, white, waxen, guttering in the atmospherics over the North Sea, the Baltic, the local storms on the East Prussian plains, rain beating on Tannenberg, autumn lightning over Westminster, a whistle on the ether.

'You can always tell Paris,' Anthony said, '*aimer, aimer, aimer*.'

'Your deal, Mr Farrant,' Hall said.

'But it was a good voice,' Gullie said reverently, 'a good voice.'

'I'm out of this,' Kate said. 'I've lost enough. Do you sing yourself, Captain Gullie?'

'Among friends, just among friends. I'm trying to get up a little opera company among the English here. Nothing difficult. *The Mikado. Merrie England.* All good propaganda.'

'Eena, meena, mina, mo,' Anthony said, dealing four cards. 'Stand behind and bring me luck, Kate. Cross your fingers, twiddle your toes, that's the way the money goes. I'll join you at the workhouse after this deal.'

Hall staked five crowns.

'Do you know a soprano, Miss Farrant? I'm held up for a soprano. Mrs Wisecock hasn't the stage sense.'

'Thank the Lord,' Anthony said, 'I've bought my tickets.'

'Bought your tickets?' Hall said sharply.

'Otherwise there'd be no London for yours truly. Do they include food with the fare?'

'No drinks, my boy,' Gullie said.

Kate said, 'You've bought the tickets?' She thought: He's beaten them after all: only this tune to remember then, because it would never be repeated. Tony happy, the mist rising, the firelight doubled by the panes, the thin hum of the electric power. 'Give me five'; in his hand a straight flush. 'I'll double you.' He'll remember this, Kate thought; year after year he'll talk about tonight, playing poker with Krogh, drawing five cards, drawing a straight flush. The story going round the world, in how many clubs, always unbelieved. 'Double.'

'I go down,' Gullie said.

But already she had begun to plan how they might be together again. She knew she might have prayed; the temptation was there, to fall back on eternity, on other people's God, the emotional cry in the dumb breast, the nudity of confession: I love him more than anything in the world; no, inexact, go nearer truth: I love no one, nothing but him; therefore give him me, let me keep him; never mind what he wants, save me, the all-important me, from pain: do I call it pain, agony, parting here, parting there, messages on post-cards, the storm, the wires down, no more thoughts in common? But she wouldn't pray, she took what comfort and credit she could for not praying; it wasn't that one disbelieved in prayer; one never lost all one's belief in magic. It was that she preferred to plan, it was fairer, it wasn't loading the dice.

'Double again.'

'I'll put you up five.'

'I'll go down,' Krogh said.

'Double.'

'I'll call you,' Hall said.

'Well, you can't beat a straight flush.'

'No,' Hall said, 'I can't beat that.'

Anthony said, 'This'll take me across. I'll be able to have a good blind on this.'

Hall began to shuffle the cards again.

'I'm out,' Gullie said.

'We've had enough,' Kate said. 'It'll take you all night to win that back, Mr Hall. Let's have another drink and go to bed.' Something in the sight of him sitting there, his prominent cuffs, his thin hands clutching the cards, irritated her. She said, 'Cheer up. You'll win it back another day. Was he always like this, Erik?' she asked. 'Always so serious?' She explained to Captain Gullie, 'They were almost boys together.'

'I've seen him in a false nose,' Krogh said, 'but I don't think it altered him.'

'Were the police after you, Mr Hall?'

Hall said sullenly, 'It was those festas they have. I believe in doing in Rome as the Romans——'

'Mr Hall's getting classical,' Kate said. His malice across the table, like a small oppressive flame, danced in the corner of the eye. One wanted either to put it out or fan it to something larger.

Hall said, 'I'm going home. Good night, Miss Farrant.'

'I'll walk back with you,' Anthony said.

'Stay a bit, Captain Gullie. It's still quite early. Have another drink. Tell me, tell me,' Kate said, 'oh, tell me about tartans, Captain Gullie.'

'That reminds me,' Gullie said, dropping his voice, 'of something that fellow Minty was telling me.'

'Minty?' Krogh asked. He rose from the table and joined them. 'What's that about Minty?'

Hall stood in the doorway buttoning his coat. It was a little too tight in the waist; it constrained him. He said sharply, 'Don't you worry, Mr Krogh.'

'An odd untrustworthy fellow. Runs the old Harrovian Club here. Don't know how it got into his hands. The Minister can't stand him. He was trying to make out you were MacDonalds. Well of course, I looked it up.'

'Good old Minty,' Anthony said. 'Good-bye, Kate. I'm off early.'

'Good-bye.'

'Good-bye, Mr Krogh, and thanks for your help. You didn't really need me here. Good-bye, Gullie. See you in London one of these days, I expect.'

But she had no plan, and she couldn't let him go. She caught him up by the lift. Hall went down before him and he waited for her.

'What's up, old thing?'

Kate said, 'There are things I want to talk to you about.' She thought: Every day he'll forget her, but the idea gave her no comfort. (Every day he'll forget me.) She said, 'I haven't seen much of you. There was a lot I wanted to say to you,' with desperate sentiment, 'about the old days.'

'This time,' Anthony said, 'I'll be a faithful correspondent. Three pages every Sunday.'

His bonhomie infuriated her; it flashed back at her from the long mirror-lined corridor, it grimaced sideways at her from the mirrored stairs, it sparkled from the lift's chromium doors. She said, 'That's the best I get, three weekly pages, when I've worked for you for years. Everything I've done was to help you, and now because a little bitch——' she despised her own tears; they were too cheap an appeal; she wouldn't dry them, wouldn't call attention to them, just let them drip across her face as if she'd walked through a storm without her hat.

'But, Kate,' Anthony said, 'I'm fond of you.' He glanced with hurried embarrassment down the lift shaft. 'Hall's waiting for me. I must be off.' He grabbed weakly at her hand. 'I love you, Kate. Really I do. More than anyone in the world. But Loo. I'm in love with her. I'm crazy about her. You'd like her if you knew her, Kate.' He became reasonable and sententious. 'Love and in love, Kate. There's the difference.'

'Oh, go to hell,' Kate said, and ran back up the passage, smearing away her tears with her hand as she ran. She heard him shout, 'Coming, Hall,' down the shaft, ring for the lift. She stopped outside the door, cleaned and prepared her face as if she were wiping it free of Anthony.

When she opened the door, Krogh said, 'Where's Hall?' She was surprised by his sharpness and anxiety. She said, 'He's gone with Anthony.'

'It's stuffy in here,' Krogh said. 'Hall smokes such bad cigarettes.' He threw up the double panes and leant out of the window. 'I wanted Hall.'

'Well, I ought to be making tracks,' Captain Gullie remarked weakly, twisting his empty glass, drooping over the card-table, the ivory chips, the deep ash-tray crammed with damp butts.

'Don't go,' Kate said. 'Have another drink.' She poured out three glasses, but Krogh didn't come. 'Here's how,' she said like an echo of Anthony.

'Foggy,' Krogh said.

'You might have sent them home in the car.'

He said sharply, 'Hall wanted to walk. He told me he wanted to walk.' He pulled down the window.

'A car's no good in one of these fogs,' Gullie said. 'It's quicker to walk. You might drive over into the lake before you knew where you were.' He began to deal out some cards. 'Do you know the Imp of Mischief patience, Miss Farrant?'

'I don't like patience.'

'You'll like this one. You've got to cover the knaves first, do you see? They are the Imps, ha ha.'

'Whose note-case is that? Is it Anthony's?' Kate asked.

'No,' Krogh said, 'that's Hall's. I saw it too late.'

'I shouldn't have thought Hall was one to leave his money about,' Gullie said. 'Did you see how he held his cards, ha, ha. Close-fisted, what?' The idea tickled him no end; anything tickled Gullie; he enjoyed himself wherever he went with the reckless abandonment of a child; any table could set Gullie in a roar.

'There'll be tears before night,' Kate said.

'Eh, what's that?' Gullie said. He swerved gallantly away from the Imps of Mischief. 'What's that, Miss Farrant?'

'What's the matter, Erik?' Kate said. 'Have a drink. You're tired.'

'I'll buzz off,' Gullie said. 'Imp of Mischief, ha, ha.'

'No, don't go,' Krogh said. 'I don't want to go to bed yet. It's early.'

'There's the lift.'

'Hall's coming back for his money,' Gullie said. 'Let's hide it.'

Kate said with bitter irritation, 'What a little Imp of Mischief you are.'

But the lift stopped at the floor below.

'Nearly got it out that time,' Gullie said, reshuffling the cards. 'Tried to teach a Frenchman once. Wasn't a bit of good. He always cheated. Can't see the fun of playing patience if you cheat.'

Krogh suddenly slid open the great folding doors, walked through to his study, his bedroom. They could see him, past the collected editions, past the Milles sculpture, taking aspirin. 'What is it, Erik?' Kate said.

'A headache.' He turned back towards them, tooth-mug in hand, and called through the two rooms, 'What's this parcel?'

'Ties,' Kate said.

'I've got enough ties, haven't I?'

'Tony chose them for you this afternoon.'

'Tony?' he said.

'Open it. They are good ties if Tony chose them.'

'I don't need them. Send them back.'

'He paid for them.'

Krogh said, 'He shouldn't have done that. You ought to have stopped him, Kate.'

'He's grateful to you. He wanted to do something.'

Krogh said, 'Why does everyone give me things? I can buy them, can't I? Hall gives me cuff-links. I've got enough cuff-links.'

'All right,' Kate said, 'I'll send them back.' She came through to the bedroom and took the parcel. 'You've emptied the aspirin bottle. What's the matter, Erik?'

'Only a headache.'

'Let me see what he bought.' She opened the parcel; they lay there in striped discretion; he had good taste in clothes. 'You might as well wear them.'

'No. I've got enough. Send them back.'

She carried them through to her own room and laid them in a drawer between her vests. A lift-bell rang, she could hear Gullie in the drawing-room click the cards. She thought: I haven't a plan, he's gone, the last thing I said was 'Go to hell'. Sadly she reproached herself for a lack of care: from childhood she had been brought up by servants who told fortunes in tea-cups, by nurses who threw salt over the left shoulder, to be careful of last words. Quarrel if you must, but make it up before night. 'Go to hell', that was for the beginning of an evening, not the end, for greeting, not for parting. In childhood one had been more careful; death was closer; one hadn't this hard grip on life. She touched the ties tenderly, tucking them in.

'There's Hall,' Gullie said to them as they came back together, 'what did I say? I knew he'd come back.' The lift stopped; it was Hall.

He came in hat in hand, thin and cold, narrow and unfriendly, the fog like dust in his red eyes. It had got in his throat. He was hoarse when he said, 'I left my note-case.'

'There it is, Hall,' Krogh said. He didn't seem to want to take it, smoothing his throat with his yellow-gloved hand; it was as if he wanted to say something, but no one would give him the cue.

'I'll walk home with you, Hall,' Gullie said, but it wasn't that.

'Did Anthony come back with you?' Kate asked. She had the impression as he smoothed his throat of some great pain hopelessly demanding sympathy even from her, but she distrusted him and wouldn't give it. 'Isn't he here?'

'No,' Hall said, 'I left him and came back.'

'Have a drink, Hall,' Krogh said.

'Thank you,' Hall said. 'It gets your throat, out there. But here, with a drink,' he sketched a smile at them, roughly, unconvincingly, 'everything's all right again, everything's O.K.'

'He'll be home now,' Kate said. 'I'll just give him a ring.'

'Do you play patience, Hall?' Gullie asked, laying out the Imps of Mischief.

'Patience? No,' Hall said, and 'no,' the voice said, coming up the wire, 'Captain Farrant's not come in.'

'Tell him,' she said, 'to give me a ring when he comes in. His sister. Even if he's late. Tell him I'm waiting up to speak to him. Yes, however late.' She excused herself to them. 'It's a superstition.' She said with sad affection, 'It beats all. He's calling himself a captain now.'

# PART VII

Minty stood at the door, took the names, noted the wreaths: the huge wreath from Krogh, the small one from Laurin; he noticed that there was none from Kate, none from Hall. The coffin slid smoothly along its runway beneath the angular crucifix. The doors opened to receive it; the flapping of the flames was picked up by the microphone beside the altar and dispersed through the great bleak building. Minty crossed himself: they might just as well have left the body in the water. He had a horror of this death by fire.

Kate and Krogh stood together in the first row; behind was old Bergsten and Hall and Gullie; the Minister had sent a wreath. One or two clerks, a woman from the hotel, stood near the door; outside a crowd had collected to see Krogh come out. A child had been taken to its first funeral; it didn't understand the standing still, the long wait, the silence, the nothing to look at; its thin bored wail troubled Minty. He felt like a dumb man for whom another acts as interpreter and falsifies his meaning.

For Minty suffered, noting the wreaths he suffered, noting names, vexed by the crying, wanting a cigarette he suffered. He thought: I'll borrow a crown from Nils: and suffered. This was the fourth friend. There wouldn't be many more.

Sparrow, outcast Sparrow because he never washed behind the ears: they went for walks together every Sunday, trudging stolidly along the high road, avoiding the favourite field paths, seldom talking. They had no interests in common: Sparrow in the holidays blew birds' eggs without success, smashing the shell, spattering his mouth; Minty collected butterflies. During term, collecting only dust from cars along the high road, they were friends because they had no other friends; they were ashamed of each other, were grateful to each other, sometimes escaping together from the wet towels in the changing-room, loved each other.

Connell died in a week. Was popular for a week, put a drawing-pin on a master's chair, gave Minty a bar of chocolate, said he'd ask him to tea, went home early during the French hour and died of scarlet fever.

A voice behind him said, 'So sad. Poor young man. A week too in the water.' It was Hammarsten, late as usual, slipping in with his note-book. He whispered beneath his hand, 'The rehearsals are going well. All except Gower. I need another Gower.' He said, 'Any relatives?'

'No, no relatives,' Minty said. He thought of his mother, of old Aunt Ella; he thought, we don't run to much in the way of relatives.

And there was Baxter who let him down when it came to the point, who would have nothing to do with the package of assorted goods from the Charing Cross chemist.

'To think,' the blonde whispered at Hammarsten's elbow, 'that only last week he held me in his arms.'

Minty winced. He wanted incense to take out the odour of Chanel. He wanted candles to light before the saints. He wanted every possible aid for his fantastic belief that his fourth friend perfected had joined Connell in some place of no pain, no failure, no sex.

He said, 'You aren't the only one.'

'He had such a way with him.'

'He had a girl. He introduced me.' He made his proudest claim. 'No one else knew about her but me – and his sister.'

'Poor, poor young thing,' Hammarsten said. 'Where is she?' peering into the bright hard glittering church through his steel-rimmed, black-ribboned eye-glasses.

'In England. She doesn't know. Nobody knows her address.' But all the time he knew, Minty knew, remembered Coventry. It was the one secret he would preserve from this friendship (the morning in his room he tried to forget, tried to forget the lack of milk, the lack of a cup, the starveling hospitality). The secret of friendship he kept as carefully as he would have kept the relic of saints, the Saxon thighbone, the holy bandied splinter itself: the bar of chocolate which he never ate, preserved for years, until at last it was lost in one of his innumerable moves through no carelessness of his own: the Brownie snap of himself with a butterfly-net taken by Sparrow: a copy of *The Bushman's Vade-Mecum* Baxter gave him: now to be added, the name Coventry.

Hammarsten said, 'You slipped up badly over the marriage announcement. Lucky not to lose your job.'

Minty laughed: lucky! he couldn't help himself: lucky still to be here to count the wreaths, tot up the names, write out his paragraph, and then up the stairs, the fifty-six stairs, fourteen to the Ekman's home, twenty-eight to the empty flat, the single umbrella, the engraving of Gustavus, and at last the brown dressing-gown, the cocoa in the cupboard, the Madonna on the mantel. But yes, on second thoughts, lucky: things might have been so much worse.

'And today,' Hammarsten said, 'the great new American issue was subscribed. Life and death, life and

251

death,' he began to cough, throwing up a little old phlegm on to his grey stubble, his frock-coat, and up in the air behind him, wheeling over the lake, zooming down towards the City Hall, rising and falling like a flight of swallows, the sun catching their aluminium wings as they turned, came the aeroplanes, a dozen at least, making the air noisy with their engines as the sound of the organ died away.

The child stopped crying. 'Look,' she cried, 'look.' Something was happening at last.

The woman from the hotel slipped out, looking here and there at everybody with her narrowed gleaming commercial eyes; the clerks hurried out (they had to be back at work). Old Bergsten was supported by his chauffeur down the steps into the street; he wasn't certain why he was there (you could tell it by the cross way he looked about him; he was prepared at any moment to be put upon). Gullie stayed a moment, said something appropriate to Kate, waited until he was outside to put in his monocle. When he saw Minty he tried to avoid him, but Minty caught his sleeve. 'You'll be at the Harrow dinner?'

'Of course. Of course.'

'I had an idea,' Minty said. 'One gets so tired of the old toasts, the school, the headmaster, all the rest. I thought if the Minister replied for Literature and you for Art——'

'Well,' Gullie said, 'well. It's worth consideration, my dear fellow.'

'Of course, you're so many-sided. You could reply for Music, for Drama – not to speak of the Services.'

'Just let me know,' Gullie said, pulling away, 'send a card.'

'You were there, weren't you, that last night?' Minty said.

'What do you mean? Where?'

'Playing cards with them.'

'Oh yes. Yes.'

'You've heard what people have been saying, that he couldn't, even in the fog, have just walked into the water.'

'People will always talk.'

'Was he drunk?'

'He'd had a few. My dear fellow, you can't imagine how foggy it was. It took me an hour to get to the Legation.'

'I know how foggy it was,' Minty said. 'I was out in it.' He coughed. 'It's in my throat still. Standing around all the evening.' He put his hand in his pocket and pulled out a silver match-box. 'I wanted to give him this.' He twisted it to show the engraved arms. 'I was really at Harrow, so it's no good to me. He'd have liked it.'

'Well then, you know how foggy it was.'

'He came out with Hall. I couldn't speak to him then. I thought I'd follow them, but I lost them at once. It was about ten minutes later I heard him shout.'

'Poor devil.'

'Yes, but it was after the shout that Hall came back. He must have been nearer to it than I was, but he'd heard nothing.'

'You're imagining things, Minty.' Minty turned to watch Hall come down the church, and Gullie pulled himself free. 'Send me a card about the dinner like a good chap.'

'Yes,' Minty said, 'yes. The dinner,' and watched Hall coming to the door; took in with extravagant and useless hatred the wasp waist, the brown velvet lapels; if I could do anything: he stood, a small yellow avenging fury between Hall and the street, the cold clear sun, the crowd, the arabesque of aeroplanes across the sky.

'Excuse me, Mr Hall.' He barred the way, scraping his sore tobacco-bitten tongue along his teeth, aware of revenge wilting in the common everyday air until it became no more than the will to vex, to tease. 'Have you a statement to make?'

Hall said, 'What do you mean? A statement?'

'Surely,' Minty said, blowing his fumy breath in Hall's face as he blew his coffee to cool it, 'surely you must be one of the new directors? With all your experience you'll be managing the New York end?'

'No,' Hall said, 'Laurin is going there.'

'But Mr Krogh owes you so much.'

'Listen,' Hall said. 'Get this straight. He owes me nothing. It's me who does the owing.' He slipped on his tight brown gloves. 'And if we don't see eye to eye about the way I manage things, that's my funeral.' He said, 'You'd better not worry Mr Krogh while I'm round.'

'You didn't send a wreath,' Minty said. 'Didn't you and he get on together?'

'No,' Hall said.

He waited in the entrance for Krogh to appear, and the two men went off together to the car, side by side, with several feet between, saying nothing. The crowd was silent because it was a funeral. The brain and the hand: the heavy peasant body uneasy in the morning coat, cramped by the collar; and the hand, destruction with a wasp waist and jewelled cuff-links flashing like ice. They had nothing to say to each other; what lay between them, held them apart, left them lonely as they drove

254

away together, was nothing so simple as a death, it was as complicated as the love between a man and a woman.

When they had gone the crowd began to leave. There was nothing to wait for. There was nothing further to see. 'Look,' the child said, 'look,' dragged along the pavement, tripping on the edge of the paving, watching the aeroplanes.

'Well,' Minty said, 'I'll have to go to the office, get this in.' He didn't know how to talk to her; she was a woman, and just because she was a woman she woke his malice. 'He let me down badly over your wedding.'

'We were going to be married.'

'Well,' Minty said, 'I must be pushing along. See you some time, I suppose. If you'd like to come to an arrangement——' He wanted to escape; he despised scent, silk stockings, powder, salve; like a small smoky Savonarola his nostrils shrank with distaste; he would not feel clean again until he was drinking his cocoa by the meter, under his house photograph. He jumped when she spoke to him; he was not used to be held in conversation: he was ready to suspect the worst of any woman who troubled to talk to him.

Kate said, 'You heard him shout. I didn't hear a thing. I didn't *feel* a thing.'

'Yes, but I didn't know.' He said, 'I couldn't see. And when Hall came back I thought it must be all right.'

'They've had a quarrel,' Kate said. 'Erik and Hall.'

'You think——' Minty said, 'Hall——'

'Think,' Kate said, 'I know it.' He flinched from her certainty, for if one was sure, one ought to do something, and what, he thought, with sour self-pity, can Minty do?

'So Laurin's going to New York,' Kate said.

'You'll stay, of course?' he asked, with contempt.

255

'No,' Kate said, 'I'm leaving.'

'Oh fine,' Minty said, 'fine. How it'll hurt them. Couldn't you think up anything better than that? After all, he was your brother; he was only my——' he sheered away from the word 'friend'. Standing there she awed him with her quiet, her moneyed mourning; he couldn't claim more than acquaintanceship; she robbed him a little of Anthony with every sight of her gloves, her shoes, her model dress. 'Oh,' she said, 'a few days ago I could have ruined them. A word to Batterson's. But what would have been the use? There's honour among thieves. We're all in the same boat.'

'He wasn't a thief,' Minty said, defending Sparrow, Connell, Baxter. . . .

'We're all thieves,' Kate said. 'Stealing a livelihood here and there and everywhere, giving nothing back.'

Minty sneered: 'Socialism.'

'Oh no,' Kate said. 'That's not for us. No brotherhood in our boat. Only who can cut the biggest dash and who can swim.'

The aeroplanes drove back above the lake, leaving a plumy trail: 'Krogh's. Krogh's,' over Stockholm, a thin trellis-work of smoke, the 'K' fading as the 'S' was drawn.

'So you're going back to England?' Minty said, remembering the fifty-six stairs, the empty flat, the Italian woman on the third floor,

'No,' Kate said, 'I'm simply moving on. Like Anthony.'

the incense cones, the condensed milk, the cup (I've forgotten the cup),

'A job in Copenhagen.'

the missal in the cupboard, the Madonna, the spider withering under the glass, a home from home.